# THE BITTERROOT FIRE

DONALD F. AVERILL

ISBN 978-1-954941-55-7 (softcover)
ISBN 978-1-954941-56-4 (hardcover)
ISBN 978-1-954941-57-1 (ebook)



Printed in the United States of America.

Book Vine Press
2516 Highland Dr.
Palatine, IL 60067

# ACKNOWLEDGEMENTS

Many thanks to Mary Stebbins for her work as editor.
Thanks to Efren Sifuentes for proofreading the manuscript.

# PROLOGUE

"All three of them wore masks, Lieutenant; the kind you can get at Home Depot for working with drywall or where sawdust is flying around."

"You're familiar with those dust masks?"

"Uh-huh. My husband bought a couple of packages. We're remodeling our bathroom. We use them almost every day. We work on the house after dinner if we're not too tired. He works on microwave relay towers during the day."

The police arrived at the bank, just off the freeway, five minutes after the holdup men fled. It was the third robbery at the branch in the last six months. Detective James Jarvis, a fourteen year veteran of the St. Louis Police, questioned all three cashiers and the branch manager as they sat around the supervisor's desk in the small open lobby. Jarvis scribbled with a bank's ballpoint pen in a small spiral-bound notebook. He wrote 6/11/08 at the top of the page below City Bank Robbery (branch #5).

The youngest, but most experienced cashier, Joyce Nevers, had just mentioned the robbers had all worn masks. An older gentleman and middle-aged woman, the two other cashiers, were listening attentively and seemed anxious to contribute what they thought was vital information. The manager, Stanley Rivers, had already told the detective he hadn't seen a thing. He had hit the floor and closed his eyes when the robbery commenced. He had a wife and child at home and wasn't going to get killed because of money, especially when none of it was his. During the previous holdup, a gun was poked in his ear. He remembered that feeling of cold steel and that menacing voice, "*Move and I'll kill you.*"

Bespectacled Frank Sievers, today working the drive through window, was wringing his hands nervously and glancing out the branch bank windows waiting to talk. He frequently adjusted his glasses and looked outside, perhaps wondering if the robbers would return to punish the staff for activating the silent alarm. He had been at the drive-up window with a wall at his back and hadn't seen the men enter the bank, but he had seen them leave the parking lot.

"Mr. Sievers, by any chance, did you notice the car they were driving; the make and model?"

Before Frank could answer, Rhoda Tomask, the third cashier, spoke up, "They didn't have a car that I could see." Rhoda, mid-forties, was slightly over-weight, about five foot six with silver streaks through shoulder-length auburn hair. She was watching the detective's every move.

"They were on foot?" Jarvis asked.

Sievers grinned and answered quickly, "No, they were riding bicycles." He removed his glasses and began cleaning the lenses with a breast pocket handkerchief. "They were riding girl's bikes; two blue and one green and white. They all had saddle bags, couldn't see any licenses." He sighed, leaned back in his chair, put his glasses back on and smiled, proud of his contribution.

Detective Jarvis scanned the faces of the cashiers, "Describe the height and weight of each robber. You first, Mrs. Nevers, and tell me if they were male or female."

"Okay, I'll try." Furrows appeared in her brow as she concentrated. "The tallest one was a bit over six feet. I could tell by the scale on the door. The other two were about five-nine or ten. They moved pretty fast so it's hard to say exactly. They were all men; two white guys and one black. The black guy was one of the shorter ones. He was very muscular. He reminded me of a weightlifter, but perhaps a football player." She motioned with her arms at her sides, elbows bent.

Jarvis shifted his eyes to Rhoda Tomask. "Mrs. Tomask, tell me what you saw."

She said, "It's Ms. Tomask, detective; I'm divorced. My first name is Rhoda." She smiled and paused to let the statement sink in. "I can't add much to what Joyce said. That's about what I noticed, lieutenant. The tallest one had black socks and wore New Balance sneakers. They didn't say a thing to each other, not a peep. The short white guy was keeping time and stomped on the floor when it was time to go. I think it was after about three minutes. Say, are you married?" She smiled and brushed her hair back from her pierced ears showing her tiny gold flower petal earrings.

Jarvis frowned, took a step back and stammered slightly, "Ah, yes, I'm married…to my job. I'm divorced in the sense you mean. My ex-wife remarried a rich man in the oil business. She moved to Texas five years ago. And no, I don't have any children."

Another officer, in plain clothes, entered the bank and swiftly approached Jarvis.

"Hey, Jim, we just got an update."

Jarvis turned away from the employees, "Yeah? Whatcha got, Ted?"

"A woman down the street noticed three grown men on girl's bicycles, thought it was strange and called the police station. She figured the men took the bikes from some girls playing at the park."

"Tell me she saw a car."

"She did, a white four-door sedan, didn't know the make. She perked up, thought something was funny when they dropped the bikes in a pile and got in the car."

"That's all?"

"Nope. She got the tag. I already reported it. The APB just came out."

"Good work. It's conceivable we'll have this one taken care of before dinner."

Rhoda approached Jarvis and touched his wrist, "I'd like to make you dinner, detective. Let's say…seven thirty. You will come, won't you?" She smiled and shrugged her shoulders. "If you're reluctant, you can bring a friend for support. You can come armed."

Jarvis chuckled, "Thanks for the invitation, I was going to catch a burger on my way home from the office. Give me your address, I'll be there. What kind of wine do you like?"

Rhoda's face lit up, "A Merlot or Riesling would be nice."

The detective looked at Mr. Sievers and raised his eyebrows. Sievers winked.

Jarvis gave the group a quick survey and said, "That's all I need from you. I assume the bank will be closed for the remainder of the day. Thank you for your cooperation. I'll let you know if there's anything else. I'll get everyone's contact numbers and addresses from your manager, Mr. Rivers."

The group began dispersing and Ted, the other plain clothes officer yelled to Jarvis, "The three suspects were just stopped on the freeway and taken into custody. Looks like all the money has been recovered."

Jarvis gave a thumbs up and replied, "Looks like I'll have a relaxed dinner tonight. Hopefully, I won't get called away." He winked at Ted.

# CHAPTER 1

Jay, early forties, prematurely gray, was riding with nine other rough-looking men. The youngest member of the group was in his thirties and the oldest was pushing fifty. They were riding in back of an older GMC flatbed truck fitted with side panels. A wooden slat of the panel Jay was leaning against irritated his shoulders, but not enough to cause him to adjust his otherwise comfortable position. He was enjoying the irregular massage as the sun began to shine through the upper limbs of the mature trees that crowded the hills. The group had travelled over an hour since six o'clock and had yet to eat breakfast. They were twenty miles out of Dillon, designated the stop for a pancake breakfast.

Nine of the workers were asleep or appeared to be, their heads rolling with the bumps the truck seemed to be seeking out on Interstate 15. State road crews were still out patching the carnage on the roads from the freezing temperatures of the long winter, but they were currently tending the East-West Interstate 90. Route 15, a North-South road was being ignored for the time being, but mountain dirt roads were receiving attention, the reason the prison crew was being taken into the mountains. The dirt roads had to be cleared to allow easy access of firefighting equipment.

The motley assemblage of personnel had been mustered out of bed at the Montana correction facility, provided work clothes, and loaded into the truck before the sun was up. They were to leave Butte by 6:00 a.m. in early July, for the sun was going to be heating up the countryside before they had arrived to establish camp. Their destination was six miles north-northwest of Suddenly, a small community with limited road access in the Bitterroot Mountains. By two in the afternoon the temperature would be pushing ninety, the humidity hovering around ten percent, ideal conditions for forest fires. Carelessly tended campfires and lightning strikes were the leading causes of destructive fires, but smoldering cigarettes and fireworks also contributed to the statistics of summer forest fire blazes.

Jay and Guns sat facing each other on opposite sides of the fully loaded state truck. Their feet might have touched but for the firefighting equipment boxes piled in the center of the truck bed. Jay's feet were resting on top of a sturdy red box packed with six axes. His neck and shoulders were pressed against a side panel that telegraphed every bump in the road through his wiry six-foot muscular body. The rigid panel had taken the place of a soft pillow placed against a concrete wall in cell 242.

He was beginning to get the feeling of liberation from his fifteen year sentence having eleven years invested. Volunteering for the fire brigade had involved three months of rigorous training. Jay's taste of freedom was punctuated with fresh mountain air and scenic vistas. He had kicked himself repeatedly over the years for getting involved in the robbery that netted the three beer-drinking buddies only a few thousand bucks and terms in the Missouri Penitentiary from ten to twenty years. The men had been caught so quickly; they hadn't spent a cent. All the money had been recovered.

The net take from the holdup netted the three men nothing but prison sentences. The idea of some quick money had been only a pipe dream, but one with good intentions. Erica, his wife of nine years, had been diagnosed with metastatic breast cancer and was expected to live approximately two more years if proper care was given. That was the problem, the drugs and care were expensive. His regular job as a car mechanic wasn't going to pay enough to meet medical expenses and they had no insurance. John, Sr., began to look for some easy money.

Near the end of his first year in prison, his older brother, Tom, and Erica were returning home from visiting him and were killed in a freak freeway accident. Eight year old John Junior was to live with Grandma until he was eighteen.

Jay had been given a choice to attend either his brother's or Erica's funeral, but not both. After speaking with his mother, Jay chose to attend Erica's funeral where he and his mother, Loretta, had created the story of Erica's and his death, not his brother's. Loretta was vehement about not letting Junior know his father was in prison. She was afraid it would do irreputable harm to the youngster. Jay agreed that it was best that his son be kept from visiting his father and not revealing the lie. When he became of age, Junior would be told the truth about his father, but it never happened. Loretta died before she told her grandson about his father.

Jay and two other inmates at the Montana Correction Facility had been offered a reduction in their sentences if they would volunteer to be part of the Montana Forest Fire Brigade. The team was to be composed of ten inmates from Missouri, Montana, South Dakota, and Washington minimum security prisons.

As the fully loaded vehicle slowed when entering the outskirts of Dillon, the occupants began to stir and were jarred completely awake when the truck stopped for a red light. Jay could see the sign for the pancake house restaurant, and he wondered when they would get something to eat. His stomach had been growling for the last thirty minutes.

The two guards in the cab had planned for the crew to get fed at the Dillon Sausage and Flapjack House before continuing on to Suddenly, still more than thirty miles away. The turnoff to Suddenly was about twenty-five miles from Dillon. After Suddenly, the truck was to follow dirt roads through the densely forested mountains to Fire Tower 32, where the team would camp overnight. Another meal would be prepared by one of the guards and the eldest crewman, Pops Curtis, who liked to cook and was good at it.

The truck squeaked to a stop behind the restaurant and the crew entered through a side door, marched down a narrow hallway past the bathrooms to the lobby and eating area. Tables were arranged to seat twelve men and each position had a meal ready to eat. The food wasn't hot, but not cold either. The plates had been warmed to keep the food at a reasonable temperature. Twenty minutes were allowed for eating and the crew was ushered back to the truck. The men were quiet and ate rapidly. They had been warned if any outburst occurred, they would all suffer, any uneaten food would be thrown in the garbage. Other patrons noticed the men but after a few quick glances, the brigade was ignored.

Jay noticed his former position was taken when he vaulted into the truck, so he sat beside Guns instead. Guns was a giant among the crew, standing nearly six-six and rarely said more than a few words unless provoked. Today he nodded to Jay as the smaller man joined the bodybuilder with the massive biceps. Guns had been an over-aggressive bouncer at a tavern, had crippled one patron and accidently killed a drunk in a parking lot when he threw a full trash can at some inebriated patrons taunting the big guy. Though remorseful, he was given ten years due to an inexperienced defense attorney and a harsh judge. The other members of the crew maintained their distance from Guns. Gun's biceps were so large he had to remove the sleeves of his shirts to put them on.

The third man from Missouri was Manny Chicon. Initially, Jay didn't understand what Manny had done to deserve his twelve year sentence, but illegal border crossing and drugs had been involved. Later, during training Jay was told Manny, a US citizen, made the mistake of helping a friend cross the southern border with illegal drugs. He would be back among the public population in another year. The other crewmen had maintained anonymity. Jay was unaware of their past or whether they could be depended on in a pinch in spite of their training.

While eating breakfast the crew obtained more information about the nearby area they would be patrolling. From Tower 32, three single lane dirt roads radiated through the forest for from eleven to fifteen miles to towers 31, 37, and 40. Tower 40 was located at the top of an eight thousand foot peak only a hundred yards from the Idaho border. The brigade was to make certain all the forest roads of the designated area were free of debris, open for vehicular traffic through the wilderness areas. They were also assigned to guarantee helicopter landing sites were free of obstacles and accessible from the roads.

The truck slowed and made a right turn to the west exiting Route 15 and began a slow climb in elevation travelling at 25 miles per hour. Jay felt the gears shift and heard a brief grind as the vehicle began moving on the two-lane road. Within a few minutes he noticed the density of trees was increasing. After nearly an hour of meandering through the forested area on the partially paved road, the vehicle made a sharp turn to the left on a graveled path. A small sign said Suddenly: 2 miles.

Jay said, "Someone does live out here; seems pretty isolated." He chuckled, "Could be a ghost town. Wonder if we'll stop."

Guns grunted his agreement, "Hope so, my ass is gettin' sore."

The truck slowed again as a car approached, pulled over and stopped, blocking the road. Jay glanced through the slats in the side panels and saw bright-yellow SHERIFF written across the side of the dark-green four-door sedan.

Another worker announced, "It's a cop. What's his problem?"

When Jay saw the officer walking toward the truck driver, he motioned to Brian Potts, the worker nearest where the cop was headed, "Hey Potts, listen and tell us what's goin' on."

Potts gave Jay a thumbs up and turned his head to listen, leaning against the panels. A hush came over the brigade when the deputy began talking with the driver. In a few seconds, the deputy sheriff walked back to his car and turned his cruiser around.

Potts turned back to the others and said, "It's nothin'. We're spose to follow the cop. There's a road crew redoing the main drag so we gotta detour."

Near the back of the truck, Sam Winters commented, "Damn. I wanted to see main street and all the pretty ladies. Maybe a ghost or two."

"Sure, Sam. You just wanted to see where the jail is." Fred James winked, elbowed Sam, and everyone adjacent to them laughed.

The truck's gears ground and they lurched forward following the green cruiser at a leisurely pace. The edge of town was abrupt, houses appeared after the truck passed about a hundred yards of shrubs and towering pines and firs. Perhaps it was only the eastern part of town, but the large trees seemed to be guarding the community from intruders. Jay looked at the surrounding forest as the walls of a prison, the truck just entering into the prison complex.

The men sat silently, watching the few cars passing by with passengers rubber-necking, probably wondering what the truckload of men was doing coming into Suddenly following the sheriff's car. The truck continued on for six blocks, made a right turn and crossed seven streets before taking a left one block to Main Street. The loaded flatbed stopped at a red light, signaled right, made the turn, and continued on, but without the police car. It had vanished. Jay could smell hot asphalt and could hear the muffled engines of road equipment as the brigade left the central part of the little town.

The gears were shifted again, this time more smoothly, and the truck picked up speed to what Jay estimated was the posted limit. He saw a sign that read 25 miles per hour. As the density of trees increased and no more buildings were present, another sign indicated that they had exited the Suddenly city limits. The sign thanked them for their visit. Jay saluted the sign and thought he might return when he was a free man.

The next signpost appeared about five minutes later. It read Hadley with an arrow pointing to the left. A nice looking log home could be seen from the road with two vehicles parked near the structure: a jeep, and a small flatbed truck. Jay shifted his eyes forward to the road and could see two older boys tossing a football on the remote two-lane road. Clearly unconcerned with sporadic traffic, the nearer kid had just thrown a pass to his friend about thirty yards ahead of the brigade's truck. The driver slowed and shifted to the other lane to avoid any accidents with the boys.

The nearer boy caught a return throw but when he glanced at the passing truck, he dropped the ball. Jay heard, "Nice catch, David!"

David called back, "See if you can snag this one!"

Jay watched the distant boy wind-up and throw the ball again, but the truck and the receiver were side by side and the ball dropped into the back of the vehicle, striking Guns on the left thigh. Guns shoved the ball away, saying, "Damn kids. Toss it out, Jay."

The kid that would have caught the ball, had the truck not been there, called out, "Sorry about that." Jay grabbed the ball, stood up and yelled, "Go long!"

Dexter paused for a second and then took off running toward David. The guy in the truck reared back and launched the ball high into the air, a perfect spiral. Dexter thought for a moment the ball would go over his head, but he continued running flat out and extended his arms. The ball struck his forearms and he latched onto it, stopped running, turned, and yelled at the guy standing in the truck, "Great throw!"

Jay yelled back at the young receiver, "Great catch!" He waved to the boy that caught the ball and sat beside Guns as the truck rolled away from the teenagers.

Jay rubbed his throwing arm and commented, "Those boys look to be about the age of my son. I wonder what he's up to these days."

Guns glanced at Jay, "You gonna look him up when you get released?"

"I don't think so. It's better that he thinks his dad is dead. I'm not much of an example of a responsible father."

"Not even curious to see what he looks like?"

"Well, yeah. I might find him but not tell him who I am; just spy on him to see if he's doing all right."

"You can do what you want, but we'll both be out in four years, maybe less if we don't get burned up in a forest fire. I'm hoping for at least a couple of years will be knocked off my sentence."

"You gonna go back to work as a bouncer?"

"Nope. I'm lookin' to be a physical trainer; work in a gym. That's less dangerous than being a bouncer. What about you?"

"Motorcycles. I wanta fix bikes; at least long enough so I can buy one for myself. I want to tour the country, do some fishin'. I'm gonna try to avoid people and trouble; prison isn't my style."

Guns sat and pondered for a few seconds, nodded, "I get ya."

# CHAPTER 2

Dexter pondered, staring after the departing truck. The two boys walked back to Dexter's recently acquired real estate, an old barn that needed major repairs, but he bought it at a bargain price. It was something he could afford. He had made a down payment with money he had earned as a package delivery boy in Saint Louis. Dexter tossed the football back and forth from one hand to the other as they sauntered down the lane adjacent to the Hadleys' side yard.

David commented, "I guess that answers one question I had about you. You can catch the ball on a dead run, plus, you've got plenty of speed. You've got to come out for ball this September. With Chase and me in the backfield and you as a receiver, we'll terrorize our opponents."

Dex wasn't thinking about football. "I wonder who that guy was; the one that threw the ball to me. He's got quite an arm."

"That was a state truck; I noticed the license plate. Those guys are probably one of the bunches that helps with forest fire prevention. I don't think they were firefighters, but I'll ask Scott; maybe he'll know."

"Don't go to any trouble. We'll probably never see them again."

David chuckled, "Yeah, I'll probably forget to ask anyway. Let's get the insulation and drywall unloaded from my car. There's room for it in your side room. It won't get wet in there. We can start modifying your barn in a day or two. Have you sketched what you want to do?"

"I have some ideas, but I need to talk with Jenny, I can't draw a lick. I want to make the barn into a one story house. Do you think there's enough wood in the barn to do it?"

"The only problem I can see is the trusses. Some of what's in the barn will have to be replaced and we'll have to fix the roof; there are a lot of shingles to replace. Course, you could redo the entire roof and put composition shingles on instead of cedar. I think you need to wait to see how much cash you'll have from the diamond recovery insurance and also find out what Jenny can sketch for you."

"Yeah. It's going to be more of a project than I originally thought. A barn is one thing, a livable house is another."

"And you'll want a portion of the structure for your bicycle business, too."

"Yeah. I want to keep that side room where the potbellied stove is."

David rubbed his chin, "You'll have to fireproof the walls, the ceiling where the chimney vents, and build a brick hearth underneath. Your neighbor, Mr. Hadley, can give us some tips. He's a surprisingly good builder. As soon as we get this stuff stored, I need to see how Megan is doing with Rick and then go do some painting with Jenny."

Dexter and I spent about fifteen minutes unloading sheets of plywood and drywall from my Forester before I left to see how Megan was progressing with Rick Hadley. Over a year ago, Rick had been working with his dad to clear timber from a nearby farm and had been hurt. A snapped cable had devastated his legs and he had almost lost hope of being able to walk again. His days as a star athlete had abruptly ended and so had college scholarship offers.

My girlfriend, Megan Isaacs, and I were trying to help with his recuperation. She worked afternoons at the hospital as a candy striper. In order to earn money for college, I ran a yard maintenance service in the mornings to avoid the afternoon heat, but today Megan and I came out to the Hadleys' ranch. I went next door to see Dexter. This first visit to the Hadleys' to begin helping Rick was Megan's chance to see what equipment the Hadleys' had for Rick's rehab. After Dex and I unloaded my car, I started to the Hadleys' to meet with Meg.

As I approached the main road on the single lane to Dexter's, two cyclists came riding toward me. I slowed and pulled a little to the side so they could pass, but they stopped, blocking the road. I lowered my window while the dust settled and heard, "Hey, is this the way to Dexter Young's place?"

I nodded and then called out, "Yes, just follow the path you're on. I just left him." Then I recognized the two riders. They were the honeymooners that were renting one of the fire lookout towers for a month. I wondered why they wanted Dexter. Perhaps they were checking on his sprained ankle. They had helped get him out of the ditch he had fallen into when a truck ran him off the road outside of Suddenly. I had forgotten their names. Straddling his bike, the male came closer and removed his helmet.

"You're David, right?"

I was surprised that he remembered my name. "That's right. I've forgotten your names. Sorry."

"Devin and Clair Springs. We've been renting tower twenty, but we're headed back home, our time is up day after tomorrow. Our bikes need servicing before we return to Helena. We're hoping Dexter has some extra spokes and a tire he can loan us."

I thought about telling the couple that Dexter was thinking of starting a bicycle repair business, but he was going to make his barn into a habitable home first. But I hesitated in going into more details of Dexter's plans. I felt it would be better for him to inform people of his plans and I should worry about my own business.

"I think you'll have to talk to him about spare parts. I don't know what extras he has."

Not to be left out of the conversation, Clair chimed in, "How is Skimmer doing? He's such a cute little dog."

"I didn't see him today, but if he weren't doing okay, Dex would have said something." I thought I should tell them why I hadn't seen Dex's sidekick. "Dex and I were playing catch with a football and were out here on the road. I was at Dex's barn for only a few minutes – for unloading some building materials. Skimmer is too little to help."

Devin smiled at his wife, "Building materials? Is he adding something to his house?"

"Oh. I guess you don't know. Dex bought a barn, not a house, it's part of an old farm. We're doing a conversion, so he'll have a place to live during the winter. There's no heat in the barn; he also doesn't have any electricity or running water, but he does have an outhouse. Be ready to jump back in time about a century and a half."

Devin commented, "I'll be able to give him a hand procuring materials. I'm the assistant manager at High-West Hardware in Helena. Thanks for the information. Now I'll have something to trade for the bicycle parts."

Clair looked up at her husband. "It might be feasible to bring down a load of lumber and hardware next time we come south. We're not that far away. I kind of like Suddenly."

"I'm sure Dex will want to talk with you about materials, but I have to get back on the road. Maybe we'll meet again. Bye."

I slid my foot off the brake and pressed on the accelerator when the Springs continued toward Dex's barn. I got back on the highway and drove the short distance, about one hundred yards, to the Hadleys'. All the time while I talked to Clair and Devin, I was thinking Megan would be completing her visit with Rick and going back home. I had hoped to talk with her at the Hadleys'. I wanted to talk to Rick with Megan present so we could plan our next visit when I could help steady Rick as he exercised. He had to start getting out of his wheelchair.

I was expected to help Jenny and her grandmother paint their living room after I had lunch at home. Mrs. Kincaid had finally decided on a color, light-yellow with white trim. The old light-gray smoke and humidity stained walls should cover nicely. That new color should liven up the big drab room.

I parked directly behind Megan's jeep so she wouldn't leave the Hadley's without me. I knocked and Mrs. Hadley came to the door. She wore a big smile and pushed the screen door open with her foot. Mrs. Hadley was always so glad to see us come to the house to see Rick. I believed his climbing free from depression was a result of Megan and me volunteering to help Rick with his rehabilitation. We made her day.

I had never seen her wearing boots before and had to ask if she was going riding.

"A little horseback today?"

She seemed surprised. "Oh, no, I was cleaning my bedroom closet and found these old cowboy boots. Thought I'd see if they still fit. We don't have horses anymore, David." She continued to smile. I couldn't remember Mrs. Hadley being in such good spirits before. Perhaps it was a result of Megan and me working with Rick to get him walking again.

"Come in, David. Megan said you would be here. Megan and Rick are in the rehab room going over the apparatus Rick has been using for rebuilding his muscles. Down the hall and to the left. I think they're waiting for you."

"Thanks, Mrs. Hadley."

I followed her directions and found Rick moving around the large room talking to Megan. She was trailing a few steps behind him. He was very adept at moving in his wheelchair, snaking through the rehab apparatus. The room opened onto a red brick patio at the rear of the house through a sliding glass door. He stopped and attempted to push the door to the side so he could exit the room, but he was having some difficulty. I reached over him and gave the glass partition a good shove.

He looked up, smiled, and said, "Thanks, David. When did you get here?"

"About two minutes ago. I came to rescue Megan from your clutches."

"You mean my crutches, don't you?"

"Good one, Rick." We all laughed.

I glanced at Megan, "Have you gotten all the info we need?"

Megan and I and the physical therapist at the hospital, Gerry Irwin, were going to devise a program for Rick to follow with Megan and my assistance. We figured the plan would take up most of the remainder of the summer. When classes start at the end of August we would have to cut back on the program. So, we had six weeks to get something positive accomplished with Rick. He seemed to have a good attitude. I had to conclude that from his joking around.

"Uh-huh. I have to be at the hospital at one o'clock. What time is it?"

"You've plenty of time, it's not quite eleven."

Mrs. Hadley called me from the house.

"David, you have a phone call. It's Jenny Kincaid. She said it's not an emergency. The phone is in the living room." Mrs. Hadley disappeared into the house.

"Mom will probably listen from the kitchen, David. Be careful what you say."

I gave Rick a questioning look and he grinned.

Megan laughed, "He's just kidding."

I couldn't help but joke with Megan. "I'll be careful, anyway. I wouldn't want our conversation to be made public."

It took about ten seconds for me to get to the phone. "Hey, Jen. Where are you calling from? Did you come into town?"

Jennifer chuckled, "I'm calling from home; we got a phone installed. Two guys put it in this morning. I had to call you to make sure you'll be here at one."

"I'll be there, just like we planned."

"Okay. Good. Grams wants me to take her in to the bank to see Mr. Isaacs about something and we have to be there at one. I don't want to leave the door unlocked if you won't be here. Someone might steal the paint. That's the only thing of value we have."

I could tell Jen was smiling when she said that about the paint; she was joking with me almost as much as Megan. Jen and I had known each other for only a couple of months but Megan and I had known each other for our entire lives. I couldn't think about one of them without the other intruding into my thoughts. I wasn't complaining.

"You can lock the house. I'll work on the porch railing until you return. It would be a pity if you broke another collarbone."

"Yeah, you'd have to do all the painting yourself. I'm not sure when we'll get back from the bank. Don't work too hard."

# CHAPTER 3

Megan grabbed my arm and began pulling me away from the phone. "Hey, come on. I have to eat and change clothes to go to work. Your car's blocking me." I put the phone back on the wall cradle and followed her out to our cars. Mrs. Hadley was talking to Rick, so I just waved. We'd be back tomorrow.

I glanced at Megan as she got in the jeep. "Will I see you tonight?" I asked as I opened my car door.

"Maybe." She didn't smile or even look my way.

I backed out so she could maneuver her jeep and she took off toward town without another word. I wondered if she was mad about Jennifer calling me at the Hadley's. I'll have to straighten that out later.

I drove slowly, heading home for lunch, trying not to let Megan's mood bother me, but that always stirs up my emotions. Hopefully, she would be more civil tonight. Since we were next-door neighbors, I had to walk about twenty yards to be at her front door. As I moved through the streets, I planned the reconstruction of the Kincaids' porch railing where Jennifer had fallen through and broken her left collarbone. Jen was now free of that sling and tape that had been her companions for the last four weeks. Painting the living room walls was going to be her first project with her rejuvenated left shoulder. I was going to have to make sure she didn't overdue as she rebuilt her muscles after nearly a month of inactivity.

Mom was working half-days now and baby Gwen was being taken care of by Mrs. Weems who had a four-year-old to watch over, too. Gwen was taken to the Weems' at eight o'clock and picked up at noon when Mom returned from the Ranger Station at the north end of town. She hadn't wanted to take the full ninety days of maternity leave from her normal duties as a ranger. She couldn't sit at home for hours; Gwen didn't need constant supervision.

Dad, or more officially, my stepdad, as sheriff of Suddenly, was working on a program to facilitate communications with the forest fire fighters. Suddenly was not, in any stretch of the imagination, the center of crime in the Bitterroot mountains. Most of the policing was to rescue pets stuck in tall trees or sewage pipes. Deputy Doureline occasionally wrote a speeding ticket for an out-of-towner, but most of his time was spent talking to lonely older women and running off wildlife that meandered into town. Suddenly had an occasional visit by a bear, but most often a skunk or two created a minor problem. The two-man police force routinely assisted the local rangers when the need arose.

I rolled into the Kincaids' driveway a couple of minutes before one o'clock. Jen's pickup was gone as I expected. Originally, I had no idea when Mrs. Kincaid and Jen would return from meeting with Mr. Isaacs, but after thinking about it, I figured they would return from the bank before two-thirty.

When it comes to banking matters, Isaacs can be exceptionally long winded. He could probably teach banking to a kindergarten class. I parked at the side of the dirt driveway and grabbed my handsaw and hammer from the back seat. I hoped to get some of the porch railing replaced by the time the women returned. The old balusters were going to be reused, saving me several hours of measuring, sawing, sanding, and painting. The horizontal pieces had to be new and I just had to cut them to size from studs, do some sanding and paint the assemblage.

Jen's Ford pickup chugged into the driveway at about a quarter after two. I had finished with half the railing and needed a break, so I dropped the tools and met the ladies in the driveway. Mrs. Kincaid seemed to be having difficulty releasing her seatbelt, so I opened the passenger door and helped her to the ground.

"Thank you, David. I can get seated without problems, but I have trouble getting back out. I don't like that drop to the ground. Why do pickups have to be so high off the ground, anyway?"

"No problem. I've done some work on your porch railing while you were gone."

"Yes, Jennifer said you would be doing that. It looks good."

As I assisted Mrs. Kincaid up the three porch steps, Jen was right behind us with a sack of groceries. She looked like she was hiding behind the big bag.

I looked back and smiled, "Hi, Jen. Ready to paint?"

"Not yet. We didn't have lunch yet. Grams wanted to be early for her meeting and afterward, we went to the store." She smiled, "We were out of peanut butter and dill pickles. Come in and have a pickle with us."

I stood by the front door and watched Mrs. Kincaid walk into the kitchen, Jenny following. The older woman seemed to be laboring to move down the hallway and through the kitchen doorway. I noticed she hadn't smiled since arriving home. That seemed a bit unusual to me; she was normally a cheerful woman.

I could have imagined something. Mrs. Kincaid called out to me, "Come in here, David, so I can talk to you." She sounded like her normal self. I stood in the kitchen doorway and watched as the women made sandwiches and set paper plates and napkins on the small table in the kitchen. The space could only accommodate three seated bodies without moving into the more formal dining area. The larger dining room table was covered with banker's boxes and several stacks of papers. It looked like Mrs. Kincaid was sorting some things or perhaps looking for something specific. When I was invited for lunch before, we sat at the dining table, but it didn't make any difference to me. I never felt as if I were there as a guest, more like family.

We ate quietly without much conversation for about five minutes. Mrs. Kincaid took a drink of lemonade, her favorite beverage, cleared her throat and said, "I want to go to the top of lookout tower seventeen. If you recall, after you found all those pesky diamonds, you said we would go. Remember?"

I looked at Jen and she grinned. She had said her grandmother wouldn't forget that I was supposed to take her to the tower for a picnic.

"When do you want to go?" I knew the weather was going to be nice for at least the next week, maybe longer. I had only two customers for my lawn service over the next few days; only a couple of hours work. I could drive out to the fire lookout tower almost any time.

Mrs. Kincaid knew what she wanted. "Tomorrow morning, if that's all right with you."

I didn't have anything planned for the next day except to paint another room of the Kincaids' farmhouse. Jen and I were going to paint the kitchen and the hallway leading to the bedrooms next. We had done the living room in record time. Jen's expression was one of surprise when she heard her grandmother's request. Jen and I had planned to paint in the morning. But I could take the ladies to the tower at any time, except at night, of course.

"Okay. When do you want to leave?"

Mrs. Kincaid didn't hesitate, "About ten o'clock. Can you do that?"

I gave Jen a glance, but she hadn't reacted negatively and then I looked at her grandmother, "Sure. I'll bring some water and one of my dogs, if you don't mind having an animal along."

Mrs. Kincaid replied, "That's all right." She resumed eating without further comment. Jen and I chatted about the earlier installation of the phone. She was happy to get a link to the outside world.

Jenny and I got busy with painting and within an hour, the long hallway had been completely changed to a new color. We took the brushes and empty paint cans outside to use the hose for cleanup.

As we washed the brushes, I asked Jen, "How did your meeting with Mr. Isaacs go?" It really wasn't any of my business, but I was curious.

"I don't know. Grams went in his office and closed the door. I just waited in the lobby. The bank had a little table with a coffee dispenser and some dried out cookies. I read some of the investment brochures on the table. Real exciting, kind of like reading the phone book. Oh! The coffee was awfully bad."

I was amused with Jen's take on the coffee. I think the bank had the same supplier as the hospital. One sip of the hospital coffee and you began to think about going to the emergency room. I jokingly asked, "Did you finish the coffee?"

Jen shook her head. "No way, but the cookie wasn't too bad, a little scratchy."

I had to drop my inquiry about Mrs. Kincaid's meeting with the bank president. It really wasn't any of my business anyway. Still curious though, Megan might know about it from her dad. She might tell me about it if it had been anything important.

"You want to paint some more today?" I hoped Jen's arms were tired, I need to mow the Farnhams' lawn and trim their hedges. Bonnie, Mrs. Farnham, told me if I had time, I could cut back her roses, too. Bonnie and Mom were good friends, she had a two-year-old. Bonnie's husband was also a ranger but was in charge of an area farther north.

"No, my arm is getting sore. I'm working on some clothing designs and I've started a painting. I'll take my sketch book with us tomorrow so I can rough out some views from the tower. That's the one we repaired, isn't it?"

"Uh-huh, that's the one. Do you think your grandmother will be able to make it to the top?"

"She's tougher than you think, David. She will take some time, but I think she'll be able to climb all those steps. Do you think you could carry her if she can make it halfway?"

"I know I could carry *you*, but she's heavier than you are, isn't she?"

Jenny smiled, "She's rounder, but shorter. I think we weigh about the same. I'll tell her to eat a light breakfast." We both laughed and Jen tried to squirt me with the hose. I flipped a wet paintbrush at her, but she sidestepped, and I barely got her with a few drops of water.

"You'd better give up, buddy. I've got more ammunition than you." She walked over to the faucet as she kept the hose pointed at me. I didn't mind getting wet, but I was afraid if we got into a tussling match for the hose, she might hurt her collarbone again. I gave up. We had a good laugh and finished cleaning up.

Midafternoon signaled time to go and do some work for the Farnhams' before it was time for dinner. I helped Jenny store the painting materials, told her I'd be back in the morning and left to do some yardwork. I didn't have to go home; all my equipment was in the cargo portion of my car.

I drove to my job site, and when parking at the curb at the Farnhams', I saw three bike riders approaching at a leisurely pace. They were talking, two large riders with one diminutive in the middle. I looked closer and recognized the biker closest to me near the center of the street; it was Dexter. As they got closer, I saw the other riders were the Springs, Devin, and Clair. I hadn't recognized them with their helmets on. They pulled up beside me as I got out of the car. After we all said hi, I asked what they were doing in town. Clair spoke up, "We're riding around town to get some ideas for Dex's remodel."

Dex asked, "Know of any new construction around Suddenly? I'm trying to get some ideas for roof construction. The Springs are helping with their thoughts."

I only knew of one home being constructed and the builders had just started putting up rafters, in the form of manufactured trusses. I had stopped to watch for a few minutes as a crane lifted each supporting structure from a large truck and swung it over to the builders.

"There's a roof being built over on Noble, about six blocks from here: ride straight ahead. You'll see and hear the activity. You can't miss it."

"Thanks. What are you doing here?"

"Oh, yardwork. Can't depend on rewards for finding diamonds to pay for tuition."

Clair and Devin glanced at each other and shrugged their shoulders. They didn't know what Dex and David were talking about, having been in the woods for a month without contact with anyone from Suddenly.

David noticed their reaction, "I'm sure Dex will fill you in."

Dex looked at David, "Yeah, it's kind of a long story. Has anyone received a check from the insurance company yet?"

"I don't think so, but Mrs. Kincaid met with Bruce Isaacs at the bank earlier today. Maybe she got something. I'll ask Jen." David looked at the shrubs, "Well, I've got to get to work. I might see you guys tomorrow. Bye."

The three bike riders rode down the street towards Noble Avenue. David began trimming shrubs after checking the ground for objects that might damage his mower when he later cut the lawn. He didn't want a repeat of the problems he had at the Kincaids about a month ago.

Working efficiently, David completed the job at half past four. He loaded his equipment into his SUV, sat in the front seat to write a bill, and taped the invoice to the Farnhams' screen door. It had been an uneventful job; the family hadn't been around for any interaction. He drove home, went directly upstairs, showered, and got ready for dinner.

Scott got home late from the sheriff's office, but the family was still at the dinner table. David and Danny were talking and trying to entertain Gwen as she squirmed a bit in her mother's arms. Julie was trying to eat and hold the baby, but the two operations were not very compatible. She knew if she put the baby down, screaming would ensue.

Scott kissed Julie and Gwen, took the baby from Julie, and said, "I have some news for you guys." He glanced at the boys as he sat down at the table. "A truck of workers came through town today, heading for the tower thirty-two area northwest of town. They're clearing debris from fire roads."

"Yeah, Dex and I saw them this morning out by the Hadleys'. They were riding in a flatbed truck with a bunch of equipment."

"Did you talk with any of them?"

"Kind of."

"What's that mean?"

"Well, I threw the football to Dex, but it landed in the back of the truck. One of the men told Dex to go long and he threw the ball, almost fifty yards. It was a perfect spiral. Dex caught it and yelled nice throw. The guy yelled back nice catch."

"That was it?"

"Yeah. Why?"

"The guys in that truck are convicts from the state prison."

# CHAPTER 4

I was surprised at Scott's statement, but not really concerned. Those men wouldn't be out and about if they were dangerous. I figured they were in the pen for petty charges, and besides, they wouldn't be coming into Suddenly unless they needed medical treatment. That made me think of Megan, working as a hospital volunteer, but she's too bright to get outsmarted by a convict.

I put the thoughts of convicts in my mind closet, shut the door, and began to consider what I would need to take in the car for tomorrow's visit to tower seventeen. I had to check my medical kit, to make sure it was stocked adequately and see if I would need any gas. I decided the amount of gas was not a problem since we were going only a few miles out of town. I didn't need any food, but I put some bottled water in the fridge. I didn't know if Mrs. Kincaid would bring drinks with her picnic basket.

Although the chances were nil, if I ran out of gas, the walk would be a short one and the weather was nice, but I would be embarrassed. Then it occurred to me that Mrs. Kincaid probably couldn't walk that far. Jen could stay with her while I walked into town to get a gallon of gas. I'd check the tank in the morning.

I woke up at seven o'clock. I heard Scott leave for the office and I could hear the clinking of dishes as Mom loaded the washer. Gwen was sitting in her chair by the kitchen table watching Mom. Danny was stuffing his face with toast and scrambled eggs. I joined him, loaded a plate with the last of the scrambled eggs and dropped two slices of bread in the toaster.

I sat down and asked, "What's going on today, Danny?"

He glanced at Mom; her back was turned as she rinsed some dishes in the sink. "Carl Majors and I are going to ride around and see if we can locate some of those convicts."

Mom raised her voice, "You are not!"

Danny and I laughed. Danny responded, "Just kidding, Mom. Carl and I are going to ride out to Dexter's barn and talk to him about bikes. He should be there, shouldn't he, David?"

"I guess. I saw him with the Springs yesterday. They were going to check out that new construction on Noble."

Mom asked, "What are you up to today, David?"

"Jenny and I are taking Mrs. Kincaid out to tower seventeen. We promised her we'd drive out there for a picnic after the diamond search was over."

"Gosh, that was over two weeks ago. I guess she wasn't in any hurry, huh?"

"She's been deciding on paint colors for her rooms. Everything was white and was in bad shape. She said she couldn't remember the last time the interior was painted."

"Okay, have fun at the tower. I have to deliver Gwen across the street to Mrs. Weems and go to work. Please take care of your own dishes. See you this afternoon."

Mom scooped up Gwen and headed for the front door loaded with the baby and a pink laundry bag full of Gwen's essentials. I think that bag contained much that Gwen could do without, but I'll never be a mom, so what do I know?

Danny carried his dishes to the sink, said, "See you later," and went out the back door to retrieve his bike from the garage. I bussed my dishes, felt my pocket for my keys, grabbed a six-pack of bottled water from the icebox, locked up and headed for my car at the front curb. When I started the engine, the dash showed that I had gas for one hundred thirty miles, so I put getting fuel out of my mind. We wouldn't be running low on gas driving to the tower and back, the round trip was less than twenty miles.

I got to the Kincaids' at eight thirty. I left my dog, Suzy, home; she's doing a lot of scratching and I don't need more dog hair in the car, it sticks to everything, especially passenger's clothing. Jenny was sitting on the porch sketching something. Drawing was her noticeable interest and activity since the diamond hunt had ended. She was already an exceptionally good artist when she arrived in Suddenly and in my opinion, was getting better all the time. I wish I could draw the way she can, so effortlessly.

We both said "Hi," had a few words of small talk, and I began working on the railing. She didn't have much to say and was concentrating on her sketching, so I left her alone. I figured I'd get about an hour's work done before we shoved off for the tower. I heard Mrs. Kincaid rummaging around in the house, but she didn't come outside. I assumed she was preparing things for the picnic. I did hear something different; the radio was on. Music was playing.

I glanced at Jenny and wondered if she was going to take her cigar box of drawing materials with us. Previously, she had indicated she could perch on the deck at tower seventeen and draw for hours, thinking of nothing else, but this time her grandmother would be dictating activities at the tower. I'd wait and see.

When I tried to see what Jenny's subject was, she turned her sketch pad away to keep my prying eyes off her scribbles.

"You're keeping me from seeing what you're sketching, so I'm assuming it's me."

"You wish." She grinned.

"Make me handsome."

She ignored me so I got to work. After nearly a-half-hour of sawing and hammering, I sanded a few rough spots and gave the railing a quick coat of white satin enamel. The label indicated there was primer in the paint. I was using an old brush that was probably on its last application when Mrs. Kincaid appeared on the porch carrying a picnic basket.

"Ready, David?"

I replied, "Hi, Mrs. Kincaid. I'm ready when you are."

She pointed at my brush. "Are you going to clean that brush?"

"Nope, it's a throw-away." I put the lid on the paint can and tossed the brush on the ground at the side of the house.

I glanced at the sketcher, "You ready, Jen?".

Jenny said, "Think we'll need jackets this morning?"

I answered, "Wouldn't hurt to take them. It's pretty cool in the morning shadows. Goosebumps have been known to appear."

Jenny laid her cigar box on the porch and darted into the house. A minute later, she reappeared with two fluffy jackets.

I smiled and volunteered, "Let me take those, you won't need them in the car." I tossed them on the back seat and put the basket on the floor. Then, I assisted Mrs. Kincaid down the steps and helped her in the front passenger seat. "Do you need to lock up the house?" I asked.

"The door's locked, just pull it shut, dear."

I leaped onto the porch and saw that Jenny was in the back seat behind her grandmother. They both had their seatbelts latched. I made sure the house front door was closed and locked, jumped down from the porch and climbed in the driver's seat. After backing to the road, I maneuvered to the right and we were on our way to the tower Jenny and I knew so well from our renovations.

As soon as we left the city limits, the road changed from asphalt to gravel and it seemed in the past month, since Jen and I had rebuilt the tower's interior, the lane into the forest had gotten much rougher. Jenny didn't comment, so I figured it was just my imagination, or she had something else on her mind. When we had gone about a mile, Jen leaned forward and tapped her grandmother's shoulder.

"Put your window down, Gram. The forest smells wonderful out here."

Mrs. Kincaid appeared to be ignoring her granddaughter for about ten seconds, but then I heard the passenger window go down about halfway. I could feel the outside air flowing into the car and then I heard Jenny's window descend all the way. I grinned, thinking I had determined what had taken place. Mrs. Kincaid had taken a few seconds to figure out how to operate the window from the buttons on the arm rest.

At twenty miles per hour, it took about thirty minutes to reach the tower. I never drove much faster on the rutted forest roads for two reasons: to spare my suspension and to prevent hitting wildlife, especially deer and an occasional moose. As we approached the structure, I slowed the car to a crawl, hoping we would see something special. When I could see the tower, I looked at the top, and there it was, an eagle perched on the peak of the roof. I stopped the car and said, "Look out your window, Jenny. Something on top of the tower will catch your eyes."

"Oh! Is that an eagle? Gram! You have to see this!"

Mrs. Kincaid couldn't possibly see through my window or the windshield to see the majestic bird. Our windows were down, so I whispered to her, "Open your door as quietly as possible, slip out and look at the top of the tower. Try not to make any noise."

She nodded and followed my suggestions. I could hear the static discharge as she slid off the seat to the ground. Jenny and I watched the majestic bird from the car, hoping Mrs. Kincaid would at least see the bird take to the air if it were startled.

We watched for nearly a minute before the bird of prey suddenly moved and took to the air, flying over the treetops in the valley below the tower. It was gone in a split second. Then I heard Mrs. Kincaid gasping for air. At first, I thought she would need help, maybe after fainting, but she was smiling and said, "I was holding my breath. I used to be able to swim a long distance underwater, but not anymore. I didn't scare you, did I?"

"I was a little worried when I heard you gasp for air."

"She does that when she gets into the bathtub, David."

"Oh, I do not. Be nice to an old woman. Now show me the tower."

Jenny snickered and said, "I'll bring the picnic basket."

We closed up the car but I left my window down a couple of inches. The summer sun could make the interior unbearably hot. I let Mrs. Kincaid begin walking toward the tower unaided, but I joined Jenny and commented, "Let's escort her to the steps; one of us on each side."

"Yeah. There's a couple of rough spots on the trail. I don't want her to trip and fall. Grams might break something. We'd have to take her to the hospital."

We made it to the stairs without mishap and stopped. Jenny and I wanted her grandmother to see what she had in store if she was going to climb to the top. She looked up the first flight of stairs and said, "I think I can make it up this first section. Then, I'll reevaluate. You might have to go slow, but I'll try to keep up."

"Don't worry Mrs. K, we've got plenty of time. We can rest anytime you want. I'll be right beside you – all the way."

Jenny announced, "I'm going ahead to get some air flowing into the cabin; it's probably very stuffy. Is the door locked?" She zoomed ahead, two steps at a time, not waiting for my reply.

Standing next to Mrs. Kincaid, I didn't want to yell to Jenny. "Shouldn't be. Last time I checked it wasn't." I hoped she heard me.

I took Mrs. Kincaid's arm and we started up the stairs. About halfway up the first flight, she said, "I'd never seen a live eagle like that, only pictures. Oh, I might have seen one at a zoo once. It was a real treat today. Will we see it again?"

"Only at a distance. It won't come back with us here. There are binoculars in the cabin. If its nest is nearby, we might see a couple of them overhead."

I could tell Mrs. Kincaid was getting winded and tired by the time we were midway between the third and fourth landings, but we still had a flight and a half to go. I began to wonder if she was going to make it to the top by herself, or was I going to have to carry her up the remaining steps. I felt certain I could carry her, but it would be slow going uphill.

"I'll have to rest at the next landing, David. My legs are getting tired."

"That's all right. I'll carry you the rest of the way. I want you to see what's in the cabin and be able to see what lookouts can see from the tower. You know, I've never seen the valley during the winter, but I bet it's a spectacular sight with all the snow and no signs of humans. It would be difficult to get out here in the snow."

# CHAPTER 5

We reached the landing at the foot of the fourth flight of stairs with Mrs. Kincaid showing discomfort in breathing and leg weakness. Jenny came down from the cabin and made a face at me when she saw her grandmother's condition.

"How are you doing, Grams?"

"Just give me a few minutes, I'll be okay after I've rested a bit." Her breathing was labored, and her cheeks were red from the exertion. Beads of perspiration were running down her forehead. Jenny mimed mopping her face and I pulled a handkerchief from my back pocket and handed it to Mrs. Kincaid."

"Thank you." She unfolded the square of cloth and mopped her brow as she leaned against the heavy-duty railing.

Jenny whispered into my ear, "She needs to sit down, her heart isn't strong. Can you carry her the rest of the way?"

I murmured back, "If she'll let me."

I moved closer to Mrs. Kincaid and asked, "Would you let me carry you up to the cabin? There are some places to sit up there, and you will be able to see out the windows; maybe catch sight of that eagle again."

"You're trying to talk me into it, aren't you? All right, but I'm a heavy load."

"Not anymore than a tackling dummy." I reflected on what I had said and quickly added, "Not that you're a dummy, Mrs. Kincaid."

She laughed, "I know what you meant, don't worry."

Mrs. Kincaid didn't look heavy, but the number of pounds packaged in her short body had me completely fooled. However, I was able to get her off the ground with a bit of straining, probably starting a case of hemorrhoids. I had never purchased a tube of Preparation H, but I new where it was located at the drug store, in the aisle adjacent to the prophylactics. Every teenage and older male knew that location. Jen got behind me placing one hand on my lower back and the other grasping the railing. She had positioned herself to help me if I stumbled.

We made it to the top of the tower without any problems, but I was happy to put her down and shake off the burn in my arms. Jenny joined us and took her grandmother's arms, clearly concerned about the strain on the old woman. Following a short breather, they started walking around the deck while I went inside the station to make sure everything was in order.

I had been in there for about ten seconds when I heard Jenny call, "David! Come here!"

From the sound of Jenny's voice, her grandmother was in some kind of trouble, possibly a heart attack. I burst out on the deck and found the two women gripping the railing and excitedly pointing to the east. I relaxed when I saw they weren't in any danger.

As I slowly approached them, I asked, "What are you looking at, another eagle?"

I turned my head and tried to find what had attracted their attention. I couldn't pick out anything they were focusing on.

"I don't see anything. What do you see?"

"Grams saw it first and pointed it out to me. It's darting around over the trees. We're wondering if it's some kind of bird looking for dinner."

I scanned the trees and still couldn't see anything moving. "How far out is it?"

Jenny sounded a bit frustrated, "David, it's about the length of a football field out there and moving around those tall trees. Come here and I'll show you. Look where I'm pointing."

I moved close to Jenny. She smelled great. I avoided putting my hands on her waist by concentrating on the area where her outstretched arm was pointing.

"Do you see it?"

"Oh, now I see it. It's a drone."

"Really? You're teasing!"

"No, I'm not. Some forest service management group is probably searching for beetles or something else that might be damaging trees. I'll get the binoculars so you can see it better."

I still hadn't seen what the Kincaids were describing, but I made a guess at what the object was. There weren't any birds that darted around the way they had mentioned. I got the binoculars from the cabin and returned to the women. They were watching the object and were fascinated. I hoped I was right; for the morning, I was lord of the forest in the vicinity of tower seventeen.

I focused the field glasses and watched for the movement. A couple of seconds passed and there it was, five propellers keeping the small unit in the air. It looked like there was a camera attached on the bottom. From this distance, I could see why the ladies thought it might be a bird, but the motions were more like those of a hummingbird than the motions of a bird large enough to be seen at that great distance.

I gave the field glasses to Mrs. Kincaid and went back into the observation room to check the phone and the alidade. It only required a couple of minutes to determine the essential smoke reporting equipment was in good shape. I plopped down on one of the cots and stared at the floor thinking about the drone. I'll ask Mom what it was being used for out near tower seventeen. She'd know all the details.

Jenny's voice brought me out of my short trance. The two women were entering the cabin. "Have a seat, Grams."

Mrs. Kincaid joined me on the cot and kicked off her shoes.

I glanced sideways, "Does the view live up to your expectations, Mrs. Kincaid?"

She sighed with contentment. "Yes, David, it is even more thrilling than I had imagined and I've seen many captivating things over the years." We sat there in silence for a minute, then she turned toward me, "From now on, I'd like you to use my first name instead of Mrs. Kincaid. Maud is much less formal, and since we know each other quite well, I think first names should be used all around."

If I called Mrs. Kincaid, Maud, I felt like I was going to break a cardinal rule of Mom's. To converse with an elderly person, I was told to always use the family name. I was a little hesitant to call Mrs. Kincaid by her given name, but I would follow her request for now. I'd have to consult with Mom and Scott. They'd know what I should do.

We gabbed for about fifteen minutes, sipping on bottled water, when Maud suggested we open the picnic basket and have lunch. She said the fresh forest air and climb up the stairs had triggered her appetite. Jen and I agreed enthusiastically. We spread out a tablecloth on another cot. My hunger grew as we began unpacking the treats. Maud sure knew how to make a picnic lunch.

"Grams, you can cross another item off your bucket list, you've made a visit to a fire prevention tower."

"Well, I wouldn't call it a bucket list; it's more of a small aluminum can list. I also saw an eagle that was nearby. Those birds are majestic when they soar above the trees."

Maud finished eating, struggled to her feet, moved slowly to the door, and went outside. Grabbing the guard rail, she slowly swiveled her head around taking in the forest and began deep breathing the pine scented air.

Jen and I tidied up the picnic things, packed leftovers in the basket and joined Maud. She took another deep breath, gave us a weak smile, and said, "Are you young people ready to return to the dungeon?"

Jenny and I laughed, and we started down the stairs, Jenny carrying the lunch basket. Maud steadied herself with the railing on one side and I took her other arm and descended alongside her. As we went down the steps, I wondered how many years would pass before I would need help navigating multiple flights of stairs. I hoped it would be at least sixty years in the future, about 2080.

Twenty minutes later, we were back at the Kincaids' two story farmhouse. Every time I drove up to that old building, I had the feeling it was unoccupied, even though I knew Jenny and Maud were living there and had been at the old place for nearly four months.

The only changes noticeable from the front driveway were the freshly painted porch railing and a new metal telephone pole standing about fifty feet from the house.

The new telephone line stretched from the pole to the peak of the second story roof and disappeared into the attic. I wondered if the phone company had tacked on extra charges because the Kincaids' home was slightly outside city limits; I imagined Maud had to pay extra for the new service. The first time I talked with Jenny on the phone, I could tell from the sound of her voice she was happy with the new convenience. Land lines were a must in our area where no cell towers existed. Satellite service wasn't yet available in Suddenly, I wasn't sure why not.

I helped Maud up the porch steps and to the front door. Jenny had gone inside and was probably visiting the bathroom. Maud wanted to sit down and when I turned to go, she said, "Thank you so much for the exciting visit to the fire tower. The eagle and drone sightings were unexpected extras."

"You're welcome, Mrs. K Is it all right to call you Mrs. K? I'd feel better than using your first name.?"

She paused for a moment and said, "That's fine with me. I don't want you to feel uncomfortable."

"Awesome. If you ever want to go out there again, just give me a call. Tell Jenny I'll see her tomorrow, I have to take care of a lawn this afternoon. That was a great picnic lunch. Bye."

I turned, made my way out the front door and walked to my car. As I got in, I heard Jenny yell from the house, "Bye, David. See you tomorrow!" I waved, beeped my horn twice, backed out into the street, and drove home, a little sorry I didn't say goodbye to her before driving away. Even though I enjoyed time spent with Jenny, I didn't want to be at the Kincaids' any longer; I was afraid I'd be late getting to the Lawsons' to mow their lawn. I was looking forward to the job, they were a new customer, had a riding mower, and a large flat yard. It was cool that I didn't have to take my own mower.

Cutting lawn grown in the mountains with a riding mower was less fun than I had expected. The expanse of grass of some yards was full of ruts, a few rocks, and little potholes making the mower ride somewhat uncomfortable: the bumps propagating all the way to my teeth. As I started mowing, I wished I had my football mouth guard. The nice thing about the experience was the short mowing time; a normal hour mowing was done in about fifteen minutes. When finished with the rider, I trimmed around the edges with my weed eater. I billed the Lawsons' at fifty percent of my regular fee and headed home for a shower and clean clothes.

I had skipped lunch at home because the picnic at the tower had filled me to the brim. If I had eaten again before riding that mower, I probably would have barfed on the Lawsons' lawn. When I arrived at home, Mom was feeding Gwen in the living room and the little kitchen radio was playing light classical music in the background. Gwen appeared to be asleep and Mom raised a finger to her lips so I would be quiet.

I was gonna tell her what Mrs. Kincaid asked me to call her from now on, but that could wait 'til later. Since Mrs. Kincaid and I had settled with Mrs. K, instead of Maud, I didn't think it was particularly important. I got a couple of cookies from the big jar on the kitchen counter and went up to my room.

I removed my greenish-tinged sneakers without unlacing them and dropped them beside my bed. I heard Danny moving around in his bedroom next to mine and then he wandered in my room. He didn't knock, the door was open, and he just barged in; we both did that, what was there to be private about?

He plopped down on my bed with his dirty shoes hanging over in the air. He knew enough not to dirty up my blanket.

"What's up, Davie?" He knew Davie irritated me.

I grinned and shot back, "Nothing, Danny boy. What'd you do today?"

He leaned back on my pillow with his hands behind his head, "I put about five miles on my bike. Tim Evans and I rode the path around the edge of the golf course and found eleven golf balls in the tall grass. Most of them were in good shape and Mr. Stanley gave us three bucks for 'em. He gave five of them to his friend, some guy from out of town, I think from Dillon. Mr. Stanley said his friend was here on business and they were taking a break to hit some balls around."

"So, what'd you do with the money?"

Danny smiled, "We ate it at the Dairy Queen."

I told Danny about taking care of the Lawsons' yard, but I didn't comment about going to the tower.

# CHAPTER 6

About eleven o'clock, I set my alarm for 7:00 am and crawled into bed. I was reading Moby-Dick by Herman Melville and I was in the boring chapter that discusses the different types of whales around the world, but I couldn't hold my eyes open. Rather than fall asleep and lose my place, I marked the page, turned off my light and closed my eyes.

What seemed like seconds later, Mom was shaking me.

"David! Jenny's on the phone."

At first, I thought I was dreaming, but Mom's voice forced me to open my eyes. I didn't even see Mom and my clock showed 6:51. I told myself to stay in bed until my alarm sounded in nine more minutes.

"David! Jenny says she needs you. Get on the phone. She's crying!"

That statement made no sense and I figured I was still dreaming. When I heard Mom say, "David!", the third time, I flew down the stairs to the phone in the kitchen. On the way down the stairs, I thought, *why would Jenny be crying?*

As soon as I got the phone to my ear, I could hear crying.

"Jenny, are you okay? Are you hurt? Did you call 911?"

She didn't answer immediately, but I heard her sobbing.

"What's wrong, Jen, tell me."

"It's...it's grandma, she's dead. Can you come over?" She stuttered, "I...I don't know what to do."

"Okay, I'll be right over. Go out on the porch. I'll get Megan and we'll be right there."

"No! Don't bring Megan, just you. Come now."

"All right, I'll be there in a few. Hang tight." I heard the click of the phone and I hung up. I didn't know why she only wanted me, but I didn't want to upset her any more than she already was. It was no time to argue. I was standing in the kitchen in my undershorts, barefoot. I had to get dressed.

"Mom!"

Mom was standing in the hall holding baby Gwen and she stepped into the kitchen. "Yes, David. What's going on?"

"Mrs. Kincaid died. I'm going over to be with Jenny. She's really shook up."

"Look at you, David. You need to get dressed. I'll pour a glass of OJ. You can get it as you go out the door."

"Thanks, Mom."

I got dressed as fast as I could and grabbed the OJ as I streaked to my car. I broke the city speed limit getting to Jenny's house in about three minutes. She was sitting on the top porch step and ran toward me as I turned into her driveway.

I popped open the door and she wrapped her arms around me as I stepped out of my Subaru.

"Oh, David, what took you so long? I've been going crazy; I don't know what to do. I didn't call 911, I don't know those people."

"Don't worry about 911, it's not an emergency. We'll call the hospital in a few minutes when an ambulance driver will be on duty. The EMT's are a little poky unless the sheriff calls them. Let's sit on the porch and you can tell me what happened. How did you discover she had died?" We walked to the porch and sat facing each other.

"Okay. Grams wanted to get up early and watch the sunrise, so I set my clock for five a.m. When I got up, dressed, and called out to her, she didn't answer, so I knocked on her door. There was no answer, so I cracked the door and sneaked a look. She was just lying there, and I called to her, thinking she was just sleeping soundly. When she didn't respond, I went to her and felt her forehead. She was cold, so I checked for a pulse and couldn't find any. I even listened for sounds of breathing, there was nothing. She had died in her sleep. What should I do?"

I looked at my watch. It was too early for the hospital to be fully staffed for a new day. The ambulance would take at least twenty minutes, maybe longer, so I asked, "Do you know if she left any instructions if she passed? From her recent activities and wanting to see the sunrise, it's feasible she knew she didn't have long."

"I don't know; she didn't tell me about stuff like that. She seemed her regular self."

I thought for a few seconds, "What did she do at the bank when she saw Mr. Isaacs?"

"She didn't tell me; she acted kind of secretly. She was that way with important things."

"I'll bet she knew she didn't have long and was preparing a will. We need to see Mr. Isaacs." I thought further for a few seconds, "Did she leave a note for you? Like a diary, or something?"

"I really don't know." She tossed her hands in the air. "I have no idea, David."

"Let's go in her bedroom and see if there's something written down."

"You go, I'm not going back in there. I don't even want to go back in the house knowing Grams is in there dead."

"All right. I'll go in and check for a note."

I stood up, touched Jenny's shoulder and said, "It will only take a minute. I won't disturb anything."

I entered the house quietly and made my way to Mrs. K's bedroom and paused at the closed door. I wanted to believe what Jenny had said, but she could be pulling a prank. Mrs. K could be in on it; she was capable of pulling off a joke. I half expected her to throw back her covers and yell "Surprise!" when I entered her room.

I stood there for what I thought was a minute before deciding to venture into Mrs. K's space, even if it was all a ruse. I had never gone inside a mausoleum but that is what I was imagining; a burial site containing a dead person. When I turned the knob and pushed the door wide open, it squeaked, reminding me of a horror movie scene.

Jenny had covered Mrs. K with her bedsheet, so I didn't have to look at the body. I stared at the bed, hoping I wouldn't hear "surprise" and get the hell scared out of me, but I didn't want Mrs. K to be dead either. I waited, but nothing happened. I looked around and saw a drawer in the nightstand next to the bed. There was a half-full glass of water and a small white pill next to the alarm clock. In addition, a little brass lamp on top of the night table probably provided enough light for reading.

I pulled out the drawer and under a small container of tissues was a pocket sized dark-gray notebook. I picked it up and scanned the rest of the room. There was a suitcase standing on end, but it was half open and empty. I didn't see anything else worth investigating, so I left the woman at peace and rejoined Jenny on the porch.

"Did you find anything?"

"Just this," I held out what I had found. I hadn't wanted to open the notebook, so I gave it to Jenny to examine. She laid it on the porch and stared at it for some time before she picked it up and gave a big sigh. I think she was afraid to look inside; it was her grandmother's personal possession. Would Gram have objected?

I sat beside Jenny and waited for what seemed at least a minute before I asked, "Are you going to look inside her diary?" I didn't know what else to call the little booklet. I didn't know if Jenny wanted to share her grandmother's thoughts with me, so I didn't say more.

She looked inside and slowly nodded after reading the first page. She turned the page, then another and quickly flipped through the rest of the diary.

"There's writing on only one page, David. She says if I'm reading it, she must have passed on. I'm supposed to see Mr. Isaacs at the bank. He has her will and power of attorney." She closed the book and held it to her chest like it was sacred. Jenny looked at me and asked, "Should I call the hospital?"

I checked the time. I had spent nearly fifteen minutes in Maud's room, but I thought it had been a much shorter time.

"Yeah, someone will be on duty now. Where's your phone?"

Jenny pointed at the house, "In the living room. You call, please."

It was obvious to me, she didn't want to go back in the house, so I did what she requested. I knew the hospital number and dialed it on the rotary phone. I think Mrs. K had selected the rotary cause she was familiar with using it. Two rings and I heard Nurse Berg's voice.

"This is the Suddenly hospital. How may I help you?"

"This is David Drum, Nurse Berg. I'm out at the Kincaids' place. Mrs. Kincaid died last night in her sleep. Can you send the ambulance? Jenny and I are here. Jenny's a little shook up about it."

"I recommend you take Jenny to your place for breakfast if you haven't eaten. I'll take care of everything in the house and lock up. Make sure Jenny has a key."

"That sounds awesome, Mrs. Berg. I'm glad you were there to take my call."

"I'll phone you at home or call Megan when we're finished at Kincaids'. All right?"

"Sure. That's fine with me. We found a note about Mrs. Kincaid's will. We'll be going to see Mr. Isaacs at the bank, so we night not be home when you call."

"Well, I'll leave a message with someone. You take care, David."

"Thanks, Mrs. Berg."

The voice was gone. Nurse Berg had hung up. I placed the phone in its cradle and went outside to talk with Jenny.

She looked up at me and said, "What's going to happen?"

"I talked with nurse Berg and she wants you to go to my place while the ambulance is here. Do you have a house key?"

Jenny tapped the pocket of her jeans, "Uh-huh. They're going to take Grandma and lock up?"

"That's right. We'll have some breakfast at my place and then visit with Mr. Isaacs. Hopefully, he'll know your grandma's wishes. He'll make all the arrangements."

Jenny stood and asked me to lock the front door. I pressed the button on the handle and pulled the door shut."

Jenny frowned. "And how will the ambulance people get in?"

An obvious question. I thought for a second, "Let's leave a key inside the notebook here on the porch. Where's your grandmother's key?"

"I don't know. Let's just leave the door unlocked. Who's going to rob Grams?"

"Yeah, good question." Jenny gave me her key; I unlocked the door and returned the key. We walked slowly to my car and started back to my place.

On the way, Jenny said, "I don't want to stay in that old place all alone. What am I going to do?"

I didn't have to think. "You can stay at our place in the apartment over the garage. It's pretty nice."

Jenny was quiet for a second and then uttered, "Okay. Think one of your dogs could keep me company?"

"Sure. But let's go to the bank and talk with Mr. Isaacs after breakfast, then we'll go back to your place and get some of your things."

I glanced at Jenny and she was leaning back with her hands clasped in her lap and her eyes closed. I decided to shut up.

# CHAPTER 7

When I entered my driveway, and slowed to a stop, I saw Megan get up from her front porch swing and coming toward us across the lawn. As I opened my door, Meg leaned forward and whispered, "Your mom told me about Mrs. Kincaid."

Jenny was still sitting with her eyes shut and I replied to Megan, "Maybe you can give her your shoulder to cry on; she hasn't displayed much emotion yet. I guess she's in shock." We went around to the passenger side and I opened the door, reached in, and released Jen's seatbelt. Thinking she might be a little unsteady, I helped her out.

Megan took Jenny's right hand to steady her and said, "I'm so sorry to hear about your grandmother. What can I do to help?"

They hugged tightly and for the first time, I saw tears flowing down Jen's cheeks. As Jenny cried openly, the two women walked slowly toward my front door. I darted ahead and made way into the house. After Jenny and Megan were seated on the sofa, I noticed a small Post-it pad containing a note. Mom had written that Danny was off to see a friend and wouldn't be home for lunch. That was good news for me. I wouldn't have to explain what had happened.

Megan had her arm around Jenny's shoulders and Jenny had her head bent forward with her hands in her lap, eyes closed, completely deflated. I guessed she had realized the enormity of what had happened. She was barely holding things together.

I asked them if they wanted to have some lunch. Megan looked up and nodded, but Jenny shook her head. I think she wanted to be left alone. I motioned for Megan to come into the kitchen. Meg stood, swung Jen's legs onto the sofa, getting her lying down.

Megan and I ate sandwiches and drank ice water, every so often checking on Jenny. After about ten minutes, I asked Megan, "Is she asleep?"

Meg check and replied, "No, she just wiped her eyes. I think the crying is over."

"I wanted to know because we're going to see your dad at the bank."

"My dad?"

"Yeah. Apparently he has Mrs. K's will and power of attorney."

"He's busy in the morning but should be available at one o'clock unless he has some other appointment. I'll call him right now, so he'll know you're coming."

Meg grabbed the phone and talked with someone at the bank, but I could tell by the conversation it wasn't her father, probably his secretary. Placing the phone back on its cradle, she said, "Dad will be expecting you soon after one p.m."

"Thanks, Meg. I'm glad you were here to help."

"You're welcome. I'd better go home and change; I've got to be at the hospital at one o'clock. You gonna be all right with Jenny?"

"Yeah. When we get to the bank, I think she will perk up. She'll be curious about what her grandmother said in her will."

"Okay, I'll talk to you later this evening. Thanks for the sandwich, it was very tasty." She grinned, gave me a kiss, and left me with Jenny. It was 12:38."

I cleaned up the lunch plates and utensils in about five minutes before sitting down on the edge of the sofa beside Jenny. She reached out and gripped my left hand and squeezed.

"Thank you, David. Are you ready to take me to the bank?"

"I was just about to ask you that."

"Let me up to visit the bathroom. Then, we'll visit with Mr. Isaacs and see what he can tell me."

"Okay. You're sure you don't want something to eat?"

"I'm sure. Ask me again after we find out what Grams said in her will."

I stood up and she swung her legs from the sofa and got to her feet. A few minutes in the bathroom and she appeared in fairly good spirits. She gave me a weak smile, pulled on my arm and we left the house. I shut the door, made sure it was locked and we got in my car.

We arrived in the bank lobby at a couple of minutes past one. There were several patrons at the counter taking care of business and we sat down in the waiting area. I guess Mr. Isaacs was waiting because he appeared immediately, nodded to me, and approached Jenny.

"Miss Kincaid, I'm so sorry about your grandmother." He took her hands in his. "I only dealt with her once, but I was impressed. She seemed to be an exceptionally fine woman. Come into my office and I will go over some things with you. Would you like David to join you?"

Jenny nodded and said, "Yes, sir. Is that all right?"

"No problem at all. David is welcome and should be present if that's what you want."

Mr. Isaacs led the way as we walked about twenty feet to the president's office.

I could see why depositors received such a small interest on their savings accounts. Everything in the room was high class, from the rugs to the light fixtures. Isaacs extracted a file from a large cabinet that occupied one entire wall and sat behind his massive, polished desk. He occupied one of those high back executive chairs that I imagined cost as much as all the furniture in my living room.

A large red desk pad trimmed in leather took up nearly half the desktop and computer equipment the other half. I envisioned the red pad was from the blood of the bank's customers. Fictional stories had left a negative view of banks in my mind. He flipped open a file folder and looked at Jenny. "Shall we get started?" He didn't wait for a response, reached forward to his phone console, pressed a button, and said, "Please hold my calls, Phyllis." I guessed Phyllis was his secretary.

He began to read; *These are my final wishes. Jenny Kincaid, daughter of my only son, James Edward Kincaid, is to receive my home in Suddenly, Montana. She will also inherit all of my bank holdings and any money received from the recent diamond recovery, with the following restrictions:*

*Twenty thousand dollars will be available to care for the farmhouse, she will receive a monthly allowance of four hundred dollars for living expenses, and the remainder of my estate is to be used for her college tuition. Mr. Isaacs has power of attorney and will monitor all of my granddaughter's expenses until she reaches the age of twenty one. At this time, my estate is valued at four hundred twenty eight thousand dollars. Mr. Isaacs has agreed to a one thousand dollar stipend per year for monitoring the various account's activities. James Edward Kincaid will not receive any benefits from my estate.*

Jenny and I looked at each with our mouths open; we didn't know what to say.

A few seconds later, I smiled and said, "It looks like art school is in the cards for sure, Jen."

She grabbed my hands, "I'd rather have Grams back. I can always find a way to go to college."

"Well, she thought a lot of you, Jen. She really loved you."

Mr. Isaacs followed up with, "Today, the bank received a cashier's check from Diamond Insurance Brokers in the amount of fifteen thousand dollars. If it is agreeable to you, Jenny, I will use that money to establish the farmhouse care fund and add five thousand more from Mrs. Kincaid's estate funds." He looked questioningly at Jen.

"Um, sure. That sounds fine with me. Thank you, Mr. Isaacs. Is there anything else?" Jenny stood, "Oh! What about my grandmother's funeral? Did she make any requests?"

"She did. She wants to be cremated and David Drum to disperse her ashes at the location where he sees another eagle. She believed the sight of an eagle guaranteed luck for the Kincaids."

Jenny didn't know how to react to her grandmother's request. She frowned and looked at David, "Would you do that?"

"Wow, I didn't know she had such confidence in me. Of course, I'll do it. We'll do it together."

"But you might have to haul her ashes around for some time, David. Do you really want to do it? You don't have to, she'd never know, and I won't hold you to it."

"I'll do it; it's her last request, Jen. If she had asked me, I'd have promised. Besides, when I drive out there again, it won't take long before I see an eagle."

I glanced at Mr. Isaacs and he was smiling. "I told Mrs. Kincaid you would agree. She thought you would, but she asked for my opinion."

I felt a little uneasy, but I was determined to carry out Mrs. K's last wish. She had grown on me and I treated her like she was my own grandmother.

He was still smiling, "I'll notify you after final preparations. Mrs. Kincaid didn't want any kind of service. She said all her acquaintances are dead or wouldn't come back to Suddenly to remember her. If they did, they'd be lying. If someone that knew her returned, it would just be a coincidence."

I had to admit that sounded like Mrs. K. She was a no-nonsense lady.

We left the bank with confidence that Mr. Isaacs would handle all the details of Maud's last wishes. We buckled our seat belts and sat there at the curb for a minute, digesting what we had just experienced.

Jen broke the silence, "God, all my financial worries have evaporated in just a few minutes. I had no idea Grams had such belief in me. Now I have to be a success." She sighed and looked at me for a second, "I'm hungry. Take me somewhere to get something good to eat."

I said the first thing that came to mind, "Dairy Queen here we come." We both started laughing, Jenny first, and I joined in after I realized she would be happy with some soft ice cream. My only worry was the possibility of brain freeze.

It was 2:13 when we began attacking two large vanilla cones while sitting in a booth watching customers, mostly youngsters, come and go at the DQ. I was consumed with thinking about Jenny being a rich young woman. I was happy Jenny's near future was assured by her inheritance. And then I had a second thought. Mrs. K had received an insurance check, so I should soon be getting one, too. I hope it's a big one. I put in quite a few hours recovering those stolen diamonds.

Jenny was blinking and reached for some water. Then she grabbed my hand, closed her eyes, and breathed hard through her mouth. She stopped with the ice cream for a moment, took another drink of water, and asked, "Do you think Grams has been removed from the house by now? I don't want to see somebody hauling her off like a sack of potatoes."

My watch read 2:25. Plenty of time had passed since I had contacted Nurse Berg. Her efficiency was well known, so I was certain Mrs. K had been moved from her bedroom and the Kincaid residence. There wouldn't be any sign of the ambulance.

"Everything should be okay now. Let's get your things and move you into our apartment."

We sat opposite each other in that red vinyl upholstered booth finishing off the ice cream, then we visited the restrooms before getting in the car. Jenny removed traces of tears from her light makeup and any sticky evidence spots left from the cone. I washed my hands and wiped my face with a wet paper towel. I didn't want stuff running down my forearm as I drove back to Kincaids'. I had to admit being sloppier than Jenny.

Jenny was starting to stress out as we made our way through the half-mile drive to her farmhouse. I pulled up behind her pickup, no other vehicles were there. We climbed the steps and stopped at the front door. Jenny pulled her key from her jeans and opened the entranceway. She hesitantly entered, looked around suspiciously, and pointed down the hallway. "Would you go in there and see if Grams is gone?"

I nodded and walked to Mrs. K's open bedroom door, so I knew Nurse Berg had been there. I had shut the door earlier when I found the notebook containing the message to Jenny about the will. I looked in and saw the bed had been stripped down to the bare mattress. It looked as if Maud had never been there, a sad image, but Jenny would be free of worry about seeing her dead grandmother. I wondered if that image would fade from Jen's memory, or be stuck there forever. I shut the door quietly and went back into the living room.

Jenny had an expectant look, "Is it all right?"

"It's okay, she's gone. Pack up your things and let's get out of here."

I didn't want to be in that house where Maud had recently passed any more than Jenny did. That's how I felt. I began to wonder how long Jenny would want to stay at our apartment before she would decide to return to the farmhouse. Would she want to come back and be alone in that old farmhouse?

That last thought gave me an idea. Somehow, I had to plant the idea that Megan and Jenny could room together at the Kincaid farmhouse. But how was I going to get that notion in the thoughts of at least one of the women? As the concept ruminated, I realized I might suffer the consequences, I would probably have less time with both the girls. Could my hormones be out of adjustment?

# CHAPTER 8

Twenty-three miles northwest of Suddenly, near shouting distance of the Idaho border, the cleanup crew from the state pen had been busy clearing roads for two days straight. In some cases, firefighting and logging roads hadn't been traversed in months and required major attention. Much of the work entailed removing vegetation from the shoulders of, for the most part, old logging roads, used frequently sixty or more years ago but now only occasionally by rangers.

Three of the men were filling potholes, two were manning chainsaws, and the others were trimming vegetation and tossing it into pick-up piles to be gathered later by another crew. Jay manned a chainsaw, as did Guns. They forged ahead of the others, trimming large fallen branches, and sectioning downed trees that blocked portions, if not the entire road. The majority of the roadways were single lanes with occasional turnouts to permit small vehicles to pass the large slow moving logging trucks on the winding mountain trails bulldozed from the mountainsides. Many of the roads were made for one purpose, getting logs to the mills.

Jay and Guns were attacking a fifty foot dead tree that had fallen across the road blocking passage. One of the prison guards, Todd Grimsby, six feet tall, built like a prize fighter and with facial scars, was giving directions; he had worked a forest fire fighting crew in his younger years, twenty-two years previously when he was in his late twenties. However, he had been a helicopter pilot, carrying fire retardant and water to help hotshot crews extinguish forest fires. Grimsby had little experience working with men at ground level. That was a potential problem.

Guns, six feet-six and weighing nearly three hundred pounds, was one of the men on a chainsaw operators. The training team had assigned him a chainsaw thinking the big guy could man-handle it. A tree stood no chance of fighting back. But knowledge of the forest and logging were things that Guns lacked.

Jay had just removed most of the dead branches from the trunk except for a four-inch stub touching the ground in the roadway. Sweating profusely, he shut off his saw and walked toward the drinking water container. He had to have a drink to replace some of the water he had lost at work during the hottest part of the day.

He called back to Guns, "Shut'er down and get a drink." But Guns had one last limb in his sights, and he was unaware of any danger. He reached under the trunk with the twenty-two inch bar and gunned the engine making quick work of that four inch diameter limb holding the massive tree slightly above the ground. Jay heard the splintering wood and Guns cry out when the big guy was knocked to the ground, the tree pinning his leg to the roadway.

Jay dropped the half-filled paper cup and ran to see how badly Guns was hurt.

The guard, unable to see what happened, walked over slowly, "He'll be all right; he just got knocked on his ass."

Jay could see Guns was really injured. The big man was clinching his teeth and grabbing at his leg.

"It's broke, Jay. I heard somethin' crack and it hurts like hell."

Jay looked at Todd and said, "We'll need the truck jack to lift that damn tree and Guns will need a doctor. We'll have to take him in to the Suddenly Hospital. If we don't, he could lose his leg."

"Think it's that bad?" Todd looked down at Guns and scratched his jaw.

"Damn right. He'll need a doctor." Jay's frustration with Todd was evident in his voice. "Call the Sheriff to come out here and get Guns. That ambulance might get high-centered."

Todd stated, "Radio's in the truck. You go back. I'll stay here with Guns."

The guard had made a good call, the truck was only a few minutes away; they weren't far ahead of the others, half a mile at most. Jay figured if he carried the truck jack it would take extra time. Maybe he could get one of the other workers to assist. They could alternate carrying the jack, shortening the time Guns would be pinned under the dead tree. Jay knew that Guns had about fifteen minutes before the lack of circulation in his leg might require an amputation. He broke into a run; it was going to be a close call.

As Jay ran through stretches of sunlight and shade, he kept thinking what he would tell the other guard, Demetrius Duncan, or DD, as the prisoners referred to him. DD was medium height and muscular, but a bit slow mentally, compared to Todd. Most prisons tolerated him.

Jay's wind was beginning to dwindle, and his mouth felt stuffed with cotton as he began to hear men working but couldn't yet see them. The clank of shovels against rock and occasional voices meant he was getting close. They should be around the next bend.

Then he saw the truck, moving slowly toward him. The driver must have seen Jay, since he blinked the headlights. The truck stopped and DD, the short but muscular guard stepped down from the cab. Jay could see his frown.

DD yelled, "What's the matter, Jay?"

"Guns is pinned under a log. I need the truck jack — and call the sheriff. Guns will need to see a doc; we think his leg is busted."

DD clambered into the cab and got on the phone. Jay was bent over with his hands on his knees taking deep gulps of air and looking on the truck bed to find the jack.

He couldn't see it.

"Where's the damn jack!"

"Take it easy, Jay. It's below the bed in that metal box." DD pointed underneath the truck bed behind the cab. The box was locked.

"Where's the key, DD? Come on, we're losing time. I've got to get that jack back so we can lift that tree off Guns."

"It's the ignition key. How far did you come?"

"Half a mile."

DD shook his head, "That jack is old-school; you can't carry it half a mile in less than ten, maybe fifteen minutes. It's too damn heavy."

Jay paused for a second, "Take the truck, DD. Do what's right."

"Hell, Jay. I can't leave these guys."

"Okay. I'll take the truck. You stay here."

"You don't have a license, Jay. I can't let you take the truck anyway. It's against regulations."

"Who's gonna know, DD? Come on, let me drive the truck and save Guns' leg." Jay stared at DD and was near the boiling point. "Come on, DD. Let me have the truck."

The other prisoners had clustered around Jay and DD and were beginning to chant, "Give him the truck!"

"Oh, all right. Take the GoDDamned truck. If you wreck it, we'll all go to hell."

The guys whistled and cheered. Jay vaulted into the cab, started the engine, and stepped on the gas, showering the men in a cloud of debris. Jay was back at the accident site in about one minute. The truck skidded to a stop and Jay pulled the key from the dash and dropped to the ground. He had the jack out in a few seconds and was positioning it under the tree about ten feet from Guns. Apparently, Guns was unaware of Jay's actions. He laid there with his right arm covering his eyes blocking the sun.

"Hang in there, Guns. I'm gonna lift the tree. When you're freed, Todd will pull you out. I think it's gonna hurt like hell." Jay glanced at Todd and asked, "How long has it been?"

"About eleven minutes. Will we need a tourniquet?"

"Hell, I don't know. See any blood?"

"No, but what if an artery is leaking internally?"

"Jesus, Todd, you would have to think of that. We'll have to watch the leg and apply a tourniquet if we think it will help. Hopefully, the sheriff will be here in a few minutes, maybe with a nurse or doctor. We can use Gun's belt to apply pressure."

"Well, here goes." Jay started moving the log slowly. When the trunk had begun to rise off his leg, Guns grabbed at his leg and screamed in pain. Jay rapidly pumped the jack and got the dead tree above Gun's leg far enough so Todd could pull the big man from under the dead weight.

Jay wrestled a large rock under the tree and recovered the jack. Guns appeared to be unconscious, unable to tolerate the severe pain when circulation began to return to his leg or motion of the broken thigh bone. Jay didn't know if those were the only causes of Gun's succumbing to pain. Jay had never suffered a broken bone nor had a tree ever fallen on him, not even a small tree limb.

Jay placed the truck jack back in the box beneath the bed and locked the metal case. He looked over at Guns, frustrated that he couldn't help the big man any further. He could hear a siren in the distance; the sheriff was on his way, hopefully accompanied by a nurse or doctor.

Guns was stirring and trying to sit up, but as soon as he tried to move his damaged leg, he flopped back to the ground in pain. Jay imagined the medical aid would be administered with a shot and Jay grinned when he recalled Guns stating that he hated needles. This was going to be interesting.

Todd had gotten a paper cup of water for Guns and was trying to get the big guy to take the container and help himself to a drink. Guns was able to roll so one elbow was planted and he accepted the water with his other hand.

Jay determined from the loudness of the siren; medical aid was getting close. In another minute or two, a nurse or doctor would arrive. Todd and Jay couldn't do anything more for Guns but wait for help. The siren stopped abruptly, and Jay commented, "I wonder if they stopped where the other guys are?"

Todd tipped up his cup and swallowed, "Don't worry, they'll send them along."

Jay knew Todd was right, Guns was only a couple of minutes from getting assistance. "It seems like it's taking forever."

Todd yawned, "Yeah, kind of like a kid waiting for Christmas."

It was a mild surprise when a vehicle approached that was not a police cruiser, but a rather large ambulance with a woman driver.

Jay said, "What the hell?"

Both doors of the ambulance swung open and two women got out. Jay's first impression was that the driver was about his age, a bit overweight, probably had several kids, and the passenger appeared to be a teenager, a strikingly pretty young woman with long dark hair. All business, they opened the rear doors, pulled out a medical bag and a gurney. The young lady was trying to push the gurney but was having difficulty getting the wheels to cooperate, they seemed to have their own idea as to direction of travel.

Jay quickly stepped over to help, "Here, miss, I'll give you a hand."

"Thank you," replied the pretty one, keeping her eyes on the gurney.

The older woman was crouched beside Guns and was squeezing his broken leg behind the knee. Jay wondered what she was doing. He pointed towards Guns,

"What's she doing?"

"Nurse Berg is checking for a pulse on his leg. Who are you?"

"I'm Jay. That's Guns on the ground and that guy's Todd. He's a prison guard. Are you a nurse, too?"

"No, I'm a student volunteer." She didn't say her name.

"How are you gonna get Guns on that contraption, he's big, almost three hundred pounds."

"Don't worry, it lowers to about a foot off the ground. Listen."

Megan turned slightly and looked down the road. A police cruiser came speeding up behind the ambulance and skidded in the dirt as it stopped. A low cloud of dust drifted off the road into the trees. The driver got out, slammed his door, and started toward Nurse Berg. He gave a slight wave to Megan and said, "You all right, daughter?"

Megan smiled and replied, "I'm fine. Glad you're here to help." She looked back at Jay and said, "That's Sheriff Wilson. He'll help get the patient into the ambulance."

"He's your father?"

"Kind of. It's complicated."

Jay and Megan rolled the gurney across the bumpy dirt road to where Guns was on the ground. Nurse Berg was talking to Guns.

"I don't think you have an arterial problem; you have a strong pulse in your lower leg but I think your femur is fractured."

Guns squinted, "Femur?"

"Yes, that's the upper bone of your leg, your thigh bone. I'll give you something for the pain. We'll have to move you to get you in the ambulance." She reached into the medical kit and prepared a small syringe with morphine. She moved the syringe toward Guns, but he shoved her hand aside.

"No needles!"

"Look, you big sissy, it's a tiny needle and you won't feel a thing. I promise."

"Nope, no damn needles!"

"Okay, but you'll probably pass out when we move you. We can't hold your leg in a fixed position out here. You're just too big."

Guns responded, "Just do the best you can, but no needles."

Todd, Sheriff Wilson, Jay and the two women struggled with the three hundred pound patient and succeeded with positioning him on the gurney, however, it took all three able bodied men to get Guns and the gurney into the ambulance.

# CHAPTER 9

Thirty minutes later, Nurse Berg backed the ambulance up to the emergency room doors at the rear of the hospital. The quick response doors swung open and Frank Nivens, the five-foot seven orderly, a slender man wearing glasses, stepped up to the ambulance and accessed the gurney carrying Guns. When he saw the size of the patient, he hesitated, thinking he better wait for assistance.

Mrs. Berg joined Frank and said, "The sheriff and this gentleman's partner will be here in just a minute. When you get some help, take the patient into the x-ray room. We need a picture of his left femur. Oh, by the way, he's a state prisoner and was working on a road crew. A large tree fell on him."

Frank nodded, stepped back inside the hospital, and leaned against the wall counting floor tiles. He was used to waiting for someone in authority to give him directions. He watched the patient on the gurney but couldn't detect any movement. He wondered if the large man was deceased. Why would Nurse Berg want an x-ray of a dead man's leg? He heard a car drive up and two doors slam. He pushed away from the wall and moved beside the ambulance and looked outside to the parking lot. Two men were approaching, one was the sheriff, the man following was wearing clothes like the man in the ambulance.

Nurse Berg scurried past Frank to greet the approaching men and said, "We need some help, Sheriff. Can you gentlemen give us a hand with the gurney?"

The extra crew helped Frank get Guns into the x-ray room for a picture of his left femur. A clean break was evident, but the bone had been twisted and traction was going to be necessary to realign the segments. Dr. Rennick and Nurse Berg were talking with Guns. The doctor started explaining the procedure.

"In order to get your bone aligned, we'll have to pull on your leg, put it in traction. Then, we'll have to attach a metal plate to the bone to maintain alignment."

Guns was getting upset, frowning, glancing around for some kind of assistance, not seeming to comprehend what was going to take place. He interrupted, "Hey, Doc, can Jay come in here and listen?"

"Sure, if you like." Rennick opened the curtain to the hallway and said, "Is Jay here?"

Jay was talking to Sheriff Wilson and Megan in the hall, explaining how the accident occurred. He was in mid-sentence when he heard his name.

"Right here." He raised his hand and stepped toward the doctor.

"The patient would like you to be present as I go over the procedure that is planned. Please join us in the x-ray lab."

"All…all right, but I don't know anything about fixing broken bones."

Jay stood beside Guns and tried to relax, expecting the medical terms to be confusing. When Dr. Rennick explained things in layman's terms, he was surprised.

As the procedure of attaching a metal plate to the bone was explained, Guns reacted, "You gonna cut open my leg?"

"We have to, or you'll never heal properly, and you'll have a limp until you die."

Jay understood Gun's hesitancy, "Hey, Guns, you'll have a scar about six inches long. It'll look like you were in a knife fight."

Guns thought for a moment and then asked, "Will I watch what you're doing when you cut on me?"

Dr. Rennick glanced at Jay and winked, "Sure, you'll see everything we do."

"Okay, but no…no needles. All right?"

"We'll give you a pill before the operation and you won't feel a thing. How does that sound?"

Guns nodded, "Sounds good. When you gonna do it?"

"In about half an hour. We have to remove your pants and scrub your leg."

"You have a male nurse?"

"Sure. Whatever you want. We'll move you to another room where the light is better. In a minute, a nurse will bring in a pill for you to take."

Guns leaned his head back, "Thanks, Doc."

Jay stepped out of the room into the hallway and talked with the doctor.

"Hey, Doc. He's gonna go postal when you give him a needle. I won't be able to help; he's as strong as five men put together when he gets mad."

Dr. Rennick smiled, "After he swallows that pill, he won't cause any trouble. He'll be awake, but he won't remember a thing. We'll give him anesthesia, but he'll be able to move his leg if we need him to. What's his real name, anyway? It surely isn't Guns."

Jay grinned, "He's Eugene Tanner, but don't call him Eugene. The other prisoners will find out, razz him and he'll start a fight, even with a broken leg. He made me promise not to tell anyone at the prison his real name."

"I won't say a word. What about your last name? Is Jay your real first name?"

"My first name is John; no one needs to know the rest, but it's not a secret. I just don't want people bringing up my past life. I want it dead and buried; better for everyone."

"All right. I'd better get ready for surgery; it's going to take a while."

"Say, Doc, would it be okay for me to watch the operation?"

Dr. Rennick hesitated, looked at Jay seriously for a few seconds, and replied, "Are you squeamish when you see blood and open wounds? We don't want to have to take care of another patient in the operating room."

"I've been studying surgical techniques in the prison library so I don't think it will bother me. I've seen some open wounds before, you know, during prison riots."

An hour later, the doctor was drilling holes in Gun's femur and attaching a metal plate to hold the bone segments in the proper orientation. Megan was sitting near Jay, also observing the surgery. She was curious why Jay was in prison and wondered why he had volunteered to fight forest fires, too. Knowing Dr. Rennick didn't like observers to talk during surgery, assisting nurses being an exception, she motioned for Jay to leave the room so they could talk. Jay frowned, wondering why the pretty girl wanted him to follow her into the hall, but his curiosity ruled, and he decided to find out what she was up to.

Megan had stopped at the coffee machine and purchased a cup of high test. She noticed Jay was eyeing the choices available, but he made no attempt to buy anything. He looked away from the machine at Megan, "What is it, young lady?"

"I don't want to embarrass you or anything, but I've been wondering why you have been in prison, but you don't have to tell me. I just had to ask."

"Do you mind if I call you Megan? It's monogrammed on your pocket."

"No, I don't mind. I heard someone call you Jay. Is that your first name?"

Jay thought for a few seconds before answering, "No. Actually, my first name is John. Not many of us behind bars use our real name, mostly nick names. When we get out it's harder to contact former prisoners that way. You know, keeps us going straight."

"I guess that makes sense. I would never have thought of that."

"Well, I'll tell you how I got in prison. Two other guys and me robbed a bank and got caught the same day. We didn't even have time to count the money."

Megan almost laughed, tried to hold back a grin, but was unsuccessful.

"Did I say something funny?"

"No, not at all. My father is the president of the local bank. I just thought it was humorous that I'm talking to a former bank robber."

Jay winked, "I guess I'd better not stick up your father's bank, then. I'd be a chief suspect." Jay was watching Megan drink her coffee. Megan noticed and realized the prisoner had no money.

"Oh, I'm sorry. Can I buy you coffee?" She reached into her pocket, pulled out a dollar bill, and handed it to Jay.

"Thanks. All I had to drink today is warm tap water where we were working. No ice, either. Just the basics for prisoners. There's not much for rewards when you're in lockup."

Jay fed the dollar into the machine and pressed a couple of buttons. A cup fell into position and hot liquid filled the container. He laughed, "Sounds like a horse taking a pee." He looked at Megan and blushed, "Sorry, I didn't think of present company. Did that embarrass you?"

Megan chuckled, "No. That didn't bother me. We hear all kinds of crazy things about body functions at the hospital, some are funny, some are gross." As they talked, she got the feeling she had seen Jay before, but that was impossible. Yet the way he held his cup and moved his hands as he conversed, reminded her of someone, but she couldn't think of who it was. She decided that it was a case of déjà vu and dropped the notion.

"I have one last question. Do you have a family, a wife, and children? Are they waiting for you when you get out?" Megan thought she had overstepped, but Jay seemed willing to reveal some of his background. Maybe he was willing to talk about things because in his years in prison, he had very few conversations with people from the outside world.

"I have a son. My wife had cancer. She didn't die of cancer, though, she died in an auto accident. My wife and brother had come to visit me at the pen in Missouri and on the way home a drunk smashed into them. My son was told I had died. My mother didn't want him to know I was in prison; it might cause more harm than losing us in an accident."

"So, your mother and son live together?"

"She died a few years ago. He's on his own. I don't know where he is now."

"Are you going to get in touch with him?"

Jay began to feel that he had told the girl too much already and besides, she had wanted to ask only one more question. The conversation with this young woman was getting too personal and too complicated. He decided not to answer and changed the topic.

"I'd like to know how Guns is doing. Do you think the doc is through operating?"

"Stay here, I'll check."

Megan returned to the operating room and Dr. Rennick was discussing post-operative instructions with the nurses. Guns had been transferred to a regular hospital bed but was in recovery sleeping.

Nurse Wallace motioned for Megan to move to the foot of the bed. She took the opposite end and began guiding the mobile apparatus out into the hallway. Jay saw the bed rolling down the hallway away from him and he hustled to catch up.

The nurse saw Jay and said, "Your friend will be in room 127 for a couple of days."

Noting the concern on Jay's face, the nurse commented, "Mr. Tanner won't be working with you for the remainder of the summer. He'll be transferred to the local jail until he can be transported to the prison hospital. He'll remain in Suddenly for the next two days."

"He's not gonna like being put in a jail cell. Do you think I can come visit him?"

Nurse Wallace replied, "You'll have to talk with the supervisory guards about that. I'm sure something can be arranged. I take it you gentlemen are good friends?"

Jay nodded, "Guns has been showing me the fundamentals of weightlifting and body building and I've been teaching him how to read. We've spent a lot of time in the prison library over the last year or so. Our cells are in different parts of the pen."

Sheriff Wilson appeared in the hallway outside the operating room. As he approached the nurse and Jay, he said, "Mrs. Wallace, do you know anything about that maroon sedan in the parking lot?"

"Yes, Sheriff. It was left there last week by a woman named Kendra Hughes. She had a sprained ankle and said they'd be back for the car in a few days."

"They? She was with somebody?"

"Uh-huh. She was with her husband. They left on a motorcycle, pulling a little trailer. They looked like they had been camping. She needed a shower and some deodorant."

"Did she say how the ankle got sprained?"

"Her husband seemed a little irritated. He said they were wading across a stream and she slipped on a mossy rock and tumbled in the water. Her clothes were dry though. I think she drove the car and he was on the bike, but I didn't see them arrive. I just saw them leave."

Sheriff Wilson rubbed his chin and thought for a second. "Please give me a call when they return. If they don't pick up the car in a few days, we'll impound it as a derelict." He smiled, "We can't let abandoned vehicles take up space in the hospital parking lot, can we?"

# CHAPTER 10

Sheriff Wilson asked Jay to come outside the emergency entrance to talk. Jay drained the last few drops from his coffee cup, tossed the empty in the trash and followed the sheriff. Jay was prepared for some type of third degree and was ready to clam up.

"Have you heard any scuttlebutt from the other workers about escaping the work detail?"

"Nope, nothing. What leads you to suspect a break is planned?" Jay was going to be cooperative, and not be involved in any foolishness at this stage in his life. He wanted to serve his time and go straight.

"See that maroon car over there?"

Jay turned his head and scanned the seven parked cars, quickly skipping over the police cruiser, wrong color. The car in question was parked at the end of the lot next to a small jeep.

"Yeah, I see it. What about it?"

"Ever see it before?"

Jay shook his head, "Nope."

"Do you know a woman named Kendra Hughes?"

Jay hardly thought for a second, "Nope. Who is she?"

"That's what I'd like to know. Come on, let's take a look."

The two men walked about thirty yards to the maroon vehicle and peered through the windows. It was difficult to see through the tinted glass, but Jay could see a beer can with a bullet hole in it, some heavily stained wadded up napkins, and several paper targets on the floor behind the front seats.

"Does it remind you of anyone?" the sheriff asked.

Jay shook his head, "Afraid not, Sheriff. Seen dirty cars before, but not this one."

"The people that showed up with this car are about our age. Still doesn't register?"

"Sorry, Sheriff. I can't think of anyone."

"Okay. Thank you. I'll take you and the guard back to your work crew. Wait for me at my cruiser, I'll get the guard."

Sheriff Wilson reentered the hospital and found the prison guard sitting in Guns' room looking through a *National Geographic* magazine. The sheriff smiled, wondering if the guard could read, or was only interested in the pictures. When the sheriff approached the bed, the guard stood up and put the magazine in the wall rack.

The guard stated, "The nurse told me you would keep the prisoner in the local jail until a car can come from the prison."

"Yes, I spoke with Nurse Berg and asked her to inform you. My deputy or I will stay with him at night until transportation arrives. It should only take a day or two. I've contacted the prison and they'll be sending Eddy Singleton to get Guns."

"I know Eddy. He'll guarantee Guns gets back in one piece. He was a medic in the first gulf war, back in ninety-one."

"Jay's waiting for us at my cruiser. Let's not make him cool his heels any longer. He'll probably want to get back to work with the others," the sheriff grinned.

"I'm not sure about that. Jay and Guns have been friends for some time and seem to get along. Jay ain't that friendly with the other men. He's lookin' forward to getting out and back to civilization. He's learned his lesson."

Thirty minutes later, Jay and the guard were back at the location of the road crew. The workers were past the tree that had fallen on Guns and were sitting in the shade in groups of two or three eating lunch. The tree had been cut into four sections and pushed to the sides of the road.

The three men exited the car. The guard and Jay headed for the truck to get lunches and Sheriff Wilson walked towards one group of three crewmen. The three looked at Scott with evil eyes, expecting to be accused of some wrongdoing. He surprised them with an unexpected question, "Have any of you heard gunfire recently, say in the past two or three days?"

The guys looked at each other and the eldest answered, "Yesterday, we heard some rifle fire. Figured it was some hunters. It was way off in the distance, southeast." Carl briefly pointed in the direction he had referenced.

"Thank you, gentlemen. That's all I wanted to know. Say, you're doing a good job on the road."

Carl nodded and said, "Thanks, Sheriff."

Sheriff Wilson turned his cruiser around and started back towards Suddenly but couldn't erase the report of gunfire from his mind. When he came to a sideroad that led towards the southeast he turned and drove about two miles before seeing a camping site next to a meandering shallow creek. His map indicated the water was Indian Creek that fed Lake Ionawa about ten miles north of Suddenly.

He pulled off the road to investigate and parked. The campers might know more about the gunshots the roadcrew reported. When he got out of the car, he slammed the door with extra effort. He wanted any campers to hear him coming.

Passing by a blue plastic tent, large enough to sleep a family of six, he saw the campfire had been extinguished properly. The adult campers were sitting on a log next to the creek. He could hear the shallow water swirling around and cascading over rocks. Two youngsters were skipping rocks across the water, each boy calling out the number of skips, and the man and woman, late twenties, or early thirties, were eating and talking quietly.

The sheriff approached the adults. "Hello. I'm Sheriff Wilson from Suddenly. Would you mind answering a few questions?"

The adults stood and the man said, "We don't mind. We're the Timbers family on a summer outing. This is my wife, Lilly, and I'm

Dave. Our boys are Jim and Steve. Steve's ten and Jimmy is seven." They shook hands and Dave asked, "What can we do for you, Sheriff?"

"Do you own a rifle?"

"Yes, sir. It's in the tent. You want to see it?"

"Sure, if you don't mind."

"Steve, would you get the Winchester for the sheriff?"

The older, bigger boy dropped a rock and strode to the tent, entered and a few seconds later, appeared holding a rifle. The bolt was open, and the boy carried the gun with both hands, barrel pointed at the ground. He handed the long gun to Sheriff Wilson.

"Thank you, Steve." The boy nodded and returned to the stream.

Dave volunteered, "We only have it for protection in case we run into any bears. The boys know how to shoot, so does my wife."

Sheriff Wilson sniffed the gun and said, "You haven't used it recently. No target practicing?"

"No sir. We only shoot on a range at the reservation or during legal deer hunting season in allowed districts, but deer season doesn't start until late October."

Sheriff Wilson gave the Winchester back to Dave and said, "Looks like you know all the rules. Have you heard any rifle fire around here recently?"

"No, we haven't, but we just got here today. We like the quiet and would have heard some shooting around here."

"Okay, I'll get out of your hair. Have a good time in the woods."

"Thanks, Sheriff. Bye." Lilly spoke for the first time, "Bye, Sheriff."

Sheriff Wilson retraced the road to the turnoff and continued back to Suddenly still wondering who had been out shooting in the forest. Scott drove straight home to tell his wife about the rifle fire and grab some lunch. He also wanted to see his family. He didn't need to worry about Julie, she could handle a gun as well as anyone he knew, ranger or FBI agent. Even so, she needed to be told about the man and woman that had left a maroon car in the hospital parking lot. Was the couple just traveling through or did they have some other reason to be in Suddenly? Scott's sixth sense was starting to germinate.

One more left turn, slowly passing four homes on his right and he would turn into his driveway. But there was one small problem, the US mail truck was parked in his spot. Scott decided to pull over to the curb, wondering why the mail carrier, Molly Parker, was apparently inside the house. As he walked by the delivery van, he saw the little truck was unoccupied, except for boxes of sorted but undelivered letters, bills, and junk mail.

Scott went in the front door and found Molly getting a signature from David for a registered letter. Julie, Gwen, and Danny were sitting on the sofa watching David sign in a USPS delivery book. Molly handed the letter to David, turned to Scott, and said, "Hi, Sheriff. Sorry about parking in your driveway, but I just had to see Gwen and get David's signature."

Scott smiled, "That's all right. You're here on official business."

Danny wanted to see the letter, but David ripped open the envelope and pulled out the contents. He handed the empty envelope to Danny, who said, "Thanks a bunch, bro, just what I needed." David unfolded the paper and looked intently at it.

"It's a check from the insurance company."

Danny quizzed, "How much?"

"It's what I had hoped for."

"Come on, David, how much?"

"Six-zero-zero-zero-," I paused and looked at Mom.

She said, "Oh, David, only six thousand?"

And I continued, "another zero. Mom, it's sixty thousand dollars!"

Danny exclaimed, "Really?"

Mom smiled, "That's more like it. That's at least two years of college."

"What're you gonna get me for Christmas, bro?"

I chuckled and said, "Something less than five bucks. Maybe a box of a dozen Christmas cards, the cheap ones. That's four-ninety-nine."

"Thanks a lot, David."

Molly was standing by the door listening and chuckling. She held up another letter. "Does anybody know where Dexter Young lives? I have another registered item for him, but it's addressed to General Delivery."

I replied, "Sure, I'll see him at his place this afternoon. Can I sign for it? I'll take it to him."

"I suppose. I probably shouldn't do this, but you can sign for it. But don't open it. It's private mail for him."

"I won't open it. I'd never do that unless he asked me to."

"Okay. Well, I'd better get back to my route. I'm glad I brought good news."

I watched Molly go out towards her delivery truck and I called after her, "Thanks, Molly!" Molly was an adult, but even little kids called her by her first name, everybody did.

I rejoined the others. Everyone wanted to see the official looking check, so I let it be passed around. When Mom handed it back to me, there was a knock at the front door interrupting our family meeting.

Scott was the only one standing, "I'll get it," and he went to the door. Molly had returned, holding another envelope. Dad cracked the screen door and Molly stuck the thin cover through the opening, "It's for Danny. It's not registered."

"Thanks, Molly."

"You bet. I'll get out of your driveway now."

She said something else, but I couldn't hear what it was. I heard her drive away. That delivery truck makes a distinctive sound as it moves from address to address up and down the street, taillights blinking. I usually hear the mail being delivered when I'm in the back yard or the garage and by the time I get to the mailbox, the truck is nowhere in sight.

Scott handed the envelope to Danny and he tore it open like he had been waiting his entire life for an important message. I had to smile as he fumbled with the folded sheet of paper trying to see what it was all about. I think he thought it was just a letter.

He almost shouted, "It's a check for a thousand bucks! The note says it's for my expertise with the drone when looking for the yard ornaments."

I think Danny was prouder of his thousand dollar check than I was with my payment of a much larger amount. I heard a knock at our kitchen screen door and hustled to see who it was, but I was fairly sure it was Jenny. We had moved her into the apartment over the garage and she had said she wanted to sleep. She saw me coming to the door and said, "David, I need to get something to eat. Could you take me somewhere?"

"We can make you a sandwich if that's all right with you. Scott is going to eat something, too."

"Okay, but I don't want to bother you. Someone was just here visiting with your family. I hope I'm not interrupting anything."

"No, it was just Molly, the mail carrier."

Danny walked into the kitchen and said, "Jeez, David, invite her in."

I was already opening the door when Danny added, "I have to show you something, Jenny."

He was waving his check in front of her, but she couldn't tell what it was. She grabbed his arm and scanned the paper. "Awesome! It looks like you got paid for working with the drone. What are you gonna do with that much money?"

Danny's grin started to fade, "I'm starting an account at the bank. It's gonna earn interest."

"That's good, you shouldn't spend it on something foolish."

I decided to hold back with my announcement of the sixty grand I had received. I didn't want to diminish the excitement Danny was having. Jenny looked at me and I zipped my lips. She nodded as if she understood. I was sure she would ask me if I had gotten a check from the insurance company too, and for how much.

I said, "I'll bet you get a check today, too, but you don't have delivery out of the city limits. Where do you pick up your mail, at the post office?"

She nodded, "We…I mean I have a box downtown. If I got a check, it will be there waiting for me."

"I'll drive you and we can check your mail after you eat, okay?"

She smiled, nodded and we went into the kitchen.

# CHAPTER 11

When at home, Scott rarely mentioned anything about his office work, but Mom had followed him into the kitchen, and we started making sandwiches as he told us about the maroon car left at the hospital parking lot. He had broken his normal reluctance to talk about his official activities.

He asked us, "Have any of you noticed a couple riding around town on a motorcycle? They're about my age. I think the car is theirs."

Nearly simultaneously, we all answered, "No."

Mom asked, "Who does the VIN indicate the owner is?"

Scott replied, "Eliot Sanders, Albuquerque, New Mexico." After swallowing a bite of sandwich, he continued, "He's been dead for ten years."

I was curious, "What was in the car?"

"Nothing much, just some trash."

Jenny had sliced a pickle into quarters and held a knife in her right hand, looked at Scott and asked, "Is there something important about the car?"

Scott had taken a bite of pickle, chewed, and swallowed. "I'm not sure. The convict work crew heard some rifle fire a couple of days ago and there were several used paper targets on the floor of the car."

I liked Jenny's question, so I queried, "Did the targets indicate the shooter was a good shot?"

Scott took another bite, chewed, and said, "That's debatable. If the distance was great, yes, but if the shooter was close, then no. But if there were two shooters, one good and one just average, that would explain the holes in the targets.

Mom changed the subject and gave Scott a shopping list. He raised his eyebrows when she told him he was going grocery shopping. It was not one of his favorite tasks. He folded the list and stuck it in his breast pocket. Jenny looked at me and grinned.

After eating lunch, Jenny and I cleared the table and cleaned up the kitchen counter. We loaded the dishwasher while Mom, carrying Gwen, followed Scott out to his cruiser. We heard him pull away from the curb and Mom rejoined us in the kitchen.

After Mom sat down with Gwen, Jenny said, "Mrs. Wilson, I have a problem."

That was my cue to leave, so I stood next to the table and said, "When you're through, I'll be out at my car."

Jenny slugged me in the arm and ordered, "Sit down! it's not that kind of problem; I've already mentioned it to you."

Turning back to Mom, she continued, "I don't want to go back to that old farmhouse and be by myself. At night, it's kind of creepy. I hear it groaning and snapping noises come from the attic, like something is taking the house apart. Grams just laughed about the sounds, she called them squeaks and pops. They didn't bother me when she was around."

Mom sat there for a moment, patted Jenny's hand on the tabletop, and suggested, "You know what? I think you need a roommate."

I couldn't help myself and had to inject a little humor. "I volunteer." I smiled and Mom actually laughed out loud, but then quickly covered her mouth so not to upset little Gwen.

Jenny slugged me again, a little harder, and said, "Fat chance, big boy."

Mom suggested, "What about asking Megan?"

That was it, the semi-brilliant idea I had thought about earlier. I wondered if it had a prayer of taking place, but I had strong hopes.

Jenny snapped her fingers. "Oh, Mrs. Wilson, that's an awesome idea. Do you think she would want to do it?"

"It certainly wouldn't hurt to ask. You can go next door after dinner and talk with her. I'll go with you if you want."

"I think David will go with me. Maybe Megan will be swayed if David thinks it's a good idea."

I didn't tell Jenny I had thought of the idea and couldn't think of any reason it wouldn't work. It would be a sorority with two members and since their names are Kincaid and Isaacs, it could be called the Kappa-Iota house, the first Greek living group in Suddenly for high school students. I'd spring the name on the girls when we met after dinner.

The novelty might encourage the housemate living arrangement. As I cogitated, it came to me that more girls could live with them for their high school senior year. I immediately thought Mary Lynn Snyder might want to join Jenny and Megan. Mary Lynn worked at the Dairy Queen and was independent minded. She was living with an aunt and the idea could appeal to her, but I decided to keep my trap shut.

"You've been awfully quiet, David. Will you go with me to talk with Megan?"

I realized I had been on another planet for a short time and Jenny had been expecting me to say something. "Sure, I'll go with you. I think Mom has given you a good idea. Strength in numbers so those noises won't scare anyone."

Mom and Jenny didn't even smile at my last comment, they were really serious about this new living scheme, no joking around. Mom handed Gwen to Jenny and went to the stove to heat some water for tea. I was a bit surprised when Gwen didn't begin to fuss, but Jenny and the baby started a smiling contest. I could see Mom watching Jenny with Gwen. I think Mom was considering Jenny to be another babysitter, Megan wouldn't always be available.

Jenny and I went to the post office and got the Kincaid family mail. There was a check for Jenny and a couple of bills for Mrs. Kincaid. We'd take those items to Mr. Isaacs for payment. She perked up again when she discovered the insurance company had sent her a check for eight thousand bucks. We dropped off the bills at the bank and headed out to Dexter's barn to deliver his check and see what progress he had made with improvements. Both of us had volunteered to assist him, but we hadn't talked with Dex in several days, so we were unaware of any headway with remodeling.

I was waiting at one of Suddenly's two traffic lights directly behind a small black SUV. I didn't recognize the car. I was prevented from making a free right turn and continuing out to Dex's place. When the light changed, Jenny called out, "Did you see that?"

"What?"

"The black car going left just missed hitting the red light."

"Happens all the time in Suddenly. We don't have much traffic and people want to keep going." I started to turn right, but Jenny said, "Didn't you see that car that just went by was maroon."

I spun the wheel counterclockwise and hit the gas, making a wide left turn, intending to follow the maroon vehicle. Jenny reached up and grabbed the handhold on the roof to keep from banging against the door. "It's a block ahead of us, David, don't speed. I'll watch where it goes."

I could see it clearly, too. No other cars were moving on the street. Following was going to be easy and the occupants wouldn't notice us, I hadn't squealed my tires. I didn't try to gain on them. They signaled left, slowed, and made the turn. When I was about two car lengths behind them, I pulled over to the curb when they signaled to park. Jen and I watched the car pull over and stop. The woman driver and a male passenger got out, slammed the doors, and went into Erwin's Sporting Goods.

I thought about going in to see the pair up close but decided against it. I figured Ben Erwin would ask me about Scott and mention that I was the sheriff's son. Maybe it would spook them, and they would remember me.

"Jen, would you go in and look around? Find out what they're buying. If Ben asks if he can help you, tell him you are thinking about buying a handgun and are just looking. I'm sure he doesn't know you."

"But I don't know anything about guns." She glanced at me and frowned.

"Don't worry, Ben will tell you more than you need to know. As soon as you find out what the couple buys, come back."

It seemed like I had waited at least a half hour before the couple exited Irwin's with something in a paper sack. After they drove off, Jenny came back to report. In reality it had only been about twelve minutes.

She hopped in the car, exhaled as if she had been running, and sat looking at me.

"Ammunition, David, they bought two cartons of rifle bullets. Her hair is dyed, and he needs to see a barber."

I chuckled, "Thank you, agent Kincaid. Good work."

"That's kind of a scary place. I felt really ignorant in there. Next time you go in."

"Sorry, Jen. I thought you might enjoy seeing all that outdoor stuff." I was half-kidding since she was a city kid. Then she surprised me.

"When we have more time, I want you to go in there with me and explain how all that stuff is used. Why are there so many different types of guns?"

"I'll tell you what I know some other time. Let's drive out to Dexter's and deliver his mail. I want to see how Skimmer is doing, too. Tell me about the couple you watched for me at Ben's."

Ten minutes later, as we went by Hadleys' I glanced at their driveway to see if there were any cars I recognized. All I saw was Mr. Hadley's truck. No one was on the porch, but it was getting hot, so I wasn't surprised no one was outside. We passed Hadleys' and made a sharp left turn into the dusty, weed infested lane leading to Dexter's barn.

I pulled up next to the metal gate leading to the ramshackle structure and parked. Jenny and I got out slowly looking for Dex. We recognized Skimmer's bark coming from the barn. Dex had to be in there, Skimmer wouldn't be alone.

The Yorkie shot out of the barn, his tail wiggling like a flyswatter on steroids. When he saw Jenny, he made a beeline to her and jumped into her arms. She had crouched to pet him and caught him in the air. I laughed as he tried to lick her face. She turned her head away and held his writhing body at arm's length.

"Hi guys." Dexter, holding a hammer, came through the open barn doors. He was covered with a thin layer of dust and bird droppings.

"Just a minute." He walked to a bucket of water and immersed his entire head, reached for a soiled towel hanging from a nail on the barn wall and dried his face.

"Ah, that's better." He grinned and said, "Hi Jenny, David. What brings you out to the old homestead?"

Jenny and I both laughed when he said homestead. In his mind, Dex had upgraded his old barn since we last saw him about a week ago. Before I gave Dex his letter from the insurance company, I asked, "What were you doing in there when we drove up? Anything we can help you with?"

"Thanks for the offer, but I was demolishing the old animal stalls. I want to get the floor cleared before I make too many plans. I need to build a foundation, but I don't know how. I think I could jack up the walls; lift the entire building off the ground and then drop it back onto the foundation."

"Mind if we take a look?" I wanted to see what he was thinking before I gave him his check. That way Dex could decide how the whole operation should be carried out. He would now have the money to hire some professional builders get him started.

"If you don't mind getting a little dusty. When you walk inside the barn, dust and animal waste gets stirred up. Jenny, you might want to cover your mouth and nose."

We entered the barn and wandered around looking at the walls and roof. It was surprising how many holes could be seen from the interior; the building looked much better from the outside. I noticed one thing had changed, there weren't any birds flying around the inside. As I surveyed the structure, I began to estimate how difficult it would be to lift the walls if the roof were removed. I guessed about forty percent of the barn's weight was in the roof, but that was only a rough estimate. I mentioned it to Dex.

"I'll bet we could lift the walls with some car jacks. The building would be a lot lighter if the roof were taken off first."

"Good idea, Drum. I hoped you would give me some insight."

The time was right, I pulled the slightly rumpled insurance envelope from my pocket and handed it to Dex. "Molly gave me this to give to you. She can't deliver out here, only within city limits."

He checked the return address and carefully tore open the business size cover.

I had never seen Dex smile so enthusiastically before, "Eight grand! God has smiled on me; what I can do with this!" He held the check up to see the watermark. "Thank you, David, and you, too, Jenny." Dex gave us both high fives, picked up Skimmer and danced around in a circle. However, Jenny and I were just messengers. I wondered what the little Yorkie thought was happening, his tail just kept wagging at a frantic pace.

# CHAPTER 12

As I scanned the interior of the barn, I noticed in many places big nails had been used for hanging things on rough-hewn studs. I changed my mind about using car jacks; they probably wouldn't be strong enough to lift one end of the barn; it was constructed from old thick timber. Dex's next-door neighbors, the Hadleys, had logging equipment and would probably loan us what we needed. Jen and I talked with Dex about installing concrete pedestals at each corner of the building and cementing large rocks between them to construct the foundation. Dex was pondering something when I remembered to ask him about recent visitors.

"Have you seen a maroon sedan around here recently?"

"Uh, yeah. A couple stopped here yesterday. They asked me if I knew of a shooting range near town. I told them I didn't know of any and I've never shot a gun. They said they had been in South America for several years and were thinking of staying in the US. That's about all we said. Oh, I think I told them I was from St. Louis. Why do you ask?"

"Scott was asking about a maroon car. How long were they here?"

He looked at the ground for a second and then looked at me. "Hmm, maybe ten minutes. They drove off toward town. The woman waved."

I leaned closer to Dex and told him quietly that Mrs. Kincaid had passed during the night and Jenny was going to stay at my place for a couple of days. She didn't want to be alone in the farmhouse. Jenny was absorbed in play with Skimmer, so she didn't hear what we said.

Dex asked, "So what's she gonna do about living in that run down old house?"

"We're gonna talk with Megan and see if she'll room with her for a year, or at least through our senior year of high school. Maybe they'll be able to find someone else to join them."

Dex had to joke, "Better keep it quiet, Suddenly will have gossip about its first cathouse."

"Yeah, I thought of that already, but let's keep it quiet. We don't want to spoil everything with crazy rumors."

"Gotcha. To change the subject, do you know anything about digging a well?"

"Nope. Sorry Dex. Ask Mr. Hadley, he should know. I think his place was the first one out here and probably didn't have city water. They might still use their own well water, I don't know."

Jen joined us holding Skimmer and asked, "Are you guys through changing the barn into a house?"

"Sorry about your grandmother, Jenny. She was a nice lady."

Jenny put Skimmer down and said, "Thanks, Dex. She left the old farmhouse to me. If you want to borrow some of Grandpa's tools, come by and you can pick out what you can use for your renovations. Bring Skimmer with you. Have you thought about getting a car?"

"Not yet. I'll have things delivered, or someone help me until I can afford a car. I'll have to get a license, too. I've never had one."

Jen said, "Remember, I've got a pickup and can haul stuff…as long as it isn't too big."

Dex nodded, "Thanks, Jen. I'll keep that in mind. I'll let you know. I'll get a phone put in soon."

I agreed, "Good idea. If you had an accident, who would ever know? Skimmer wouldn't run for help, would he? You should at least be able to get in touch with me, Jenny, Megan, the sheriff, or the hospital."

"Jenny, you said you got a phone recently." Dex asked, "How much did Mrs. Kincaid shell out for it?"

"I have no idea; I'll check when the first bill arrives. That reminds me, I have to get the phone bill changed to my name, also, the lights, and the water. I hope that's not a problem, I'm not an adult yet." She stood there staring across the open field past the big tree at the back of the barn.

"I need to get Grams' death certificate, too. But not today; I don't want to think about it now." Jen sighed, walked to the car, got in and buckled her seat belt. "Let's go, David."

Dex and I bumped fists, and I said, "Let me know if you need a truck driver. You might not be able to get everything you need delivered. We can probably borrow Mr. Hadley's flatbed to haul long beams, just pay for the gas."

"Thanks, David, and thanks for delivering the check." Dex gave me a beaming smile.

I got in the Subaru, waved, and drove away with Jenny. When we reached the main road, she turned her shoulders and waved toward the barn, a delayed action.

The maroon sedan moved slowly through the bumpy forest roads toward tower twenty. Since winter, the state road crews had constructed a rough road to provide better access to the previously somewhat isolated tower. The tower renters were unsure of the irregular pathway that had suffered erosion from the snow melt and spring rains. The new renterss had discussed the condition of the winding dirt road and were talking about the results of their visit at the opposite end of town as they approached the limited parking area. The woman with the black hair looked at the bearded and tattooed driver. "Well, that kid's last name is Young and he's about the right age. What do you think, could he be Jay's son?"

"I don't know. I never heard of any kid named Dexter. If he's Jay's son, where in hell did that name come from?"

"Could Jay's mother have given it to him? It's probably just a stupid nickname."

"That's feasible, that old lady did some crazy stuff after John went to prison."

The brakes squeaked as they parked at the base of the tower. The woman got out and looked up at the top of the lookout station. "Damn, those stairs look a little dangerous. God, eight flights. Let's take as much as we can each trip so we can save some climbing."

"You wanted all these groceries, Mrs. Martinez."

"You know I can't ride that damn motorcycle to get groceries, Juan." She stood with hands on her hips wanting to argue, but after a second, she reached into the car, grabbed a sack of groceries, and started climbing. Juan laughed, pulled two more sacks from the backseat, and followed Maria.

When the six bulky bags were transferred to the cabin, Juan said, "Let's go back to the grocery store and retrieve my bike. You can drive, you know the road now. If you're unsure, go slow, remember, we don't have any deadlines." They both began to laugh.

"Should we lock up?" She looked around at all the food.

"Nah, who would be out here to steal anything? Plus, we won't be gone long anyway. Let's go."

Juan tossed the car keys to Maria and they descended the steep flights of stairs to the sedan. She started the engine and crept onto the road driving slowly at first, but after a couple of miles, Maria drove at the speed limit to the grocery store parking area. When she entered the parking lot, Juan said, "Stop here. I'll follow you back."

He sauntered to the bike, put on his helmet, and started the loud Harley-Davidson. He gunned the engine and waved to Maria to lead the way. Her patience was wearing thin with Juan's time-wasting and frequent criticism. He had enough faults of his own, but the main one was treating that damn motorcycle with tender gloves. She left the lot in a huff, driving all the way to the tower as fast as she considered safe on the winding road.

Juan checked his fuel, watched Maria leave the lot and decided to take a longer way than the route they had just come. He was curious to see where the police station was, so he drove to Main Street and rode through the business district. The second light went red, he could have stopped, but no cars were to the right or left, so he rolled on through. He smiled as he looked in his rearview mirror and didn't see anyone following. He made a right and heard a siren, but he thought it couldn't be for him. But Deputy Doureline had other ideas and hit his blue lights as he watched the motorcycle exceed the twenty-five miles per hour city speed limit. It was only five over, but the red light was the deciding factor. The stoplight at the intersection was there for good reason.

Juan glanced in his mirror and saw the flashing blues. "Damn! Where did he come from?" He didn't want to make things worse, so he pulled over, shut off the engine, and removed his helmet. Juan watched as the tall deputy approached with a ticket pad in his right hand.

The deputy spoke first, "You have two infractions, ignoring the red and speeding, thirty-one in a twenty-five. I have to give you a ticket for the red light, but speeding is minor, just a few miles over the limit; that's a warning. You're new in town, right?"

"Yes, Officer. My wife and I are just visiting for a couple of weeks this summer. Nice little town. Sorry about the light. I didn't see anyone else at the intersection, so I coasted right on through."

"Accidents happen when you don't see another vehicle. When was the last time you had your muffler checked? Your bike is loud enough to bust eardrums. Nearby pedestrians have to cover their ears when you roar past them. I need your name, sir."

"Juan Martinez."

"Address?"

"Tower twenty."

Deputy Doureline nodded, "New road out there." He finished filling out the form and tore the ticket from his book.

Juan admitted, "Yeah, I guess the bike is a little loud. I'll see what I can do about that. Is that all? My wife expects me back in a few minutes."

Deputy Doureline stepped closer, took another look at the bike, and handed Juan a $30 ticket. "Watch for the red lights, we only have two of them. Have a nice stay in Suddenly."

Juan folded the ticket and stuck it in his wallet, thinking he would conceal it from Maria. What she didn't know…"Thanks, officer." He watched the deputy get back in his cruiser and drive back toward the city streets. "Son of a bitch! Maria's gonna be pissed." He slapped his gas tank, started the bike, and thundered off to tower twenty. As he wound through the forest, Juan chided himself for breaking the pact he had made with Maria. Actually, it was his idea to stay under the radar. Now, he had a big apology to perform with a weak explanation.

The deputy was completing a short shift on duty and returned to the Sheriff's Office after ticketing the motorcycle rider. He could hear the

Sheriff's voice as he entered the office. He waited until it was silent, then rapped his knuckles on the door jam.

Scott looked up, "Come in, Tim. Any news about that maroon sedan?"

"No, sir. I haven't seen it yet. I just stopped a motorcycle for running the red on Oak and Main. I was a little suspicious of him. He gave his name as Juan Martinez, but he had no hint of an accent and he didn't exhibit any Mexican or South American features."

"Could be a second or third generation. The nurses at the hospital said the owners of the maroon car had a motorcycle, a big noisy one according to Mrs. Berg. Did you get an address?"

"Yeah, tower twenty."

"Call the Ranger Station and see who's renting number twenty. Then you can take off for the day."

The deputy turned away and walked to his desk, picked up his phone and speed dialed the Ranger Station.

"Ranger Station. How can I help you, Deputy Doureline?"

"Hi, Arlene. Can you tell me who is renting tower twenty?"

"Sure, just a moment." About five seconds later Arlene said, "Mr. and Mrs. Martinez for two weeks."

"Thanks, Arlene. Did they say what kind of vehicle they have?"

"Uh-huh. Motorcycle. Want the tag?"

"No, I've got it. Nothing about a maroon sedan?"

"Nope, just the motorcycle. Today was their first day at the tower."

"Thanks, Arlene."

Arlene laughed, "Ten-four, Tim. You're welcome."

The deputy returned to the Sheriff's Office, stuck his head in the doorway and said, "Arlene confirmed the renters: Mr. and Mrs. Martinez. They have a motorcycle. Nothing about a maroon car."

"Okay. Thanks. See you tomorrow."

Scott cleared the top of his desk and then checked the FAX machine for any recent notices and wanted posters. There was a notice from the State Corrections Department about the prisoners clearing the fire roads, but that was it. There was nothing to file, so Scott posted the state office note on the hallway bulletin board and returned to his desk.

He wrote *maroon car* on a pad on his desk and leaned back in his leather-upholstered executive chair, the favorite piece of furniture Sheriff Howell had left. Scott didn't know if it was something from his FBI training or just a feeling, but that car had parked itself in a prominent part of his brain. He wanted to know where the car had been purchased, something that might divulge why he had the premonition or feeling.

There was a knock on his door, it was the department secretary, Ginny Gumble.

"Sheriff?"

Scott turned toward the door, "Yes, Ginny?"

"Do you mind if I go home early today? I'm all caught up."

"I don't mind, I'm thinking the same thing. See you *mañana*."

# CHAPTER 13

"Markus! Grab three shovels from the truck. You, Gene, and Jay are gonna make a temporary latrine." Todd was looking at a handbook for out-of-door living, having just completed a discussion with his coworker, DD. The supers had picked a site to camp in a flat grassy area about thirty yards from the road. The cabin at tower thirty-two was too small to house all twelve men and the guards didn't want any squabbles over bunks, some of the men would have to sleep outside. A decision was made: the entire crew would sleep under the stars.

Todd Grimsby had worked at the prison for twenty years. This outing was his last before retirement. He had never worked with hard asses, just low level offenders.

"You men follow me. You're gonna dig a hole about three feet in diameter and over six feet deep. Then we're making a cover from logs with a one foot circular hole in the center. Jay, grab those axes that are tied together."

The three prisoners took turns digging for half an hour before Todd said, "Okay. Jay, drop in that hole and we'll see if it's deep enough. You're six foot tall, right?"

They had just pulled five-foot-six Gene Gildsmat from the hole with a rope and Jay stood at the edge peering down. "I might break something if I drop in there, boss. Let these guys lower me with that rope." Jay pointed at the short length of rope lying on the ground beside the pile of earth the men had excavated. The rope had been wrapped around the ax handles to keep the sharp equipment fairly safe in a bundle.

"All right, Gene and Markus, lower Jay into that hole. If his head sticks up, dig it a little deeper."

As Jay grabbed the end of the rope where a knot was tied, he whispered to Markus, "I'll bend my legs if it's not deep enough. That'll save us some time and sweat."

Markus nodded, wiped his dirty hands on his pants and grinned. He had been in that hole enough today. Diggin' was awkward and it was hot. He imagined he would be going through this same routine again before the summer was over.

"Markus! Get one of those fold-up camp chairs from the back of the truck and cut a six-inch diameter hole in the canvas seat. You can use my pocketknife." Todd had solved the problem of a man having to crouch over the hole to relieve himself.

Gene was holding the rope so Jay could descend into the hole. He was preventing himself from being pulled into the hole on top of Jay by leaning away from the opening still holding Jay's weight. The rope suddenly went slack, and he nearly fell backwards. As soon as he regained his balance, he could see the top of Jay's head a couple of inches below the edge of the hole. Jay was looking up and grinning, but he couldn't see anyone. He yelled, "We're done diggin'."

Gene pulled Jay from the hole and they started making a cover for the pit from three-inch logs which they split in half and nailed to shorter logs at right angles. There was one last item, a roll of toilet paper was placed in the beverage container on the chair. From start to finish the construction had taken nearly two hours. The three prisoners stood side-by-side looking at their crude toilet. Markus said, "Not bad for an outdoor motel."

Todd gave one last instruction, "Pick up the tools and get back with the others. Another hour's work and we'll get something to eat." The guard grabbed the two axes and watched the men gather up the other tools. As they began walking back towards the rest of the crew, Todd gave a slight chuckle and smiled, "You'll meet the replacement for Guns after eating."

While Jay, Gene, and Markus were making the latrine, a couple on a motorcycle stopped and the woman got off the Harley. She approached Vince Johnston and asked, "Who's in charge?"

Vince pointed, "That guy over there. Name's DD."

She walked over to DD and asked, "You got a guy named John Young working here?"

"Who's asking?"

"An old friend, but I'm not sure it's the same guy. Can you point him out?"

"We don't call him John, name's Jay." The guard pointed out to the latrine and said, "He's the tallest one of those men. He'll be in here in about an hour. You wanta wait? They're working, I can't let you go out there to disturb them."

Maria shielded her eyes and squinted, "No, that's not him. The John Young I know is short and more muscular. Thanks." She turned and walked quickly back to the bike, got on behind Juan and they left, going back towards Suddenly.

While the men ate, DD mentioned the visitor looking for John Young.

"Yeah, Jay, not a bad-looking woman. Dark hair, nice body and about five-six or so. I didn't know you had a *pen* pal."

Most of the men laughed and Jay said, "Not me, DD. I never wrote to a woman except my mother for the last eleven years. I don't know who it could have been."

DD said, "When I pointed to you, she said it wasn't you she was looking for, her John was short and more muscular. She was with some guy on a Harley. They were only here a few minutes. She seemed to know about the crew, but I didn't tell her anything. Maybe she noticed the writing on the truck. Come to think about it, she did act a little nervous."

When the men finished eating, they began to clean up and locate sites to bed down. Everyone stopped what they were doing when a state car rolled up. They focused on the vehicle; a large white SUV with Montana State Penitentiary written on the side- panels in bold black three-inch letters.

Jay and Markus were standing together and watched as the driver and his passenger exited.

Markus was the first to notice and react, "Hey, the passenger, that's a woman! How the hell does she replace Guns?"

Jay was thinking similarly. There was no way a woman was going to be a substitute for his muscular friend. What was the warden thinking?

The driver motioned for the men to gather around. They formed a semicircle around the car's driver side with the woman and driver leaning against the SUV.

The driver spoke, "Men, this is Larrea Wisdom. She's replacing Guns. The warden sent her because she's fought fires in Oregon, Idaho, and Arizona. I advise you to get to know her; she might just save your ass in a fire. A woman guard will join us in a few days."

Todd stepped up to Larrea and shook hands, did an about face and called each man's name to acquaint her with the members of the brigade. When Jay's name was called, Todd motioned for him to come closer.

"Go to the rear door of the SUV and pull out two items of equipment for Ms. Wisdom."

Jay followed directions and lifted the rear door. He was startled by a familiar voice, "Hey, Jay. Good to see you again, buddy."

Guns was strapped to a gurney, but he was able to sit up after unclipping a torso belt that secured him to the side of the cargo area.

Jay crawled into the SUV and shook hands with his powerfully built pal.

"I guess you're on your way back to the pen. We're all sorry to see you go. I guess you know who is replacing you." Jay shook his head in disappointment.

"She's not a talky woman, Jay, but she knows her stuff. She's about your age. Get to know her. She's had lots of experience and seems to know more about fighting fires than all of the rest of the brigade put together. She's one-eighth Navajo and has an eighteen-year-old daughter that is going to college part-time. That's all I could pull out of her."

"You did good, Guns. I'll look you up when we get back home and tell you about the rest of the summer. I hope your leg heals fast. Good luck."

"Right. Those two bags are hers." Guns pointed at two large canvas duffle bags.

"I think one of them is an old army cot. Treat her right and she might share." Guns laughed loudly and punched Jay on the shoulder, almost knocking him out to the ground. Jay grabbed a tie-down strap and kept himself from tumbling out of the SUV.

"Thanks pal." Jay slid the two heavy-canvas bags toward the bumper, dropped them to the ground, got out and pulled the bags away from the vehicle. He returned to the rear of the SUV and said, "Take care, big guy. Stay out of trouble." Then, he slammed the cargo door shut and walked back to talk to Todd.

"Thanks for letting me talk to Guns. Where should I put the woman's things?"

"Set 'um down for now. I gave her a few minutes to look around and then get you for help. She might be good for you. She has seen reports of all the men. The warden wanted her to know who she would be out here working with on the brigade. She seemed to pay particular attention to your file."

"So, you and the warden are in the match-making business?"

Todd chuckled, "Nah. The warden figured the two of you would be the leaders during a firefighting mission. The team could benefit if the two of you worked together."

As the group meeting broke up, the SUV moved across the bumpy field, made it back to the road and sped away. Jay watched the car as it disappeared, concealed by the forest. He started back toward the firepit and began scanning the crew for the new member.

Larrea was moving her belongings by dragging the two containers across the ground towards the campfire. Jay hustled to her and grabbed the heavier bag from her grasp.

She jerked away, "Hey! What're you doing?"

"Just giving a helping hand. Where are you going with your belongings?"

"Well, I thought I'd try to get near the fire. That bag has a cot in it. I've never used one before when firefighting, but the warden insisted I have one. He wanted me to keep away from snakes, but I think he meant the men of the brigade, not the slithering ones." She gave a wry grin, adjusted the remaining canvas bag by raising it from the ground and continued walking. Jay picked up the heavier container and followed.

Larrea stopped about ten feet from the firepit and dropped her bag. She glanced around and located Todd. "Hey, Boss, all right if I camp here?"

Todd approached and said, "Pick any spot you want. Nobody will argue. We dug a latrine today, but if you want privacy, you'll have to grab a shovel and locate a spot behind some bushes." Todd scanned the area and pointed to a small clump of shrubs and trees about forty yards from the firepit in the opposite direction of the latrine. "Over there."

For the first time, Jay took a good look at Larrea. She was tall, about five-nine, and slender, but dressed in the brigade outfit, it was somewhat difficult to tell the frame was that of a woman. Her nearly black hair, held with a rubber band, was pulled back from her oval face. He thought her facial features had just a hint of native American blood. He smiled, thinking that she could probably hold her own in a tussle with any of the guys, including himself. This was going to be an interesting summer, better than his friendship with Guns had promised.

"Drop that bag anywhere, I'll figure it out. I've assembled Army cots before."

Jay did as asked and walked over to the flatbed and grabbed his sleeping and duffle bags. He didn't feel right to stakeout a place too close to Larrea, he had just met her. Besides, he wanted to watch to see if any of the others were going to push their luck and come on to the woman. He had a feeling she would tell the first guy that got too close to buzz off. He didn't want to be the first to be sent packin'.

He dropped his belongings on the ground about ten yards from the firepit. He didn't want to inhale smoke all night if too close to smoldering wood. Waking up with a sore throat and coughing all day was to be avoided. He was close enough to Larrea to observe any interactions with the rest of the crew. Jay cleared an area of debris and kicked a couple of high spots until the ground was nearly level. He unrolled his sleeping bag and used his duffle for a pillow.

Everyone was getting settled for the night. Jay smiled as he watched several of the crew make their way to the new latrine. The sun had dropped behind the trees and the temperature was falling rapidly. The sky was clear, and he wondered what constellations would be prominent in the Montana sky at nearly seven-thousand feet.

The last thing he observed before closing his eyes was Larrea, climbing into her sleeping bag on the Army cot. He wondered what she was thinking about her new circumstance and how she would fit in.

# CHAPTER 14

Jenny was somber during dinner, but the rest of us jabbered away about the day's activities. I kind of understood how Jenny felt without any of her family around. When conversation lulled, Scott made a statement that startled all of us. A woman had joined the penitentiary fire fighters, but even when Scott elaborated about her background, I knew Mom was going to ask a few questions.

I had a feeling she was going to say, "What was the warden thinking?" But instead, Mom asked Scott how old the woman was and what was her name. I figured Mom thought she might have heard of the woman, maybe someone with whom the rangers had been in contact previously when firefighters had been around Suddenly. She might even have stayed in our apartment at one time.

When Scott said, "Larrea Wisdom, she's about forty."

Mom put down her fork, stared at Scott, and exclaimed, "I know her! I met her in Butte about ten years ago at a convention. We were investigating some new firefighting equipment. I wonder how she got put in prison, she was so nice." Mom slowly shook her head in disbelief. I felt there was a strong possibility more questions were about to erupt.

Danny opened his big mouth and jested, "Eleven men and one woman, sounds like there might be some problems." He looked at Scott and grinned, "You'll have to get some cells ready for new arrivals, Scott."

"The odds won't be that bad, Danny. The two guards will prevent any foolishness, and the inmates know if they mess up, they'll go back to the pen and lose any possibility of reduction in their sentence. I'd be willing to bet there won't be any problems at all."

Everyone had finished eating, so Mom got a wet washcloth from the kitchen and wiped Gwen's dirty face. Gwen was being fed mother's milk from a bottle when she ate with us, but the liquid was not all going down the intended route. Milk rolled down her chin and neck occasionally, accompanied with some drool.

Mom turned toward the kitchen, tossed the washcloth in the sink, and asked, "Anyone want dessert? It's chocolate ice cream."

Everybody except Jenny raised a hand. She pushed her chair back, stood, and said, "Let me give you a hand, Mrs. Wilson. I need to do something worthwhile today."

Scott took Gwen and the two women stepped into the kitchen. Five minutes later, we were scarfing up chocolate ice cream. Jenny went into the living room and sat on the sofa looking through the newest copy of National Geographic, Mom's favorite magazine.

I wanted to lick the bottom of my bowl, but didn't want to gross out the others, so I just rinsed out the bowl and put it in the washer. Then I joined Jenny and collapsed beside her on the sofa.

I noticed she was staring at a picture of Crater Lake in Oregon, but she wasn't reading the text below the picture; her eyes weren't scanning, I asked, "You've been very quiet tonight, Jen, are you okay?"

"I'm worried that Megan won't want to live with me. I can't stay there alone, I'd be isolated."

"Let's go next-door and find out. The Isaacs should be finished with dinner now. I have an idea that might persuade her. If that doesn't work, we'll ask Mom if she knows of anyone that might join you for the next school year. Scott might be able to help, too. I'm sure he knows some old men."

I expected to get hit, but all I got was a dirty look from Jenny.

A few minutes later, Jenny and I were standing on the Isaacs' front porch. I reached for the elk-head brass knocker but decided to use my knuckles instead. The knocker made such a loud sharp noise, it could raise the dead. I didn't want to scare Mrs. Isaacs.

The heavy, oak door opened slowly to reveal Mr. Isaacs in his stocking feet.

"Hi, David. Hello, Ms. Kincaid, how are you this evening? Come in, Megan's in the living room with her mother."

We stepped into the vestibule. Mr. Isaacs closed the door and led us into the big room. As we followed him, I told him, "We would like to talk to all of you, but it concerns Megan."

Mrs. Isaacs stood and greeted us as we entered the living room. Megan turned off the sound on the TV and said, "Hi, David. Hi, Jenny."

Mr. Isaacs said, "What's this all about, David? How is Megan involved?"

Jenny opened her mouth, but nothing came out. She squeezed my hand and grimaced, "Could you?" She surprised me. Jenny wanted me to ask Megan about being her roommate. I had mistakenly thought she was prepared to explain our housing idea.

"Can we sit down?" I wanted everyone to be comfortable so our brains would function appropriately. We sat down, I took a deep breath and plunged in, "You are aware of Jen's grandmother passing. Mrs. Kincaid left Jen the farmhouse, but Jen doesn't want to stay there by herself, so she and I thought Megan would be an ideal roommate during our senior school year."

All three Isaacs were frowning, Mrs. Isaacs most severely. Megan was adjusting her position on the sofa and Mr. Isaacs stood up, moved between his wife and Megan, putting his arms around them. After a couple of seconds, he responded, "Well, that is something I hadn't expected." He looked at Meg and said, "What do you think of the idea, dear?"

"Geez, Dad, I don't know. I'd have to move all my things out there and then drive farther to work. I guess I'd have to change my address, too."

I reacted, "That wouldn't be necessary, Meg. You could stop by here every day, get your mail, say hi to me and see your parents. I figured it might be a good experience for you before you go off to college maybe a thousand miles or more away." I grinned, "This could be like a practice run, living away from home, but not far away."

Mrs. Isaacs sighed, "I don't think it's a good idea. In another year, you will be more ready to move away from home and be with many other girls having the same experiences. There is a time for everything, don't you think?" She turned to Megan, expecting her daughter to agree.

Jenny finally gave her thoughts, "I guess it was too much to expect. It was just an idea. I thought it would be kind of fun." She shrugged, "Maybe we could try it for a few weeks and see if it might work out. There wouldn't be any contract and you could leave any time if you don't like the arrangement."

Megan leaned back and said, "Let me think about it for a couple of days, okay? I think it's an important decision for me. I'd like to talk to Mom and Dad some more about it, too."

Jenny and I slowly stood almost simultaneously. I couldn't think of anything else to say to try to encourage Megan to live with Jenny for about ten months. The entire discussion hadn't gone as I expected. I counted on Megan jumping to the chance to live away from home for a while. I really thought Megan would be enthusiastic and want to try the trial arrangement, but I guess I was wrong.

Jenny and I slowly walked to the front door and I opened it. Jenny lagged behind and turned to the Isaacs, "Thank you for listening. I would like you to room with me, Megan. Please give it some thought. Good night."

I was surprised that none of the Isaacs saw us to the door. I pulled the front door shut and we walked back to my house and sat on the front steps.

"Sorry about that, Jen. I expected Megan to be more venturesome, but she was only thinking of reasons to avoid rooming with you."

"That's all right, David. To tell the truth, I wasn't totally thrilled having a roommate that was your girlfriend anyway. Let's go in and talk to your parents, maybe they can come up with someone else, someone that really needs a place to stay. I've got a couple of days to figure this out, don't I?"

"Sure. You can stay as long as you want, but I'm sure you would like to get back to your place and continue fixing it up. Let's see if Mom can think of someone else that might be a suitable roommate."

Jen and I went in the house. Mom asked us to join her and Scott at the kitchen table. They were talking over drinks of some kind. I didn't ask what it was. I couldn't smell anything like beer, but it wasn't a soda either. They hardly ever had the hard stuff. We joined them and I asked Jen if she wanted something to drink. She shook her head.

Mom smiled and said, "Well, is Megan going to live with you, Jenny?"

Jen frowned slightly, "I don't think so. She wasn't very enthusiastic about the idea."

Mom interlaced her fingers behind her head. I had seen that happen before; she was thinking seriously. None of us wanted to interrupt her thoughts, so we just sat in silence. I glanced at Jenny and she shrugged her shoulders as if to say, 'I've got nothing.'

Mom picked up her glass, took a few sips and said, "Scott, is Warren Harris still the warden at the pen?"

I was taken by surprise. What did that have to do with finding a roommate for Jenny?

"Yes, ma'am. I spoke with him a day ago about returning Guns to the prison. He told me about the prisoner exchange."

"That's great! I've dealt with him before. He's a nice person. I'll phone him tomorrow. I have an idea, but I have to clear it with him first."

As Juan and Maria were eating, they discussed their plan. On the way back to the tower from visiting the prison fire brigade, they took several detours looking for a four-wheeler they could borrow for an afternoon. They needed an all-terrain vehicle to carry out the scheme they had been planning off and on for several years. Originally, they had envisioned using the Harley, but once in the mountains, they realized the heavy-duty bike was not suited for the mountainous off-road terrain they would be traversing.

"So, did you see Johnny boy?"

Maria nodded, "Sure did, he's one of the brigade from the prison. He's got short hair and looks fit. Just about like the guy in that photo you showed me."

"You're sure he wasn't suspicious?"

"You saw where he was. He has never seen me before. I would have been another curious woman looking for a guy she knew. He looked really busy. I don't think he was aware we were there watching him."

Juan said, "Yeah, I guess you're right. He might have gotten curious if he had seen me. What are we going to do about the ATV? We're gonna need a key to run the damn thing."

"Just leave that to me. I'll go into town tomorrow and visit the dealer that sells those little four-wheel bugs. I'll ask him a few questions." Maria grinned and patted Juan on the head. "I'll wear that blond wig, high heels and that short black skirt. With your knowledge of electric circuits, we'll figure something out from the info I get."

By eight o'clock the next morning, the fire brigade had eaten breakfast and had cleared debris from the roadway for a bit over an hour. When they heard a vehicle approaching and saw it was a state pickup with a Forest Ranger decal on the driver's door, they all stopped work to get a look at their visitor.

The tinted windows concealed the driver, but both guards walked over to the small truck to investigate. The driver's window descended, and Todd stepped closer.

DD turned around and yelled at the crew, "Get back to work!" Then he joined Todd.

Jay and Larrea were cutting a downed tree into eight-foot sections and their chainsaws prevented any of the crew from hearing the discussion at the pickup. The guards engaged in conversation with the driver for around five minutes before they turned away from the pickup and walked toward Jay and Larrea.

When Todd approached within three or four yards of Larrea, he put his fingers in his mouth and whistled loudly enough to be heard over the chainsaw noise. She turned around and saw Todd gesture that he wanted her to shut down the saw. She killed the motor and removed her ear plugs. Jay heard the other saw shut down and looked to see what had happened. When he saw Todd and Larrea trying to talk, he shut off his saw.

Todd said something to Larrea and pointed to the Ranger's pickup. Larrea laid her saw on the ground and started walking toward the vehicle. After a few steps, she stopped, turned around, shrugged her shoulders, and shook her head. Jay was sure she didn't know what was going on; he reacted by nodding.

Jay and most of the other inmates watched Larrea step up to the operator's window, listen to the driver for a few seconds, then move around to the passenger door and climb in the truck.

Todd stepped closer to Jay and said, "I don't know much more than you do. The ranger had a message from the warden to DD and me. She was given authority to bargain with Larrea.

Jay frowned, "She?"

"Yeah. The ranger is a good looking woman. DD and I were both surprised."

Jay shook his head, wondering what was going on with the interruption. Realizing he wasn't involved, he got back to work. Branches removed from the tree trunk were cut into smaller sections and Jay raked them into a pile. He turned around to see if Larrea was returning but saw her toss her bags into the back of the pickup. Then she ran over to him and said, "I'll be back. I have something to look into. I might be seeing my daughter in a few days." She waved, turned around and ran to the pickup. When she was in the passenger seat, the ranger's vehicle backed up, turned around and left the area.

As the two women drove back toward Suddenly, Larrea inquired, "How did you know I was out here, Julie?"

"My husband is the sheriff of Suddenly. He received a message from the prison that you were assigned to the fire brigade. When I heard your name, I realized I had met you and was surprised you were incarcerated. What happened?"

Larrea sighed, "I'll give you the short version. My ex and I had a disagreement about having a child. He didn't want the responsibility of a child, and after I became pregnant, he ran off with another woman. I divorced him and three years after having my girl, I started dating again. I guess I just can't pick a good man; I fell for his pile of crap." She shook her head, "I was so stupid. We were together, off-and-on, for several years before he started a business with a friend. When the business collapsed, the guys took off and I was left holding the bag. Since my name was on the documents, and the men had disappeared, I was sentenced to three years for the theft of over six hundred thousand dollars."

"So, what happened to your daughter?"

"Child services gave me an option, have her live in a foster home in Flagstaff or live with her grandmother on the Navajo Nation in Arizona. We talked about it for about an hour, weighing the different choices. Spring decided to stay with her grandmother on a small ranch near Cameron, in the Painted Desert. It's about an hour north of Flagstaff."

"What a beautiful name, Spring Wisdom. She's a teenager now?"

Larrea smiled, "Yes. She's eighteen and wants to be an artist. She loves the Painted Desert and sketches all the time. She's into watercolors. Her grandmother lets her drive an old pickup around in search of artistic subjects."

# CHAPTER 15

Halfway back to Suddenly, Julie explained Jenny Kincaid's dilemma, facing the thought of living by herself in that drafty old farmhouse. When Julie related Jenny's interest in art, Larrea perked up, "Wouldn't it be nice to get Spring here to live with Jenny when I'm not around. But I don't want to get ahead of myself; Jenny might not want me to live with her, since I'm an inmate."

"I believe I know Jenny, and when she meets you and hears your story, I think she's going to welcome you to her house. And the possibility of having your daughter here, also, adds even more reason for her to want you to stay with her. Oh, I forgot to tell you, she drives a small pickup. She could take you to work and get you at the end of each workday. You wouldn't have to stay out in the forest at night with all those men. That might save the warden from having to send a female guard to the brigade."

Larrea chuckled, "I'd probably have a better diet, too. I'm not worried about the men though, I've been in that situation before."

When Julie approached her house, she noticed David's Subaru was gone; instead of pulling into her driveway, she slowed, but didn't stop. She pointed out her house to Larrea and said, "We're going to the farmhouse. My son, David, and Jenny are probably there doing some interior painting. You can see Jenny, meet my son, and look over the farmhouse. I'd like to see what they've done with the place."

Five minutes later, the ranger's pickup turned into the farmhouse driveway and parked behind David's car. As they stepped on the porch, Julie pointed out the repaired section of railing where Jenny had fallen and broken her collarbone. The entrance was open but Julie knocked on the screen door and called out, "You guys in here?"

David and Jenny were starting to paint Mrs. Kincaid's bedroom. They had moved the furniture against one wall and covered it with a drop cloth.

Jenny heard the pickup, "Somebody just pulled into the driveway."

I was curious, "Let's see who it is. I didn't want to see a motorcycle." I set the gallon of light-yellow paint on the floor and headed down the hallway when I heard Mom's voice. I had taken about three steps before I was violently shoved aside, bumping into the wall of the narrow passageway. Jenny laughed as she pushed me aside, "Some football player you are." I recovered and walked to the living room.

I heard Jen say, "Hi Mrs. Wilson," before I saw my mother and the woman slightly behind her. I had never seen the woman before. She was taller than Mom by about three or four inches, slim and had short dark hair. I was guessing that she was about the same age as Mom.

"Hi, Jenny, David. I'd like you to meet Larrea Wisdom. She's an old friend of mine and a firefighter."

We were on the porch shaking hands with Mrs. Wisdom when I recalled Scott telling Mom about the new addition to the inmate fire brigade, Larrea Wisdom. This was the idea Mom was investigating, a possible roommate for Jenny. This woman would be more like a mother for Jenny than a roommate. I wondered what Jenny would think. Would Jen think my mother was crazy?

Following introductions, Jenny invited the women into the house. We sat in the living room to talk. Mom explained her thinking so everyone would understand the concept. When Mom finished, Larrea leaned forward with her forearms resting on her thighs. The whole gathering reminded me of a coach talking at halftime to the backfield when we were behind several touchdowns. When Larrea mentioned her daughter was a novice artist, I noticed Jen began to smile. Jenny was going to approve of whatever agreement was reached. I felt it was a sure thing.

Jenny glanced at me and looked directly at Mom. "Mrs. Wilson, could I talk with David?"

"Sure, we'll step outside for a minute." Mom and Ms. Wisdom went outside and sat on the porch steps. Jen and I moved into the kitchen out of earshot.

Jen grabbed my right hand with both of hers and asked, "Do you think it's a good idea?"

"It's totally up to you, Jen. Mrs. Wisdom isn't a hardened criminal, she's a victim of those two men and the system. But I don't think she can afford to bring her daughter all the way from Arizona. That's too bad. And she would only be spending nights with you. She still has to work with the brigade crew and eat with them. You would be doing her a favor, though. She would have a nice place to sleep and clean up. Do you want to be a taxi service? You'd have to drive on those back roads twice every day."

"I don't mind driving on those dirt roads, but I'd like you to come along the first time. Could you do that?"

"Not a problem, Jen."

Jenny released her vise grip on my hand and kissed my right cheek. "Thank you, David. This is going to work out great. I can tell Megan I don't need her." She paused in thought, "And, you know what? I'll send Spring and her grandmother airplane tickets to come up here from Arizona. They'll have a reunion and I'll have several roommates." Her eyes were dancing in excitement.

I don't remember Jenny being so enthusiastic about anything, except maybe finding the gnomes and diamonds in the attic. Her grandmother's death had taken so much spirit from her, I was happy to see her positive change in attitude. She hadn't given a second thought about bringing Mrs. Wisdom's family from Arizona. I guessed she will want me to go with her to see Mr. Isaacs at the bank for him to agree with spending some of her inheritance on a good cause.

We went back outside, and Jen informed Mom and Mrs. Wisdom of her decision.

Mrs. Wisdom was all smiles. "Thank you, Jenny. I think we'll get along fine. I promise I won't boss you around."

Jenny laughed, "I'll probably need some bossing. Don't worry about that."

Mom said, "David, please take Ms. Wisdom's things out of the pickup. I have to take her back to the brigade. She will be able to return about eight o'clock." Mom engaged Larrea's input with a quick glance.

"Eight o'clock will be about right. I should be ready to go then. And please call me Larrea."

I left the women talking and went to the back of the ranger truck. I saw only two things that weren't Mom's regular equipment. The two canvas bags had STATE PEN stenciled on them in yellow capital letters. I lifted the two containers from the back of the pickup and put them on the porch next to the door. Jen and Ms. Wisdom would decide where things belonged in the house. I suspected Larrea would be staying in Mrs. Kincaid's former bedroom. It should be freshly painted and free of fumes by this evening. I'm sure Jenny wants to clear her mind of the image of her grandmother's death bed. I believe that has been haunting her.

Jenny and Larrea shook hands and exchanged a few words. After Jen and Mom hugged, the two older women climbed in the state pickup. I waved to Mom as she backed to the street and turned around. She beeped the horn as they drove away.

"I really like her, David. It will be so nice to have someone staying with me. Let's get back to painting. I want that room to be ready for her. Do you know what her first name means? I've never heard Larrea before."

"I don't know. My dad mentioned her name yesterday. That was the first time I heard it. I guess you'll have to ask her if it has any special meaning."

By lunchtime, the bedroom was repainted. Fortunately, I didn't have to patch any holes or cracks in the plaster. Using rollers, we had painted quickly. Jenny used a brush to finish around the trim and corners as I cleaned up the equipment and a few drips. We opened the window and I brought in a fan from my car and to ventilate the bedroom for faster drying.

We sat on the porch eating sandwiches for lunch. Jen's excitement hadn't waned much since meeting Larrea and she remarked about such a productive morning. She was hopeful that Spring would come from Arizona. Jen would have someone about the same age for company and they had similar interests in art. We talked about which room was next for painting and decided it would be the bathroom in light-lilac, Jenny's choice. When I looked over the bathroom, I thought it needed a new tub, the clawfoot one was ancient, but I didn't mention it. I'd suggest it later.

Maria arrived in town right after lunch and visited Harley's New Cars and Trucks. The business sign was prominently displayed on a banner across the store front above the windows. When Maria waltzed to the counter, she noticed a picture under glass showing an older store name: Harley's Car and Truck Fleet. It was the same location. She surveyed the dealership and imagined why the name had been changed; only two new vehicles could be seen, a Toyota sedan and a GMC pickup, both in black and very shiny.

A slightly overweight and balding middle-aged man wearing a yellow dress shirt and brown slacks approached from the other side of the counter. She wondered, *Is this Harley?* Her uncertainty soon vanished.

He bellied up to the counter and reached across the glass top with his right hand.

"Afternoon, ma'am. I'm Harley Templin. How can I help you?"

Maria smiled as she shook hands and swept her blond hair back from her face with her left hand, exposing her fake diamond earing. She could see Harley's eyes drift to her cleavage; just what she wanted.

"I have a problem with an all-terrain vehicle, I've lost the key and start the darn thing. My teenage son wants to go for a ride with my boyfriend tomorrow. Could you loan me a master key for a Yamaha?"

"Well, pretty lady, I can't do that. There's no master key. Besides, I only carry Hondas; they're the most powerful, dependable and the best for getting around in these mountains. I do have a used model for rent. Would that help?"

Maria acted like she was considering the rental, but then said, "No, I guess not. Maybe we can figure out a way to start it without the key." She started toward the door but stopped when Harley asked, "Does your friend have a set of booster cables?"

"Gosh, I'll have to ask him." That was all she needed to know. She knew Juan would know how to use the booster cables. As she went out the door, she glanced back and smiled, "Thanks, Harley."

As she walked around the corner to her maroon sedan, she noted the temperature on the bank's sign: 92 °F. Few people were on the streets, the heat had driven nearly everyone inside to air-conditioned environments. She slid onto the hot leather seat, opened all the windows, and drove away slowly; no cops wanted.

Deputy Doureline saw the maroon vehicle and noted the driver was a good-looking blond but had no reason to stop her. He would report the observation to the sheriff. He noted the time and direction in his logbook and turned up the cruiser's AC another notch.

Maria could hardly wait to get back to the tower and out of the tight-fitting clothes and remove the ridiculous wig. She liked the looks men gave her when she wore that crazy wig and the tight skirt, but she disliked the use of the disguise. If it weren't for the promise of half a million dollars, she wouldn't even be involved in this nutty scheme.

Juan had been so convincing when they met in San Diego two years ago. He didn't tell her his real name until they had been together for six months. She was simply happy to have found a boyfriend that made good money in the electronics industry, until one day everything changed. Juan never explained what had happened but promised things would get much better. She didn't think long about the plan, she just went along for the ride, though she realized it might get dangerous. She was determined to disappear if her involvement was going to cross a moral line she had established. Murder was over that line.

She parked in her normal spot next to Juan's cycle, left the car windows down and began climbing the steep staircase. After the first twelve steps, she stopped on the landing, took off her skirt so she could move without restriction, and continued the trek to the top.

Juan was having a beer and laughed when she entered the cabin. "Geez, woman, did you have to strip to get the information?" He laughed again and took another swallow.

"A lot you care. You sit around while I do all the leg work." She pulled of her wig, kicked off her heels and put on a pair of jeans. "The guy told me all we have to do is use jumper cables. I thought you'd know how to do it. We have cables, don't we?"

"Yeah. They're also called booster cables, they're in your trunk."

"Oh! I saw those, one's red and one's black."

"Uh-huh. Those are the ones."

# CHAPTER 16

Following lunch with Jenny, David was called away from the Kincaid property to mow two lawns. Jenny worked alone, cleared the clutter from the vanity, removed a small chest of drawers from her bathroom, and began painting the walls. With the ceiling fan on, the paint dried quickly, and she was able to finish the improvement by dinnertime.

She cleaned up and changed clothes, nervousness beginning to grow as the minutes passed. What would she talk about with Larrea? As usual, Jenny was to have dinner with the Wilson family. Afterwards, David would drive ahead of her pickup leading the way to get Larrea at the brigade camp site. Jen hoped it wouldn't be too dark for the return trip to her home.

She didn't like the thought of driving those shadowy, dirt and gravel forest roads in near darkness. At least this time, David would be along for support. She had to concentrate on the route, looking for landmarks so she could drive to the brigade camp without David leading the way. All of a sudden, she realized starting tomorrow, she would be accompanied by Larrea. She wouldn't be alone.

Earlier that morning, around ten-thirty, Larrea was returned to the brigade in Julie's pickup. At Larrea's request, Julie let her out of the truck about a hundred yards short of the work site. Larrea walked the remaining distance and reported to Todd and DD. When one of the men saw her walking toward them, he whistled loudly enough for Jay to hear even with ear plugs. Everyone stopped working and watched her conferring with the guards.

Jay thought Larrea's actions were curious and wanted to find out what she had done when she left the men after breakfast. Was she receiving special treatment? He hoped she would work with him again so he could find out the facts instead of rumors spread by the others. But, before she was even working again, he heard one of the guys say, "The queen bee has returned to the hive." Jay would keep his mouth closed and his ears open. Maybe she would tell him what had happened, but that was entirely up to her, he wouldn't ask. He hoped it would be an interesting story. He noticed she didn't return with her belongings; something was up.

Todd bellowed, "All right, back to work. The sideshow is over."

Jay walked toward the flatbed to get more gas for his chainsaw. As he reached for the gas can, Larrea's voice startled him. "I'll pour, put your saw on the ground."

Larrea was holding a gas can from the other side of the truck. She looked different; her previous all-business expression was gone. She smiled and said, "I have something to tell you."

Jay lowered his saw to the ground and removed the gas cap. He watched in silence as Larrea poured fuel from the two-gallon container into both chainsaw gas tanks. He bent down and screwed the lids back on as she replaced the larger receptacle on the shelf under the truck bed.

"I'll be leaving for nights from now on. A young lady will come for me after chow this evening. I'll tell you more when we take a break."

"Good idea. The guards will start hounding us if we stand around talking. We'll have a break for lunch, then I want to hear the details."

Jay yelled at Todd, "Hey, boss, where do you want us?"

The bigger guard pointed ahead on the road. "There's a huge tree across the road about a quarter mile ahead. Cut it up. Some of the guys will come and help you move it off the road. Don't try to move it yourselves, it's too damn big. You'll bust a gut."

Jay and Larrea picked up their saws and began walking, slightly up hill for about a hundred yards and then down hill the rest of the way. They moved in silence for a few seconds before Larrea spoke, "That ranger knows me and she thought I could help a girl who just lost her grandmother. The youngster inherited a large farmhouse outside town and didn't want to live alone. She gets spooked by the night sounds out there."

"Sweet. You get to sleep in a real bed. Good for you." Jay smiled, "You'll come to work refreshed and put in a full day's work. You'll be expected to work harder than the men now." He winked at her.

"Hey, don't kid yourself. I work harder than the men anyway."

Jay grinned, "Yeah, you're probably right. Say, who's this girl you'll be mothering?"

Larrea frowned, "Not mothering, Jay, just helping out. The girl, Jenny Kincaid, is about the same age as my daughter, and like my kid, she's an artist. Actually, she's interested in designing clothes."

"So, you have a daughter. Where is she now?"

"She's with her grandmother on the Navajo reservation in Arizona, in the Painted Desert. The reservation is called the Navajo Nation."

"Well, at least you know where she is."

Larrea looked at him curiously, "What does that mean?"

"I have a son, but I don't know where he is." Jay exhaled, "He thinks I'm dead."

Jay glanced at Larrea. Her brow was furrowed. She looked back, "I'm sorry. I assume you wanted it that way when you were sent to prison."

"It was mostly my mother's idea, but I agreed. I didn't want the kid to have the knowledge of his father being in prison hanging over him. What would his friends think?"

"What about his mother?"

"She died in an auto wreck about two years into my sentence. My brother died with her. I was allowed to go to her funeral. That was a tough time for the family. She had cancer, too. It was bad."

They walked the rest of the way in silence. When they were ten yards away from the roadblock, they stopped to evaluate the position of the four-foot diameter behemoth. Todd was correct, the tree was enormous, probably seventy to eighty feet long. It was even larger than the tree that had crushed Gun's leg. Larrea walked across the road evaluating the structure of the giant as Jay stood watching her work.

She walked back to where Jay was standing and said, "I could have predicted this big boy would fall during heavy rain and wind. Growing on the side of this hill was going to be a disaster for it, when it grew this big. I'm surprised it didn't come down sooner."

Jay explained what had happened with Guns and she said, "Two mistakes, Jay. The big limbs are cut last. They are used for support while limbing. When removing limbs, keep the tree between the saw and you. Sometimes that's awkward, but necessary for safety." She stepped back and said, "One more thing, always stand uphill from the tree. Gravity is an accomplice of a killer tree."

Larrea looked at Jay and said, "Okay, ready to work?"

Jay grinned. "I'm ready, but I'll watch you start. I'll learn from the pro."

She started her saw, removed a few limbs so she could access the uphill side of the tree and started removing branches at a rapid rate, working toward the exposed roots where the limbs increased in size. Jay was amazed and shook his head at her rapid progress. He had a lot to learn from this woman. He made his way to the other side of the tree and began applying what he had just learned, moving in the opposite direction from Larrea.

When all but the largest limbs remained supporting the massive trunk, the saws were silenced. Larrea and Jay talked about the next step. Larrea explained, "We need to put some supports beneath the tree so we can remove the root structure. There's a lot of weight involved; that's why your friend was injured, the tree crashed down on him when the support limbs were removed."

They began scanning both sides of the road for smaller downed trees to be made into supports. They walked together on the uphill road with Jay carrying his saw, Larrea left hers beside the nearly naked monster. They had gone about thirty yards when Larrea cried out, "There, just what we need." She pointed to an eight inch diameter log jutting out from the right hand ditch onto the shoulder. "We need two lengths, one about three feet and the other a half-foot longer."

Jay began stepping off the three foot distance and Larrea started laughing, "What are you doing, Jay?"

He gave her a questioning look, "Measuring off three feet. My boot is twelve inches long."

"Okay, but those lengths are only approximate; they don't have to be accurate."

Jay felt a bit foolish, but said, "Hey, after eleven years of lock up, I just follow directions." He forced a smile and began cutting the log.

They wedged the support pieces under the big tree trunk, kicking them into position until the heavy posts were lodged securely in place.

Larrea inspected the entire tree before saying, "It looks good, now we can remove the root structure. This is still dangerous though, so if the tree moves as you're cutting, get the hell away as fast as you can. Drop the saw and run. I don't want a dead partner."

Jay planted his feet securely on the ground and began cutting into the tree trunk. He quickly realized his saw could cut less than halfway through the largest part of the log. When he finished the first cut, he stepped back, killed the engine, and sat on the ground. His arms needed a rest. It felt good to take a break and sit on his butt.

He expected Larrea to join him, but instead she started her saw and began removing large wedges near his first cut. He watched as she guided her saw almost effortlessly through the wood, chips and chunks falling to the ground. When they were finished, the tree was on the ground in five approximately twelve-foot sections but still too heavy for them to be removed from the road without help.

Sweating heavily, Jay and Larrea started back to the brigade for lunch. Jay commented as they walked slowly downhill, "The saws are lighter, almost all our gas is gone."

Larrea laughed, "We're lighter, too. We need to get a drink of water. I'm happy we're going downhill; my legs feel kind of rubbery."

Back in camp, the loggers shoved the chainsaws onto the truck bed and collapsed on the ground. Todd had watched them return and brought them some bottles of cold water.

"You guys lost track of time. We've all had lunch. There are sandwiches and apples in the cab, help yourselves."

"Thanks, boss. That tree is in sections, but it will take most of the men and the truck to move them off the road. There's some good wood in those big logs."

Larrea and Jay joined the rest of the brigade for the afternoon, cutting back growth that was beginning to invade the roadway. Aside from two confrontations with porcupines, the work was boring. Inmate conversation and an occasional off-color song were all they had to relieve the monotony. Gossip about Larrea didn't last long after DD explained why she was leaving the camp at night.

After dinner, a motor was heard but the expected truck did not show; an ATV appeared and passed quickly by the camp. A young boy about twelve years old on a four-wheeler went roaring up the road. A few minutes later, he returned, stopped, removed his helmet, and yelled, "Hey, the road's blocked with logs up ahead."

Todd yelled back, "Thanks, kid. We'll remove them tomorrow."

"Okay, just thought you should know. See yah." He donned his pink and black helmet and sped off down the road.

# CHAPTER 17

Long shadows were creeping across the forest floor approaching the campsite as Larrea, Jay, Markus and Todd reviewed the day's accomplishments. Jay was telling the others about Larrea's guidance to change that enormous tree into more manageable sections, when a light green SUV arrived. The crew's attention shifted to the car.

Jay asked Larrea, "Is that your ride?"

"No, I'm expecting a black pickup driven by a teenage girl. I'm not sure who that is."

David stepped out of his car and Larrea recognized him. "Oh, that's the sheriff's stepson."

A few seconds later, a small black pickup arrived and parked behind the SUV. Larrea nodded, "That's my ride. The young man knows this area. I'll bet she didn't want to get lost, so he came along."

Jenny met with David and they walked toward the campfire where Larrea was waiting. When the boy and girl got closer, Jay recognized David as one of the boys that was playing catch with a football when the brigade left Suddenly.

Larrea introduced Jenny and David to Jay, Markus, and Todd. When hand shaking was complete, Jay commented, "David, I threw the football to your buddy from the back of our truck as we drove out of town. Who is that kid? He's pretty fast and has good hands."

"He's new to Suddenly. Been in town three or four weeks. He bought a barn close to where we were that day. His name is Dexter Young."

Surprised that the kid and he had the same last name, Jay inquired, "Is that kid from around here?"

I smiled, "No way. Forests are like a foreign army of warriors to him. He's from St. Louis. He quit his job and rode a bicycle all the way out here—took him a week with a little dog."

Although Jay and this kid Dexter had the same last name, he didn't want to push his questioning any further. If he asked more questions, the teenagers would begin to get suspicious. He decided to keep quiet and, in a few days, he would see what Larrea could tell him about the kid from St. Louis. Could this Dexter kid be his son?

Larrea watched Jenny whisper something to David. She interpreted the action to be the youngsters wanting to get back on the road.

She said, "I think we'd better get going. These old roads are dangerous at night."

I agreed, "You're right about that, Mrs. Wisdom. Let's start back to Suddenly. You and Jenny can follow me to my house so Jenny can get her things from my place. I'll follow you guys to Jenny's house if you need me to help with anything."

Jenny and I started walking toward our vehicles. I noticed Larrea walking with Jay about ten feet behind us. I wondered what they were up to, maybe they were saying good night. I got in my car and watched Larrea and Jenny get in the pickup. Jay had followed and motioned for Larrea to lower the passenger window.

She reached out and placed her right index finger on Jay's lips; it wasn't a kiss; it was more like a hush, quieting a secret. I'll have to ask Jenny what had happened. Could it be that prisoners form close relationships so quickly? That's something to ask Mom and Scott tonight.

I watched Jay start back to the campfire area and Larrea close her window. I shook my head slightly, thinking inmates probably have a special way of communicating, unknown to outsiders. The automatic lights came on when I started my car; the sun had gone behind the trees. I turned my car around and waited for Jenny to get close behind me before I stepped on the gas.

I drove slowly, trying not to kick up too much dust. At twenty-five miles per hour, it took us twenty minutes to reach the outskirts of Suddenly. When we passed by Dexter's place, I looked for a light, but wasn't able to see signs of life. He was probably in bed after a tough day's work on the barn. I was going to help him in the morning.

I parked at the curb behind Mom's pickup and let Jenny use the driveway backing her truck to the garage like a pro. Scott wasn't home. I wondered where he had gone after dinner. I followed the women up the stairs to the apartment above the garage, picked up Jenny's large suitcase, and went back down the stairs. The women followed with a small suitcase and a laundry bag.

Mom had put Gwen to bed and came out to say hello to Larrea and Jenny. Mom started talking with Larrea, so I pulled Jenny aside and asked, "What did Larrea and Jay say just before we left the camp site?"

Jenny thought for a second and replied, "Oh, she told him she knew what he wanted, and she would find out for him. That's all they said. It didn't make any sense to me."

"And she didn't say anything to you about it on the way back?"

"No, nothing. Do you know what they meant?"

"Not a clue; it was probably nothing." I grinned, "Maybe he wanted her to buy some mosquito repellant."

Jen laughed, "Or sun block." She looked upward and said, "There's that bright star again. I've got to find out what it's called; I bet it has a fancy name."

I teased, "Yeah, like Jenny-O."

Jen said, "No, Star of David." We both started laughing; neither of us being Jewish, but her remark was better than mine.

Larrea said good night to Mom and got into the pickup. I heard, "Let's go home, Jenny!"

Ten seconds after Jenny and Larrea pulled out of our driveway, Scott stopped in front of the house; with the engine running, he called to me, "Please move your Mom's truck into the driveway. I'll park behind so I can be first out in the morning."

I got Mom's truck keys and parked her pickup close to the garage. Scott pulled in behind me. As we walked into the house together, I asked, "Did you go to the office after dinner?"

"That's right. An old acquaintance from the FBI wanted to talk about a case he's working on. He's in a tough spot and asked for my advice. Unfortunately, he couldn't discuss any of the details, so I wasn't of much help. How was your trip to the firefighting crew?"

"About like your talk, uneventful, although I did see something I thought was a bit curious."

I had Scott's attention. He asked, "What was that?"

I told him about the interaction between Jay and Larrea I observed. "What do you think was going on?"

Scott thought for a second and replied, "Probably something that Larrea didn't want Jenny to hear, but not earthshattering or Jay wouldn't have started to say what ever it was when Jenny could overhear."

"Well, I asked Jenny what they said, and she told me she didn't understand what they were talking about."

Scott smiled and slapped me on the back, "I don't think they're planning an escape, David."

I thought what Scott said was kind of funny. I'm reading David Baldacci's paperback: *The Escape*. I usually read in bed for about twenty minutes or until I fall asleep; I've only read a few chapters of the 470 page book.

I watched a half-hour of television, said good night, and started to my room. As I passed by Danny's bedroom I saw him on the floor studying a road map. I grinned and said, "Going on a trip this summer?"

"No, I'm memorizing the capitals of each state. I figured it might be useful information someday. Did you make some friends with the convicts?"

That was my opening. "Yeah, some of them haven't finished high school. I figured they might want to play football this coming year. We'd have an awesome team with older men on it. They'd scare the other team off the field."

Danny looked a little perplexed. "Isn't there an age limit?"

"Gotcha! You're too gullible, Dan."

He kind of whined in protest, "Geez, David, how would I know?"

I felt bad teasing him that way, but I don't pick on him very often and he gets me sometimes. Our teasing is done in good fun. Mom comes to his rescue if it gets out of hand; then I apologize.

In the morning, I got a call from Jenny as I was having breakfast.

"Hi, Jenny. What's up?"

"I need to talk to you after I take my roommate to work."

"Okay, but I'll be at Dexter's place. Stop by and see what we're doing."

"Sure, I'll see you there. I want to see Skimmer, too."

"That little guy loves you, Jen. Oh, remember? Dex wants you to make some sketches of the renovated barn, so bring your pencils and imagination."

"Oh, yeah, I remember. I'll come prepared; see you about eight-thirty."

Jen's pickup rolled down Dexter's drive and stopped directly behind my Subaru at 8:35.

Dexter saw her coming from the barn roof where he was pulling the last few boards from the old trusses. I was on a ladder in the interior taking the boards from Dex, pulling rusty nails, and stacking the wood outside the structure. As soon as we got the roof removed, we were going to jack up one end of the building and pour footings for the new foundation.

I heard the pickup door close and knew it was Jenny, without Dex saying anything. She cautiously leaned into the barn and said, "I've got some news."

I answered back, "Don't come in here, it's too dangerous. It's very dirty and there are rusty nails everywhere. What's the news?"

"Mrs. Wisdom asked me what Dexter's grandmother's name was. I told her I didn't know. I think Dex told me once, but I couldn't remember. Should I ask him?"

I watched Dex sneak behind Jen and tap her on the shoulder.

"Ask me what?"

Startled, Jen jumped, "Oh! I thought you were up there." She pointed to the open roof.

"I was, but I got the last board removed and came down. What did you want to ask me?"

Jenny looked at me, raised her eyebrows for permission and I nodded.

"My new roommate asked me what your grandmother's name was. I don't remember. I think you told me once."

"Who's your roommate?"

"A lady named Larrea Wisdom. Do you know that name? She has an eighteen-year-old daughter. Larrea's really nice."

"To answer her question, my grandmother's maiden name was Loretta Meyer. She was an only child. Her father was a farmer in Kansas, Frank Meyer."

"I don't think I ever knew that."

"Why did this woman want to know that?"

Jenny looked at me and asked, "Should I tell him about Ms. Wisdom?"

"Yeah, I guess. What would it hurt?"

"Um, Ms. Wisdom is an inmate working with the firefighting brigade. She stays with me at night. I didn't want to live in that old farmhouse by myself. I took her to work and then came here."

Dex grinned, "You could have asked me. I'd stay with you."

"Sure, Dex. Your imagination is bigger than your barn." We all laughed.

Dex gave me that inquiring look and said, "Why would an inmate want to know my grandmother's name? I don't get it."

I recalled our experience with the fake insurance agent. Could be he knew one or more of the prisoners in the brigade.

"Hey, maybe someone in the brigade knew Cyrus Whitmore, that fake insurance agent."

Dex said, "Hey, David, I'll bet that's it. Fat old Whitmore had been in prison once. He probably knew one of those guys, but why would he want to know about me?"

I chuckled, "Maybe he has a job planned for when he gets out. He must want an expert and dependable bicycle rider as a getaway member of his gang. You could ride off into the sunset with the loot, divvy it up later."

Jenny began laughing and had to put her hand over her mouth to keep from drooling spit all over. Dex saw her actions and started laughing, too. I just smiled and looked at Jenny, "Are you all right?" Then I started laughing. Jen moved closer to me and hit me in the stomach.

"David, you are too funny. I'm not sure which of you has the bigger imagination."

Dex said, "I'll be right back," and left Jenny and me standing by the barndoor.

Jen asked, "Where's he off to? I need to talk about his house."

"You got me. I don't know Dex well enough to predict what he's up to."

Dex came back holding Skimmer. He put the pup on the ground and Skimmer ran to Jenny, shaking his little body from the tip of his tail to his cute little nose. She picked him up, cuddling him in her arms. "Oh, Skimmer, I've missed you."

While Jenny and Skimmer were getting reacquainted, Dex and I were estimating how much concrete was needed for the footings. We estimated ten eighty-pound bags of cement would do one end, but I didn't want to transport eight hundred pounds of dead weight in my little SUV. I volunteered Jen's pickup. Now to ask her. Would she trade her pickup for my car for the remainder of the day?

Jen was on her knees tickling Skimmer's stomach; he was nipping at her fingers.

"Now, don't you bite me, you little scamp."

When we stood beside Jen, she looked up at Dex and said, "Give me an idea of how your house should look. I'll sketch two or three of different views. You and your chief advisor can figure out what you want, maybe combine some of my ideas."

I put my arm around her shoulders and said, "Jen, can we use your pickup? You can have my car for the afternoon."

"I wouldn't feel comfortable driving your SUV, David. What do you need to haul? I can get it for you guys while you work on the house. Okay?"

"We need eight hundred pounds of concrete."

"So, you want to trash the pickup with all that muck? I'll never get it clean again."

She didn't understand. I said, "The cement is a dry mix in paper bags, not the wet stuff. We need ten eighty-pound bags."

"Oh. I didn't know what you meant. I can get those for you, but I can't lift eighty pound bags."

"You won't have to, the guys at the building supply will load your truck. You just need to drive."

"How much will it cost? I might have to get some money from the bank."

Dex chimed in, "Here's two twenties; that should cover it." He took out his wallet and gave Jenny forty bucks.

She stuck the money in her pocket, got in her truck and waved, "I'll be back in about an hour. Have your muscles ready to unload those heavy bags."

# CHAPTER 18

I was excited about getting started on the major changes to Dex's barn. I told Dexter, "We need a wheelbarrow, a hoe and some shovels. What do you have here?"

Dexter was not prepared, and he knew it, so did I. "Nothing. Do you think the Hadleys' can help us?"

"Maybe. Let's go ask Mr. Hadley if we can get some loaners." I was fairly sure we could get most of the needed things from Mr. Hadley, but if not everything, Jenny's grandfather's old tools were another source. Dex and I started hoofing it down the lane toward the Hadleys'.

As we walked, Dex asked, "What do you think about this woman, Ms. Wisdom, staying with Jenny?"

"At first, I had some doubts, but Mom knows her and she's only in lockup because she was taken advantage of. I think she'll be a better mother to Jenny than her real one. Jen's parents are really out of touch with their daughter. I think they're in Malaysia now."

When we reached the highway and turned right, I commented, "You're feeling a bit protective of Jenny, right?"

"Yeah, I guess I am. She's sure changed since we were in St. Louis. When we were dating, I could steer her around, but not anymore. She is more decisive and has real goals in mind now. Before, she was very unsettled, kind of lost. She always asked me what she should do, but now she's a thinking woman and knows what she wants."

I replied, "Maybe that's part of inheriting the farmhouse."

Dex thought for a moment, "Maybe that's part of it. Does she have enough money to take care of that old place? That's one of my worries."

Dex didn't know that Jenny was rich, and I wasn't going to tell him. I grinned and said, "Don't worry about that, Dex."

He gave me a funny look as we turned toward the front door of Hadleys' home.

"Something I don't know about?"

I changed the subject, apparently Dex didn't know that Jenny had inherited a lot of money in addition to the farmhouse. I wasn't going to tell him; that was Jenny's business.

"Megan's jeep is here. She must be working with Rick today. She didn't mention it to me." I had seen from the road that Megan's jeep was parked in front of the flat stone sidewalk leading to the front door. We stepped around the jeep and Dex knocked.

In a few seconds, Mrs. Hadley opened the door.

"Well, hello neighbor, and you have David with you. What can I do for you young men?"

Since I knew the Hadleys' better than Dex, I explained our situation. She listened attentively and invited us into the living room.

"Please have a seat. I'll call my husband; he knows where all those things are. I'm sure he'll let you borrow them. He just wants to know where things are going."

I sat back against a pillow on the sofa and Dex sat on the edge of another cushion and scanned around the room. I guess he had never been in Hadleys' house before. We could faintly hear Mrs. Hadley talking on the phone in another room.

Megan suddenly appeared in the hallway and saw me. She called out, "David, come help me. Rick needs some support."

I jumped up and Dex followed, a short step behind me.

"Grab his arms and lift so I can get the harness better placed." Dex and I did as instructed and in a few moments, Megan had things under control.

"Thanks, guys. He's heavier than I thought. I couldn't lift and work with my hands to adjust the harness."

Rick said, "Thanks guys, you saved me. She was trying to make me a eunuch, but it isn't necessary."

I think he meant that as a joke, but I suppose it could have another meaning. Neither Dex nor I laughed, but Rick chuckled, and Megan said, "Don't kid about such things, Rick. I didn't mean to hurt you. I'm sure your swimmers are all right." She grinned and patted Rick on the back.

Mrs. Hadley came in the room and asked, "Is everything okay in here?"

"Yeah. We're okay, Mom." Rick sounded a bit irritated.

"David, you will find the tools you need in our garage, and there are a couple of barrels of rainwater out back. You can have all the water you want from them."

"Thanks, Mrs. Hadley. I guess we'd better get going. We expect a delivery of concrete before long."

Rick asked, "Did you guys order some concrete to be delivered?"

I replied, "Jenny Kincaid is getting bags of the dry mix. We came over to borrow shovels, a hoe, and a wheelbarrow if your dad could spare them. We'll bring everything back in a few days."

"No problem. Dad's out doing some logging. He won't need that stuff for some time."

Dex and I excused ourselves and exited through the front door. When we stepped from the porch to the flagstone path, the garage door opened, and Mrs. Hadley called to us.

"Boys, everything is in here, take two wheelbarrows to haul the hoes and shovels. There's a gate in the back fence so you can access the water you'll need from your place, it's only a short walk. My husband said you need to dig a well, Dexter." She flashed us a big smile and withdrew into the house.

The garage was the most well organized space I had ever seen for car storage. The tools were hanging from a wall rack and the wheelbarrows were stacked, three in all. The one most used and beat up was on top. We took the upper two and loaded each with a hoe and shovel. There was a stack of five gallon buckets. I grabbed one.

Dex took off ahead of me singing, "Off we go into the..."

He stopped singing when the hoe fell off the wheelbarrow and he had to stop to pick it up.

I advised, "Slow down and pick a less bumpy path, Dex." I doubt if he ever pushed a wheelbarrow before, his only experience with devices with wheels was with bicycles. The hoes were difficult to keep from falling to the ground, but the shovels, being heavier, stayed in place. As we arrived at the barn, Jenny beeped her horn and came down the lane from the highway. When she was about halfway to us, she suddenly stopped, backed to the highway, turned around, and drove slowly all the way to Dex's gate.

She popped right out of the pickup and said, "I see you both have heavy loads."

I laughed, "How was driving with a full load?"

"Kind of squishy, I was afraid the tires would explode, but I made it. Can you guys unload for me? I need to get back home and make some phone calls."

I looked into the truck bed and counted ten bags of cement, just what we sent her for, and in good time. She had returned in fifty-five minutes, a bit less than an hour.

Jenny opened Dex's gate and began searching for Skimmer. Dex pointed at his bicycle where Skimmer was sacking out in one of the saddlebags, his home when travelling.

Dex and I got busy and began unloading the cement. After each of us had carried five eighty-pound bags about twenty feet and stacked them, we heard a siren. It seemed to be getting louder as we looked toward town. Jenny, holding Skimmer, Dex, and I started walking down the lane toward the highway, looking toward town. In a few moments, a small Suddenly fire truck flashed by, followed by Mom in her ranger pickup. I doubt if she saw me, she was probably concentrating on staying on the narrow road aware that the firetruck could slow down any second. I had never heard of her rear-ending anyone.

We started back toward the barn. Dex commented, "I wonder what that was all about."

"It was probably a small fire, maybe a garage or a hay pile, but something not too big. That small firetruck couldn't do much during a forest fire. I'll find out later."

Jenny put Skimmer back in his saddlebag bedroom, took a look in her truck bed, and climbed in the cab. Before she started the engine, I said, "Thanks for getting the concrete, Jen. That was your good deed for the day."

She answered back, "I've got some other good deeds to do. See you later if you want to come over to paint some more."

"Okay, but my arms might be sore from mixing concrete." I grinned and waved as she stepped on the gas, leaving us behind. She beeped her horn when she turned onto the highway and accelerated toward Suddenly.

Dex and I trudged to the bags of concrete and sat down. We both looked in the air for clouds, but the sky was clear blue from horizon to horizon. There was little chance for rain this week, according to the latest weather report, but we covered the bags with a tarp, just in case.

Dex glanced at me, "Jenny has a sexy walk."

He had surprised me. "I noticed. You're still hot for her, aren't you?"

"Not like I used to be. We've both changed."

I couldn't help but laugh, "Yeah, you're both older."

"Well, that's a true statement." He was looking at the ground at the end of the barn. "We need to make some forms for the footings, don't we?"

"Just for the raised corners; we'll dig out a trough from corner to corner, eight inches deep and a foot wide. Then we'll use rocks, bricks, and mortar to fill in the space between. The barn will sit on that. Three more sides just like it, but only two more corners."

"Geez, David, that's a hell of a lot of work."

I grinned, "That's a true statement. Let's get to it and start building a house. I tossed Dex the bucket and said, "Get some water."

Larrea was apparently the first of the brigade to hear the siren. She stopped working, turned her head toward the road, and said, "Listen! I hear a siren."

Most of the brigade stood still and listened. Markus was next to hear the alarm and we all saw Todd yell, "Quiet!" He was listening to a walkie-talkie and a few seconds later, he ordered, "That was a ranger. Load shovels and hoes and get in the truck. We've got a fire to mop up." It took about twenty seconds for the brigade to be loaded and moving toward Suddenly on the dirt road the crew had been working.

Fortunately, the loaded truck didn't encounter any traffic on the winding single lane road. About two miles down the tire grooves, smoke could be seen drifting skyward and the stink from a fire was evident. Larrea stood up scanning the ground and sky, hanging on to the top of a side panel and said, "It's not bad, guys, just a little smoker." She dropped back to the truck bed beside Jay in a bare spot free of hoe and shovel handles.

"Hey, I asked about the kid's grandmother, but couldn't find out anything. Hopefully, I'll get some information tonight. Jenny, my roommate, is going to ask about his grandparents. Sorry I wasn't able to talk to you sooner."

"That's okay. I've been tussling with the idea of contacting my son. I'm not sure whether I will…or even should."

Larrea reached out and touched Jay's wrist. "I think you should. The kid deserves to know about you. It'll do you both good. Once he knows the whole story, he'll understand."

The truck pulled into an open area that had been burned off and stopped. DD and Todd met with the ranger for a minute and called out to the crew. "Everybody out and start looking for hot spots. Dig 'em and cover. Don't miss anything. Okay, get to it."

Jay and Larrea began working together. Jay said, "You were right. This isn't a large, burned area, maybe two, three acres."

"Yeah. It looks like someone got to it before it made it to those trees."

She pointed about fifty yards south to the wall of vertical green giants. "If those had gone up, we'd be in a big one. People living around here could have lost everything. Those guys must have gotten water or retardant on it soon after it started." Larrea pointed at the fire truck at the eastern edge of the burn. That's when she saw her friend, Julie.

# CHAPTER 19

Julie waved and started walking toward Larrea and Jay, kicking at the ground as she began the near one-hundred-yard distance over blackened earth. Larrea and Jay worked their way in her direction, turning over clumps of burned vegetation, looking for smoldering remains. Larrea used the hoe and Jay covered what she unearthed with a shovel full of dirt.

When Julie was about ten yards from them, Larrea asked, "What happened here? It couldn't have been a lightning strike."

"It was kids on four-wheelers, one was smoking. He hit a bump and lost his cigarette. They tried to find it but no success. A few minutes after they were gone, the dry grasses started burning. Fortunately, one of the kid's fathers came by to see how they were doing and noticed smoke. The kid confessed and they phoned it in from his home, about a mile from here."

Larrea noted, "Lucky those trees didn't catch fire. Flames might have crawled and jumped all the way to town. The forest very dry."

Julie agreed, "Your observations are right on. There aren't any easily accessible streams for us to get enough water for fighting big fires around here. I'll make a note and we'll try to get a road put in to Hawk Lake; it's about a half-mile east of us. Presently it's almost inaccessible; there's only a hiking trail through the woods."

Jay questioned, "What are your responsibilities out here, Julie?"

"Well, I have to write a report of the position, area burned, and the cause. Actually, this sector isn't my responsibility, but Lee Cook is out sick this week. I'm a fill in. How are you guys coming with the road improvement?"

Jay spoke up after glancing at Larrea, "We covered almost two miles in the last couple of days. We were slowed by an enormous tree that had fallen across the road.

Larrea showed me how to trim it with a chain saw."

Julie looked at them and said, "So, I interpret that to mean you're getting along okay?"

Larrea grinned, "Yeah, Jay's easy going and doesn't say too much."

"Hey, I can say the same for you." Jay smiled and smothered the last hoed plant remains Larrea had exposed.

"Okay, you two. I didn't want to start anything. The big reason I came over was to tell you there's going to be a practice water drop here in a few minutes. We have a new man flying a chopper and I'd like you to make a target for him."

"A target?" Jay asked.

"Uh-huh. Clear a circle about ten yards in diameter in the middle of the burn. We'll see if he can make an accurate drop. You might have a couple of your buddies help out; he should be here in about ten to fifteen minutes. He'll make one pass, return, and drop several hundred gallons of water. Don't stand to close to the target, the falling water will knock you out, or worse."

Four of the brigade, including Jay and Larrea, covered a roughly circular area of black with much lighter brown earth making a target as Julie had requested. Jay estimated ten minutes had passed before they heard the rhythmic thumping of a helicopter's rotor. The faint noise grew in strength until the chopper came into view above the distant line of Douglas fir and lodgepole pine.

Larrea yelled to the others of the brigade, "Better get back to the road and let the pilot do his thing." Everyone scurried from the burned area and watched the aircraft pass overhead. Larrea said, "That's an MD500, Jay. It can't carry much, only around two hundred gallons."

"What's MD mean, mini-drop?"

Larrea looked at Jay quizzically, "The manufacturer of the chopper, McDonnell Douglas."

"Oh, that makes sense. I'm not familiar with makers of planes and helicopters, only cars and motorcycles. I do know Boeing makes big planes."

"There's no reason you would know that. I won't hold it against you," said Larrea and flashed him a big smile. She poked Jay and pointed at Julie talking into some type of phone with a foot-long aerial extending from the device.

Everyone watched the small helicopter pass overhead and disappear behind the trees, but the rotor noise could still be heard. Less than a minute passed, and the chopper returned, flying slowly, and dropping its full load of water as it crossed directly over the burned area, but not hovering, the water raining down in about a thirty-yard path that included the quickly made target.

Larrea looked up at the chopper as it vanished over the tall trees and said, "Not bad for a beginner." Her eyes caught sight of Julie as the ranger moved toward her truck, climbed in the cab, and drove off slowly.

Todd appeared from the brigade truck and gave an order. "Police the area for any hot spots and we'll get out of here, back to our regular task. Hope you liked the show. Can any of you fly a chopper?" None of the brigade members answered. "All right, back at it. Let's finish up here." Todd started toward the truck, stopped for moment, scanned the sky, and then continued on to the vehicle.

Forty-five minutes later, the snail-paced crew, sweaty and slightly stinky, was back to work on the road. They found several downed trail markers and referred to maps to reestablish their proper indication of direction. Some of the information boards along the road informed that no vehicles of any kind could traverse the area indicated.

When Jenny arrived at the brigade camp to pick up Larrea, she noticed the workers were unusually quiet, almost acting as if sedated. After a few minutes during the drive back to Suddenly, Jenny asked her new roommate, "Did something happen today? I saw a firetruck earlier. Was one of the brigade injured?"

Larrea smiled, "Nothing like that. We're all very tired. We were transported to the fire area and spent a couple of hours making sure nothing was smoldering. Can you smell smoke from my clothes?"

Jenny started laughing, "That explains a lot. Don't take this the wrong way, but you do smell a little gamey today. A shower will take care of that, and we can wash your clothes. You'll feel like new by bedtime."

"Oh, that sounds so good. I'll sleep soundly tonight. If I wake up yelling, just tell me I'm dreaming."

"Do you do that often?"

"I did once, after I was almost toasted in a big fire. It was very scary. The dream was worse than the real thing."

The women rode in silence for a couple of minutes before Jenny commented, "I found out Dexter's grandmother's name, it was Loretta Meyer. I hope that helps. David, Dexter, and I wondered why you wanted to know that."

"Thanks for the info. Loretta Meyer, not a strange name or anything."

"Who wanted to know?"

"I can't tell you now, maybe some other time. It's confidential. It might not mean anything to the guy that asked."

As the shadows lengthened and the sky began to gray, Jenny remembered to ask about the star she and David had joked about.

"I know you've slept out at night many times. When we get home, I'll point out a star. I'd like to know if it has a special name, it's a bright one."

"I know most of the northern hemisphere constellations, but not the names of very many stars. If it's a bright one like you say, maybe I'll know. I'll try."

"I'll locate it when we get home, and later I'll point it out after you've cleaned up. It'll be darker then, too."

"Do you have a telescope?"

"No. The only one I've ever looked through was one out at tower seventeen. David and I reported a fire from there."

Passing Dexter's and the Hadleys' residences, they reached the edge of town, and continued straight to the farmhouse. David's car was parked at the side of the road, but he wasn't waiting on the porch steps, which was his normal spot when visiting. Jenny parked ten feet from the porch and the women got out. Jenny was confused, she wondered where David was. Why would he have parked so far from the house? Was he hiding and going to surprise or scare her?

Larrea stood by the front door waiting for it to be unlocked. She watched as Jenny looked past the end of the porch. "Don't worry, Jenny, if he wants to see you, he'll show up."

"I guess so. Sorry, I'm making you wait to get your shower."

Larrea began stripping off her clothes as she walked down the hallway to the bathroom. When she entered the room she gasped, "Oh, you painted the room. How nice!" She closed the door and a minute later was standing under a refreshing stream of water. She heard a knock and said, "Yes?"

Jenny stated, "I'm going to wash your clothes. I'm leaving you some of mine, we're about the same size: jeans and an old sweatshirt."

"Okay, thank you."

Jenny went to the kitchen and began preparing a pitcher of lemonade. She thought about her grandmother as she added ice to the two-quart container; lemonade was Gram's favorite. She jumped when there was a sharp knock at the front door. Jen rushed to the door; it must be David. Where had he been? She looked out the peep hole and saw David; he was grinning. She swung the door wide open.

"Where have you been? Why is your car parked on the side of the road?"

"Hey, slow down. Can I come in?"

"Oh! Yeah. Come in. Larrea's taking a shower."

I stepped in the house and drifted into the living room as I collected my breath and thoughts. As usual, Jenny looked nice. She turned away and went to the kitchen saying, "I just made some lemonade, want some?"

I was trying to breathe normally after sprinting three blocks and jogging back. When I reached my car, I saw Jenny's lights were on. I had walked down her drive, taking deep breaths, climbed the porch steps, and knocked. I was still breathing hard, slightly out of shape. I took another breath and exhaled.

"Sure, I'd like some after running. It's still hot out."

She gave me a large glass of cold lemonade and asked, "Why were you out here running?" I sat on her sofa and leaned back to relax.

I took a big gulp and answered, "When I was going to turn in your drive, I saw a man looking in your living room window. When I stopped my car and got out, he ran, so I followed him, but he had too much of a head start. I couldn't catch him. He took off on a motorcycle."

"That's scary. Should I call the police?"

"No, don't bother. I'll tell Scott about it when I get home. Since you weren't around, you weren't involved. Don't worry, I'll make a report. It might have been a peeper kid trying to get a look at you in your undies." I raised my eyebrows and grinned.

Jenny grabbed a sofa pillow and threw it at me. "I think you said that to find out if I walk around naked."

"That crossed my mind, but only *briefly*." I chuckled. Jen sat beside me.

Larrea appeared from the hallway and said, "What was that about a Peeping Tom?"

"David saw someone trying to look in our windows. He chased him but the guy got away on a motorbike."

"Can you describe him?" asked Larrea. Her hair was still wet. She looked younger than the last time I saw her. Maybe it was the jeans.

"Dark clothes, but too far away to see much. I was gaining on him before he got to his motorcycle."

"Hmm. A man and woman stopped where we were working the other day. They were riding a motorcycle, but I suppose there are a few of those around."

Jen tapped my leg, got my attention, and said, "What did you come to see me about?"

# CHAPTER 20

"I wanted to apologize for not coming over to paint. I was helping Dex with the foundation and we got involved with pouring concrete. He doesn't have a phone, so I couldn't call you. I kind of lost track of time, sorry."

"That's all right. I finished with the bathroom and then read a short story from one of Gram's magazines. I fell asleep on the sofa for about an hour."

I had to joke, "I thought it was kind of warm here when I sat down." I patted the sofa cushion.

"You are so full of it tonight, David. Let's go outside, get some fresh air, and find your star. Larrea might know if it has a name."

I smiled as we went outside, leaned against Jen's pickup, and looked at the stars.

Larrea's eyes swept the sky and then she turned to the north. She pointed out the north star and then said, "Now, scan to the south and stop at the brightest star, that's Vega."

I could hear the excitement in Jenny's voice. "That's it! That's the star of David."

"You'll have to explain that to me," said Larrea.

Jenny and I were laughing. Jenny said, "We were teasing each other the other night and David called that star Jenny-O. I said, *No, it's the star of David.* We didn't mean any disrespect to the Jewish religion."

I could barely make out the smile on Larrea's face from the light coming from the dim living room window glow that penetrated the curtains. She was looking straight up and commented, "You two have fun together, and that's a good thing. Well, I'd better get to bed, who knows what I'll be doing tomorrow."

Jenny followed with, "I'd better do the same. Thanks for coming over, David." Then, to my surprise, Jenny leaned over and kissed my right cheek. She backed toward the porch saying, "Will I see you for painting tomorrow?"

"Sure, about eight-thirty. Good night."

"Night, David."

I started down the lane to my car, only tripping twice, but not falling. Small clumps of weeds were still dangerous when walking at night in near darkness. There was no moon. I probably wouldn't have stumbled at all if I had been thinking of walking, but I was being tormented by something else. How was I going to break up with Megan?"

It was almost nine o'clock. Maria was waiting patiently in the tower for Juan. They had planned to lay on the deck and look at the heavens tonight, but Juan said he had to check something out in the dark. Without a moon to interfere, the stars were about as bright as Maria had ever seen them. She had never been this far north before, and she didn't recognize some of the constellations. Juan said he could point out some the objects in the sky, he had visited the observatory in Los Angeles more than once. Maria wondered who he'd taken there. She knew him; he wouldn't have gone there alone.

She was tiring of the solitude in the forest and was listening for the rumble of Juan's motor. What was he up to? She heard a noise from the wood in the roof cooling, a sudden snap that surprised her. She sighed and watched for the headlight beam of the motorcycle. There it is. The beam of light became brighter and flickered as the bike wheels rolled over the bumpy road to the tower. Finally, she heard the motor.

Maria saw the light reflect off her car as Juan parked and shut off the engine. It was quiet again for about a minute before she heard the sounds of boots stomping on the steps. She couldn't see him but called out, "Were you successful?"

"Yeah, I always am." Juan's faint silhouette appeared at the top of the stairs.

Juan came close to Maria and encircled her with his arms.

"Oh! You're all sweaty. What have you been doing?" Maria pushed Juan away.

"I had a footrace with a guy I met outside the grocery store. I stopped for a candy bar and this guy challenged me to a race. I won and he bought me some candy. Then I came to the tower to see you and the stars. Let's look, they're real bright tonight." He pointed skyward, changing the topic.

Maria doubted Juan's story, but she couldn't see his eyes. She could tell when he told lies when she looked at his face. They sat on the deck with their feet on the steps, leaned back and Maria exclaimed, "So many stars! There must be millions tonight."

"I think thousands. See that one?" Juan pointed to a bright star nearly overhead.

"That's Vega, twenty-five light years away."

Maria rotated her eyes to another bright star and pointed. "What's that one called?"

Juan thought for a few seconds. "That's Altair and that one is Arcturus." Those three were the brightest stars Juan could name. But then he stood, looked to the north, and pointed, "That's Polaris, the north star."

Maria felt petty, Juan knew so many things. She asked, "So, where did you go for your night visit?"

"You know I've been watching for John. I saw him earlier today at a grass fire. He was working with some woman. They seemed to be very friendly. She must also be an inmate. When I visit them at a big fire, I'll have to take more ammunition. I was making sure where she lived, but I didn't talk to her."

"You aren't going to shoot them, are you? You can't do that! That's murder!"

"For Christ's sake, Maria, I thought you understood! We've been shooting at targets to make sure we can hit our live targets, John, and this woman. They have to go. That's why I'm waiting for a big fire. Bullets will melt in the flames and tracing them won't be possible."

Maria couldn't get to sleep that night. She hadn't imagined Juan to be a killer. He had asked her to help find John, and that is what she did. She knew enough about the law to realize she would be an accomplice and could go to prison for an awfully long time. She had to find a way out of this mess. She could hear him gently snoring. In a few hours, the sun would be rising. Leaving Juan was the last thing she thought about before finally drifting off to sleep.

Larrea and Jenny got up early the next morning after both had a fitful night because of the Peeping Tom David had run off. They had a quick bite and piled into the pickup. Larrea would get more to eat at the brigade camp and Jenny was going to drop by the Wilsons' to talk to David. She knew the concrete at Dex's wouldn't be ready for carrying the weight of half the barn for another day; David should be available, just like he said last night. Plus, she'd be able to get orange juice and maybe a couple of pancakes there.

She dropped Larrea off, returned to Suddenly, and was almost sideswiped by a motorcycle. She tried to get the guy's license, but he got away too quickly. As she pulled up to the Wilsons' and parked in front of the mailbox, it suddenly occurred to her that the motorcycle rider might have been the Peeping Tom. David said the guy trying to see through the curtains got away on a motorcycle. David was on the front porch dressed in socks and jeans when she got out of the pickup and started toward the front door.

"Well, look at you! Don't you need a shirt and shoes?"

"I was on my way to a shower before eating breakfast. Come on in and have a seat at the table. Mom's making blueberry pancakes."

"Just what I hoped for. Hurry with the shower, I've got something to tell you."

"You're here early!"

"I know. Go take your shower, I don't want my paint to smell bad."

I was out of the shower and dressed in less than ten minutes. I didn't bother with shoes and socks before I got to the table and sat beside Jenny. She hadn't put any makeup on and looked slightly tired. Even so, she was still cute.

"Are you getting sick?" I asked.

"What? No! I couldn't sleep last night because of what you did, chasing that peeper away. Larrea was bothered, too. She'll have a tough day today, working hard with all those men after not sleeping well.

"Is that what you wanted to tell me?"

"No, that's not it. When I was returning from dropping Larrea off, a guy on a motorcycle almost side-swiped me. I couldn't get his license number, it happened too quickly. I'm wondering if it was the guy you chased last night."

Mom was at the stove shoveling pancakes onto a serving plate. She turned, looked at me and said, "What's this peeper thing, David? Why weren't we told?"

"You and Scott were talking when I came home last night. It sounded like a serious discussion was taking place. I didn't want to bother. I was going to mention it this morning."

"We could have been interrupted. We were discussing the fire situation; it's getting worse as the summer progresses. Those kids that started the grass fire could have started something that might have threatened Suddenly. We were extremely lucky."

I asked, "Where's Scott? His car's still here."

"He's still sleeping, he almost nodded off last night when we were talking. Poor man has been putting in some long days with few breaks. He's going to ask the town council for another officer. He and Doureline are spread too thin."

Mom had six pancakes on her serving plate. Jenny took one and I said, "Better take two, Jen, there's plenty more."

Mom looked at her watch, took the last two pancakes, buttered them, and ate quickly, drank a full glass of orange juice, and jumped up.

"I have to get out of here, David. Take over at the stove. Don't burn the hot cakes; Scott and Danny have to eat, too. I'll drop Gwen off and be home for lunch."

Mom grabbed her keys, darted out the door with Gwen and was gone.

"Wow, your mom is like a tornado this morning."

"Not just this morning, Jen. That's typical for her, once, sometimes twice a week. Today is a busy half-day though; she's meeting with the bigwig firefighting reps at the courthouse. People are coming from Idaho, too. They're reviewing schemes for the entire Bitterroot area."

Jenny twirled her fork on a last bite of pancake, and said, "I'm not sure I want to be an adult. It's a big responsibility." She added a little syrup and her lips pulled the bite from her fork. She looked at me and grinned, chewed briefly, took a drink of milk and said, "Thanks for breakfast. I'll wait until Danny and Scott are fed, then we can get some more paint. We'll need light-blue today, for my bedroom."

I grinned, "Ah, you're going to allow me in your bedroom? Have you put all your lacy things away?"

"I knew I shouldn't have said that. Don't get any funny ideas, buster."

Larrea had arrived as the brigade was having morning chow. She located Jay and stood beside him after getting a large helping of eggs and sausage.

Jay watched Larrea as she surveyed the men and said, "Morning," as she knelt with her paper plate of food and plastic utensils.

"Good morning. I found out what you wanted to know. The boy's grandmother's name was Loretta Meyer. Does that mean anything?"

Jay hung his head and sighed, "Yeah, my mother's maiden name was Loretta Meyer." He grimaced and gazed into the campfire.

"Well, Jay, Dexter is your son. Aren't you happy to know that?"

"I don't know if I should be happy to find out. I kind of hoped it was him but didn't know what I would do if it was. What I don't understand is how he got out here in western Montana. How in hell did that happen? Six months ago, I was told he was in St. Louis and had a job delivering messages in the downtown area. He was doing well."

"I assume you don't want him to know you're out here in the forest fire brigade."

"That's right. Please don't tell Jenny what we know. This isn't the right time for him to find out I'm alive and have been in prison all these years. He didn't have me or his mother as he was growing up. He's got something good going for him now, I don't want to spoil it."

Jay leaned toward Larrea and sniffed. She turned and held her plate between them. "What are you doing? Did I step in something?"

"No, just the opposite, you smell like flowers."

She laughed, "Jenny washed my clothes last night, the laundry soap has a floral scent in it."

"Nice."

Larrea leaned toward Jay and said, "Hmm, men's' locker room number two."

"Sorry about that, two more days until we get a change of clothes. We haven't found a creek for baths. We have deodorant sticks, but what's the point? You'll have to stay a safe distance away from us for a couple of days to protect your sensitive nasal membranes." He looked at Larrea and saw her smile, then he chuckled.

Juan slept until noon, ate lunch, and rode off on his bike. Maria didn't ask where he was going, not wanting to create any suspicions. She wished for a map of the trails through the mountains so she could plan her getaway, but the only place she could think of that had maps of the mountain paths was the ranger station. She had to be patient, she didn't want to leave and have an encounter with Juan, that might be the last of her.

Maria decided to take her car and drive farther up the road that led away from the tower. Where did it go? She could possibly find a route back to the Interstate without going through Suddenly. If she encountered Juan, she could say she was out exploring, looking for a creek to find some pretty rocks and maybe wash her hair.

# CHAPTER 21

Maria waited until she couldn't hear Juan's motorcycle before she took a bottle of water, her car keys, and descended the forty steps to her car. She had confidence driving on the dirt roads in the forested wilderness after some encouragement from Juan. She checked the gas, and the tank was nearly half full, plenty of gas to explore the nearby single lane roads. She would get more gas when she was leaving Suddenly for good.

Maria drove for less than eight miles when she noticed a sign for tower seventeen. She made a sharp left hand turn and started watching for the structure the sign indicated was less than a mile ahead. It wasn't what she expected, the tower was much taller than the one Juan had rented. A climb to the top where she might be able to see another route out of the forest would only take a couple of minutes, so she parked and began climbing the steps.

When Maria judged she was halfway to the top, she stopped and did a quick survey. She could see only about thirty yards of the road she had followed to the lookout, so she continued to climb. When she reached the top, she walked the deck that circled the cabin, looking for roads to follow, but she was disappointed. Breathing heavily, she went in the cabin and sat near the door. She should have brought her water; she was parched, and the cabin air was stifling.

Maria looked around once more before she was going back down all those steps.

A refrigerator caught her eyes, could there be something cool to drink inside? No luck, it was empty, unplugged. That's it, she decided to get back to her car and continue driving; with the windows down, it wasn't too bad. One last look around and she saw it, an old rotary dial telephone! It was mounted on the wall between two by four studs, kind of hidden from view from the entrance.

She placed the phone to the side of her head and listened, a dial tone! Who could she call? She had no one's number. She put the phone back on the cradle and slumped to the floor by the open door where it was slightly cooler. She closed her eyes and then it hit her! Dial 9-1-1! She picked up the phone, dialed and got nothing. Why didn't it work? Then she saw a number written on the wall. She dialed and a man answered!

"Tower seventeen, how may I help you?"

"I need to talk to the sheriff. Can you put me in touch with him?"

"Not directly, but I can give him a message. Is it an emergency?"

"Well, no, not an emergency. Tell him there is a bad man living in tower twenty. He is going to shoot some people." Maria heard a motorcycle engine. She had to hang up the phone. "I must go. Please tell the sheriff." She put the phone back and started down the top run of stairs. She thought she would meet Juan about halfway to the ground. She was mistaken, he had come up very quickly and they met at the top of the sixth flight.

"Why are you here, Maria?"

"It's good to see you, Juan. Do you know where we can find a creek? I'd like to spend some time looking for pretty rocks and maybe cool off in the water. When you leave me, I have nothing to do, and it is so hot."

"I did see a small creek, but the water was only a trickle. But maybe you can find some nice stones. I can show you."

Maria was sure Juan believed her, but then, the phone rang. Her thoughts shifted from happiness to fearful in a split second. Was that man calling back?

Juan asked, "Who did you call?"

"I asked about directions to a creek in the area. The operator couldn't help me. Maybe he found something on a map and is calling back."

Juan was ascending the steps rapidly, pulling Maria along like she was a small child. She was half his weight and just over five feet tall. Juan was over six feet and two hundred thirty pounds.

He reached the phone on the fifth ring. Someone wasn't giving up on the call.

"Hello." He listened for about ten seconds and said, "She's not here now. I'll tell her that you called." Juan hung up the phone and threw Maria to the floor.

"You little shit! You're going to spoil everything I've worked so hard for. I even married you so you could stay in the country and you thank me with a call to the sheriff!"

Juan straddled diminutive Maria, grabbed her around the throat, and started squeezing. She tried to fight, but she couldn't do anything, her arms were pinned to her sides. She tried to kick, but decided to relax, thinking he would quit choking her if he thought she was unconscious, but he kept squeezing her throat, something snapped, and everything went black.

Juan stood up, looked at lifeless Maria and said, "You little bitch, you got what you deserved." He felt for a pulse, picked Maria up, walked outside, lifted her over the railing and dropped her headfirst from the top deck. He heard a muffled thump when her body hit the ground. He closed the cabin door and started down the stairs.

When he reached ground level, he realized he had two things to get rid of, a maroon car and a dead body. He thought for a moment and decided what to do. He got a pair of gloves from his saddlebags, moved Maria's body to the trunk of her car and drove until he could pull off the road and hide the car out of sight from the road and air. He was pleased that the disposal had been so easy to accomplish.

Task completed, Juan walked the half-mile back to the tower and wiped everything down that Maria might have touched, including the hand railing on the stairs. When finished, he was confident no one would ever know Maria had been there. Before getting on his bike, he burned his gloves, and rode back to tower twenty to pack his things. He was going camping.

Juan made a small pile of the few pieces of clothing Maria had accumulated from thrift shops and garage sales as they moved across the country, stuffed the items in a pillowcase and dropped them to the ground. He packed his things into saddlebags and loaded his bike. He tied the pillowcase on top of the saddlebags and left the cabin as it had been before their arrival, without any signs of occupancy.

Travelling on the western outskirts of Suddenly to avoid people, he stopped at a church and left the pillowcase of clothes in the donation box. He rode by the house he had been chased from the night before, giving it a last brief look as he passed. It looked uninhabited, but there were two vehicles parked in the driveway: a small black pickup and a light-green SUV. He remembered the SUV belonged to the man that ran him off the property. If he had some luck when he had his rifle handy, he would see the guy again. Conditions and outcome would be totally different.

In the cubicle adjacent to the Sheriff's office, the fax machine was churning out several pages of wanted posters from Helena when Ginny's phone rang. It sat right beside the computer console that displayed the letter she was writing for the sheriff. The noise surprised her; she missed the double t's in Bitterroot typing double y's.

She scowled and answered the call.

"Hello? Yes, this is Suddenly's Sheriff's Office. One moment, I'll transfer you."

Mrs. Gumble rotated her chair and tapped on the plexiglass window separating the secretary from the sheriff. Scott looked up and listened.

"The Forest Service wants to talk to you, Sheriff."

"Thanks, Ginny." Scott waved to her and picked up his phone.

"This is Sheriff Wilson, what can I do for you?" He listened for a few seconds and said, "Tower seventeen? Who's renting that one?" He wrote some notes on a pad and stood up with his left hand on his hip, still on the phone, but inching toward the door.

"All right, I'll check it out. Thanks for the alert, Ranger Liscomb."

Scott tossed the phone on his desk and darted past Ginny saying, "Tell Tim to meet me at tower seventeen, ASAP. Tell him to bring a rifle."

Scott arrived at the turnoff to tower seventeen in record time. He had ignored the speed limit and relied on the stability of the cruiser to cling to the dirt roads. He stopped within sight of the tower and waited for his deputy, Timothy Doureline, to arrive. As he waited, he opened the trunk and extracted his rifle, attached the telescopic sight, checked it and the magazine, and estimated the distance to the cabin at two hundred fifty yards. He knew the deputy was a dead shot from that distance, as was he. They had competed on the range outside of Dillon two weeks earlier. It was a draw.

Tim rolled up and parked directly across the road from Scott, got out and said, "What have we got, Sheriff?" He had been just three minutes behind his boss.

Scott briefed Tim on the message from a woman at the outlook and said, "I haven't seen any activity around the tower. Let's approach from opposite directions. Stay behind trees as much as possible. I see you're wearing your vest, good."

Tim offered, "I'll go ahead about three hundred yards, give me a couple of minutes."

"All right, stay in visual contact as much as possible. I'll give you hand signals when I'm ready to call out to the cabin. When I go up the stairs, cover me from a position where you can see the cabin door. Whistle when you're ready."

"Ten-four." The deputy set off down the road at a half-run carrying his rifle in his right hand, his equipment belt making distinctive sounds of the police.

Scott began moving along the road, closer to the tower, maintaining cover as he watched the cabin and Deputy Doureline. No sounds came from the lookout as he approached within thirty yards of the tower base. There were twenty yards of open ground between him and the timber tower legs and first flight of steps. He scanned to his right and found Doureline taking aim at the cabin. The deputy waved and gave a short sharp whistle.

Scott ran to the bottom flight of steps and looked straight up. He called out, "This is Sheriff Wilson of Suddenly. If anyone is in the tower, come out with your hands raised. We are armed. Leave your weapons in the cabin and come down the stairway. We only want to talk."

Scott waited thirty seconds, climbed to the second level, and reiterated his demands. No reply or movement was detected, so he leaned his rifle against the corner railing and drew his sidearm. He looked at Doureline and the deputy yelled back, "I've got you covered Sheriff." Scott continued climbing toward the top deck, took a ten-second rest out of sight, and bolted up the last few steps to the cabin wall.

"If anyone is in there, make yourself known."

There was no sound of any kind issuing from the cabin. Scott crawled beneath the windowsill to the cabin door, pushed it open, and cautiously peered inside. He could see no movement or hear sounds of any kind except for slight creaks of timber. There was no one in the cabin. He stood and motioned for Tim Doureline to join him.

Scott entered the lookout cabin and sat on the cot nearest the doorway. It was extremely hot, and he was sweating profusely, from nervousness, physical activity, and from stifling cabin heat. He wiped his forehead with his handkerchief and exhaled, happy that the no one was there. He holstered his weapon as Doureline reached the cabin door.

"The place is empty, deputy. We have nothing. Let's search for any trace of the woman that called, but it could have been a crank call."

The interior walls, floor, and ceiling yielded nothing, so Scott and the deputy descended from the tower and began walking back to their cars. Scott scanned the ground as he moved toward the road beside Tim. He stopped abruptly, grabbing Doureline's arm. "Car tracks, Tim. Look at the tread, signs of backing and pulling onto the road, going the direction you walked. Let's see where they lead."

Scott and Tim followed the tread marks nearly a quarter mile before Tim commented, "Do you think a dog could be trained to follow tire tracks? It sure would make it much easier. I've seen only a few tracks."

Scott chuckled, "The problem with police work, Tim. Just when we think there are no more tracks, we find some more. Patience is a virtue."

"I guess I'll have to do some work on that."

They continued on, finding tracks now and then in the soft dirt along the edges of the depressions from truck and ATV wheel contact.

# CHAPTER 22

"Sheriff! The tire tracks leave the road over here." Tim pointed off to the right of the road. The two men followed the impressions a short, slightly uphill distance to a rocky area where the tracks disappeared. Scott's eyes swept the area and said, "We've got two reasonable routes here that a car might travel. I'll go right, you go left. Scott drew his sidearm and started walking, scanning the ground from side to side. Tim set off in the opposite direction, wary of hidden dangers, and approached a dense clump of trees with his handgun raised.

Unable to see the other side of the thicket or a way through the dense growth, Tim crouched and began slowly circling the trees and shrubs. When he was able to see between a few of the trees, an unusual color caught his eyes, maroon. He knew the sheriff was looking for a maroon vehicle, maybe this was it. Before exposing himself to anyone in or near the car, he gave a short piercing whistle. He crouched and waited.

He listened, and watched, sweeping his eyes one hundred eight degrees, from front to back for what seemed several minutes, but was actually about fifteen seconds.

Finally, Tim heard the sheriff coming closer, his boots charging across the rocks behind him.

"What have you found, Tim?"

"I think that maroon car is behind these trees. Cover me and I'll check it out."

Working together, they approached the vehicle and found it empty, the keys in the ignition. Scott inspected the interior, now cleaner than the last time he had looked inside, but just as deserted. With a vinyl glove on his right hand, Scott pulled the key from the steering post and moved to the trunk.

When the trunk lid was raised, they saw the body of a woman. Scott commented, "I'm guessing this is the woman that called the forest service. Somebody must have felt betrayed. We'll let the coroner take care of the rest of this. Let's search the area and move the car back to the tower. I'll call Ginny and have her contact Dr. Rennick."

When the two men had completed their search, finding nothing, they drove the maroon death vehicle to the tower parking area.

"Did you notice the cause of death, Sheriff?"

"Well, She wasn't shot. The bleeding from the head is nominal. I think she was killed and dropped from the tower, but that's only a guess. Looks like she has a broken neck. The doc will tell us more."

"Want me to check the rocks at the bottom of the tower?"

"Good idea. Check for blood, hair, and tissue. If you find anything, tell the doc. I'm going back to the office and see if I can identify her. Stay out here until doc Rennick arrives. I'll talk to him to see if he needs assistance getting the body out of the trunk."

"Don't bother, Sheriff, I'll help him. I'll also get some photos you can use for the data files."

"Thanks, Tim. Somebody should be out here in the next half hour. I'll be at the ranger station after I try to ID her."

After the sheriff left, Tim scoured the area beneath the tower but found nothing of importance in the dirt and weeds. It was almost to the minute, a half-hour later, when Tim heard a vehicle coming through the trees kicking up a small dust cloud. At first glance, he thought the approaching car was the Sheriff's cruiser, but it was the hospital ambulance. Dr. Rennick had come to move the body. Tim was wondering when the body would start emitting odors of death. It was a few minutes after three when he had moved the maroon car into the shade to keep the trunk from overheating in the hottest part of the day.

He held the police department camera but hadn't taken many photos yet. He had taken several shots of the car's interior but had avoided opening the trunk. He walked toward the white hearse-shaped vehicle and motioned for Dr. Rennick to park beside the death car. He was surprised when Nurse Berg got out of the driver's seat and Megan Isaacs joined them from the passenger side.

Nurse Berg said, "Dr. Rennick couldn't come, he's in surgery. Where's the body, Tim?"

"She's in the trunk of this car. Is it gonna smell?"

"How long ago did she die?"

"Hmm. About three hours or so, I think."

"This heat won't help, but it shouldn't be bad yet, if there is any odor. Perhaps blood, urine or feces might create some foul odor."

"Geez. That's gonna be bad enough."

"Well, raise the trunk and step back. I'll tell you if there's a stench."

Megan noticed Tim's camera and offered, "If you need pictures, I can help." This was her second opportunity to assist the police and her bio dad.

Tim thought for a moment and said, "I'd be grateful, the sheriff needs a few to assist with identification." He set the camera down on the top of the gurney Megan had pulled from the ambulance. She was situating it near the trunk of the death car being careful not to let the camera drop to the ground.

Nurse Berg reached into the trunk and moved the corpse's arms so the body would be easier to lift. Megan took a couple of quick pictures of the victim's face and gave the camera back to the deputy. Tim said, Thanks," and stepped back as the women put the body on the gurney and tightened the straps. Mrs. Berg motioned to Tim, "You won't smell anything, Deputy. I didn't see any blood. Help us move this contraption to the ambulance, the ground is a bit rough here."

The deceased was wrapped in dark-blue plastic sheeting and Tim couldn't see the face of the departed. The last time he had looked at a corpse, he had suffered a terrible nightmare. In the dream, he had pulled a car over for speeding and the head of the recently viewed corpse was in the driver's seat. It had given him the willies and he had never forgotten.

When he and Scott found the body in the trunk, Tim avoided looking at her face by closing his eyes.

He held his breath and assisted with the loading. When he exhaled, Nurse Berg questioned, "Are you all right, Deputy?"

"Yeah. I don't like dealing with dead people."

"I can understand. After working as a nurse for many years, I guess I've gotten used to it. But a homicide is just evil. I pray the killer will be caught and put away for life." She shut the rear door with a solid thud and said, "Thank you for the help. Let's go, Megan."

After the ambulance left, Deputy Doureline took one last look at the tower and climbed in his patrol car. He pulled away from the tall structure, leaving it isolated and uninhabited as it was earlier in the morning.

Back at his office, Scott had flipped through the wanted posters that had arrived earlier in the FAX machine. He added them to the incoming papers on his desktop and started a computer search, describing the deceased as best he could by estimating height, weight, age, and ethnicity. Eleven possibilities turned up, but none fit the woman in the maroon car. He would try a new search when he received the pictures from Deputy Doureline.

Scott shoved his chair back, told Ginny where he was going, and left the office. Ten minutes later, he walked in the Ranger Station to pay a short visit to the director, Leonard Turner. Turner had been a ranger for fifteen years, most of that duration spent in the Bitterroots. Julie had voiced a good opinion of the man. He was about six-feet tall, had short salt and pepper hair, and was ruggedly handsome. Scott noticed a one-inch jagged scar above Turner's left eyebrow.

Turner invited Scott into his office, shook hands, and said, "Have a seat." The director sat back in his swivel high-back chair and inquired, "What's in the wind, Sheriff?"

"My deputy and I discovered a body in the trunk of a car near tower seventeen. Can you tell me who's been staying there?"

Director Turner turned to his computer and opened the file for recent renters. He picked up a ballpoint pen, started to jot on a notepad, then turned back to face the sheriff. "No renters for tower seventeen this year. That's the tallest lookout in the area and few people want to climb those steep stairs."

"How about tower twenty? It's not far from seventeen."

"Devin and Clair Springs were there until about a week ago. But they came by several days ago and checked out."

"Okay, I know that couple, they're bicycle riders and the deceased is definitely not Clair. The victim is Hispanic, about forty years old."

"Hmm." The director returned to the file and jotted down more data. "A woman of that description was renting tower twenty with her husband: Mr. and Mrs. Juan Martinez. They still have a week left on their rental agreement."

"Their vehicle?"

"A hog, a Harley-Davidson, no car. You think Martinez did away with his wife?"

"It's possible, we're trying to ID her now. The biggest reason that I came out to see you is a woman made a call to the forest service about a guy that's going to hunt down a man and woman, but I don't know who the guy is or who he's after."

"I'll let our people know what's going on. Have you informed your wife?"

"Not yet. Julie's at home, I'll see her this evening."

"Good, she should know about this. I'm wondering if any of the brigade might be involved. They're advancing into the area where there are no roads or trails to follow. A hog couldn't travel out there; it's not made for off road. Besides, no vehicles of any kind should be in that area. The brigade will have to hike in. It's protected. Julie knows that region."

"If that's the case, what are the inmates doing there?"

"They're going to clear a few spots where firefighting choppers can land and take on water. There are some small lakes up there, but no access except by foot."

"I'll go out there and talk to the guards, tell them to watch for anything unusual. Whoever this guy is, he won't know the area and might get himself into trouble."

"Right. If he walks into a momma bear and her cubs, he might not get back out of the forest in one piece."

Scott stood, reached across the director's desk, and shook hands. "Thanks for meeting with me on short notice. Say hello to Deb for me."

"You're welcome and say hi to your wife, I don't always see her when she's at work."

"Will do."

Scott drove back to his office, expecting to use photos of the deceased to search for her ID. When he arrived in the parking lot, Tim was pulling out for traffic duty. They stopped next to each other, windows down. Scott asked, "Did you get those photos for me?"

"Yes. I sent the file to you as TRUNK WOMAN, but Sheriff, I didn't take the pictures, your daughter did. She offered and I let her do it. You know how I am with the faces of the deceased."

"Megan was out there? Where was Dr. Rennick?"

"Megan was with Nurse Berg. Rennick was in surgery. Oh, yeah, I didn't find anything at the bottom of the tower."

"Thanks, Tim." Scott smiled. "See if you can write some parking tickets in the next two hours."

Tim waved two fingers in a salute and drove away. Scott parked, went inside to his desk, and opened the new digital file. Thinking the deceased might have a California driver's license, Scott sent the pictures to Sacramento. While waiting, he poured the last cup of coffee from the Mr. Coffee carafe, and sat down to wait for results. His first sip was a shock. He spit the sip back in the cup, walked down the hall to the water fountain and poured the mud down the drain. After rinsing his mouth, he filled his cup with cold water and started back to his office.

When he passed Ginny's desk, she said, "I should have warned you, sorry."

Scott chuckled, "No, I should have known better, it's too late in the day."

As Scott entered his office, the FAX machine came to life. He set the cup on his desk and retrieved the page just printed. He flipped it over and saw the picture of the dead woman found in the maroon car's trunk. She had a California driver's license. Her name was Maria Martinez, forty-one years old.

Ginny was watching Scott as he looked over the FAX. "Did you get something useful, Sheriff?"

He nodded, "Uh-huh, Maria Martinez. She and her husband rented tower twenty. Mr. Juan Martinez has some questions to answer. He might have run off, but I'll put out an all points on him."

"Should I issue an APB?" She stuck a pencil in her hair as she waited for an answer.

Scott pulled up Juan's DMV records. Now they had a picture to go with the name.

"Let's do it. I'll give you the information I have on him. Tim issued him a traffic ticket the other day. He rides a Harley." Scott went back to his office and said, "Mr. Martinez is wanted for murder."

# CHAPTER 23

Juan estimated he was about twenty-five miles north of Suddenly when he recognized the surroundings. He had been here before, briefly, with his deceitful, ex-wife. He wondered how far away the convicts were. He didn't want to roll up to them and be identified by the man he was going to terminate. Although he hadn't seen the man in over eight years, eye contact would be too risky. Juan would have to keep a safe distance away. He decided four hundred yards would be satisfactory.

He continued on, watching for signs of the men working on the road. As soon as he saw or heard them, he would back off, hide his bike, and take to the woods. His saddlebags contained enough provisions for three or four days, then he would hunt if the need arose. After passing some large logs on the roadside, Juan slowed to read a prominent sign. The Forest Service had posted a caution; the road ended abruptly in a quarter mile. No vehicles of any kind were permitted in the protected area beyond the road's termination.

He sat there scanning for a location to hide his bike but saw nothing that looked promising except a copse of trees fifty yards off the road and uphill. He had to keep looking; the bike would leave deep easy to follow tracks. Two hundred yards down the road near the large logs, he spotted a dense clump of shrubs that might conceal his Harley if he did some rearranging of the foliage. It took Juan more than fifteen minutes to hide his bike.

He removed his saddlebags, climbed the slight grade to the road, and checked to see if his bike was visible. When Juan was satisfied the Harley could not be seen from the road, and no tracks were visible, he began hiking toward the road's end.

When he saw the brigade's truck parked a hundred yards ahead, he crouched and watched for human activity. Juan moved off the road, dropped his sixty pounds of gear and crept towards the flatbed. As he snuck to the truck, he found the site was deserted. A printed note was taped to the inside of the passenger window: *Hiking to Sour Lake. Back in five days.*

Juan searched the truck, but found nothing he could use, went back to his saddlebags, and changed clothes to camouflage. The camos would allow him to move through the forest with much less chance of detection. He could shadow the inmates closely, listening for their voices and footfalls as they moved among the trees.

He discarded his civies to lighten his load, burying all items he could do without, and set out following the tracks left by the brigade. Tracking twelve people would be a simple task, they had no idea someone was pursuing them. Juan had no choice but to follow their trail; his crude road maps gave no indication of a site named Sour Lake.

The first quarter mile was easy, but as the elevation increased, Juan decided to rest and rearrange his load, he was beginning to sweat profusely. Carrying an extra fifty pounds of what he had considered essential gear, was no longer realistic. He emptied his saddlebags and sorted his gear into two groups: things absolutely necessary and items questionable. As he evaluated each object, hunger pangs forced him to stop what he was doing. Juan chose to consume a high energy snack, the label stated it contained four-hundred twenty calories.

Smiling as he read the ingredients: peanut butter and honey, mixed with a variety of nuts, reminded him of eating peanut butter sandwiches as a kid. He washed the mixture down with a four-ounce pouch of fruit juice. He wished he had some water.

Hunger abated; he dropped to his knees to repack his gear. The effort used moving his saddlebags made him think; *this damned thing is way too heavy; I can cut it in half and lose about five pounds. I'll make it into a backpack.* Adept cutting with his hunting knife altered the leather saddlebags so Juan had shoulder straps and a belt carved from one of the containers. He packed his gear as efficiently as possible and set off after the brigade. He wondered how much of a head start the inmates had but felt he would catch up to them in a few hours. The dozen people surely couldn't be moving as rapidly as a single individual in pursuit.

Larrea and the rest of the brigade were following Todd who set off in the direction of the small lake indicated on the topographical map. He had never hiked through the forest before and had to follow his compass. Larrea and Jay were within a few feet of each other and alternately made way for the others as they trailed behind Todd and DD. After hiking about four hundred yards through thick vegetation without the use of machetes or hatchets, Larrea called out to Todd, "I think we could make better time if you'd let me lead, boss."

Todd ignored her comment and continued traipsing forward using his red compass arrow to point the way. After another fifty yards of climbing through bushes, around trees and nearly tripping over roots and rocks, DD stopped Todd and faced him. Larrea noticed the standstill, fifteen yards ahead of her. DD's gestures made it obvious the guards were arguing over something.

Todd looked at Larrea and motioned for her to come forward. He held out the folded topographic map and asked, "Are you familiar with this type of map?"

She took a quick glance when Todd unfolded the three foot square sketch of contour lines and nodded, "Yes, I've used that kind of map before, several times."

"Okay. I'd like you to join DD and me and guide the brigade to this lake." He pointed out Sour Lake on the map. "How far is it from here?"

She looked at the distance scale in the corner rectangle, measured with her fingers, and answered, "About four miles, three hours from here with me leading." Larrea raised her eyebrows and smiled. She knew if they continued the present pace, they would arrive at the lake when the sun was gone and hiking under a darkening sky was dangerous.

Todd inquired, "Do you need this map?"

"Only for a few minutes. I need your compass."

Todd gave her the map, she spread it out on the ground, spent a few minutes looking at the contours, folded it, and gave it back to Todd. She held out her right hand, palm up, and Todd handed her his compass. She glanced at the needle, walked past DD, and said, "Follow me, gentlemen."

Jay had been watching and listening with great interest. When Larrea walked past DD, he turned to the other men behind him, smiled, and said, "Come on, boys, we have a new guide."

Earlier in the day, when Jenny and I were picking up a gallon of paint at the hardware store, I remembered to ask her if she wanted to put some insulation in the farmhouse attic.

"Remember when we found those figurines in your attic?"

"How could I forget? That started out scary but it turned out fun."

"Well, there is no insulation in your attic, so when winter comes, you'll be losing lots of heat through your ceiling. It will cost you to keep your house warm. We can help by installing glass-wool insulation. It will save you in the long run." I didn't tell her about the cooling effect the insulation would have during the summer, keeping the heat from the hot attic from warming the rooms below.

"Is this a joke? Glass wool?"

"It's not a joke. I'll show you." I took her to the building supplies section and showed her the rolls of glass wool blanket insulation.

"Oh! It's pink!" She reached out to touch it but I grabbed her hand.

"Don't touch without gloves, it will irritate your skin. We'll use face masks to keep from breathing the stuff. Do you want to spend the money to do it?" I pointed at the price per roll and said, "We'll need at least eight rolls, maybe one or two more."

She surprised me with a big smile. "Let's get ten, the math is easier."

I laughed, "All right. That's another project, but we'll have to install it in the morning before the sun heats the attic. The temp will go over a hundred degrees during the day."

I could see a grin turning into a big smile when Jen said, "We'll have to apply suntan lotion, huh?"

We both started laughing so hard, the sales associate approaching started to laugh at us and had a difficult time saying, "How can I help you this morning?" Our laughing was contagious, especially when I explained the situation. When we calmed down, we were asked to pull around to the back of the store where the insulation could be loaded into Jen's pickup. Jen paid the bill with a credit card. Then we returned to her house and unloaded the pickup, placing the insulation on her porch. We made tentative plans to start installation in the morning when she returned from taking Larrea to the brigade site. She was going to call me when she got back.

I told Jen I'd see her in the morning and took off to mow a lawn for a new customer, Mrs. Willard, a retired librarian from Pullman, Washington. She had worked in the university library for more than twenty years. I wanted to ask her about the veterinary science program at the school. I figured she would know all about it.

It was 11:30 and I had enough time to drive by Mrs. Willard's property to estimate the time it would take to care for her yard. Then I would go home for lunch and return to do the mowing. Her address was 809 West Elm. I had never driven by before, so I went down the street slowly reading off the house numbers. The numbers were on the mailboxes along the street, the houses set back quite a distance, making it difficult to read numbers on the houses. The mailbox at 809 was bright yellow with green numbers painted in calligraphic style. I wondered if the lady was an artist, someone Jenny should meet.

When I saw a woman on her hands and knees pulling weeds from flower beds next to the cottage front door, I stopped to talk. Was this lady Mrs. Willard? I walked over to her to introduce myself. She watched me approaching, struggled to her feet, and said, "Can I help you, young man?"

"Hello, I'm David Drum. I was driving by to estimate the job to do your lawn. Are you Mrs. Willard?"

"That's right. I didn't expect you until after lunch." She tilted her head and looked at her tiny wristwatch. "It's not quite twelve o'clock."

"Yeah, I know. I had some time, so I wanted to take a look at your grass to see what I'll have to do later. I'll get some lunch and come back."

"Since you're here, why not have lunch with me? We can talk and get to know each other."

I assumed she was lonely and might want some company, so I thanked her and followed her inside. Her front room wasn't a surprise;

it resembled a small unorganized library, books piled everywhere with winding routes to get to the rest of the house.

"Don't mind the books, I've been unpacking and haven't gotten things organized yet. There is reason behind where the books are located. I'm having some shelves installed later. Please come into my kitchen."

Mrs. Willard wasn't what I expected of a retired librarian. She didn't wear glasses, was quick witted and cheerful, unexpected attributes from the gray-haired, tall, skinny woman. I noticed her long fingers and expected to see a violin or piano but saw neither. Maybe music wasn't her thing, or perhaps instruments were in other rooms.

I enjoyed our conversation and learned much about veterinary medicine in the pacific coast schools. I had a feeling she knew something about any topic I could come up with. I was a little intimidated, almost like when I met Scott for the first time. Mrs. Willard was very impressive. When I finished with her lawn, she paid me in cash and said, "I'll call you again to mow and I'll have some books for you that I think you'll enjoy." She chuckled, "I have to find them first."

"Okay. Thank you for the business and lunch. I really enjoyed talking with you. Bye."

"Bye, David."

# CHAPTER 24

Juan had tracked the brigade with ease, their trampling had destroyed ground level vegetation that Juan treated with respect. He had learned much about the forests when living in the Sierra-Nevada range in California as a commune member for three years. When a religious group took over the rural community, he went to Los Angeles, attended a junior college, and learned electronics. That was one of the few good choices he had ever made in life. Now he had bigger things on his mind, half a million of them.

He followed the inmates' trail for two hours without a break. He would hike for a quarter hour, stop, and listen. Hearing nothing but birds and flying insects, he continued moving, repeating the technique over and over. He suddenly stopped when he heard noises off to his left. Thinking he had overrun one of the brigade members, he crouched behind stunted shrubs and remained silent, breathing slowly. He drew his hunting knife and froze in place, listening. The noise was erratic, not like a person walking at a regular gait.

A mule deer was standing about ten feet from him, but facing away, eating purple berries. The animal was feasting on huckleberries. Juan could see clusters of plants containing the ripe fruit waiting to be harvested. He moved toward the animal and it bounded off, forfeiting its place to a hungry man.

Taking time to rest while munching berries, Juan thought he was fortunate the animal was a small mule deer, not a moose that might have turned and attacked. Without having his rifle assembled, he would have only had his hunting knife. He had never heard of a man with a blade killing a half-ton moose, but the opposite might have happened.

When his fingers were thoroughly stained and his hunger pangs gone, he wiped his hands on the ground to remove most of the stickiness, stretched his arm and leg muscles, and continued after the brigade at a faster pace than before. He wanted to catch them before the sun went down. They would stop for a meal, Juan would not.

At five o'clock, Larrea stopped and looked back at the rest of the brigade. She was getting tired and she could think of two reasons her strength was failing: she wasn't in particularly good shape and she hadn't slept well last night. She observed the men and noticed about half of them were also tiring. Some were starting to complain, growling at each other for unknown reasons. She let Todd catch up and said, "Let's eat something here and shove off for the lake. I believe we're about half a mile away, but the guys are getting a bit cranky."

Todd motioned for DD to join him and after a short discussion, they decided to follow Larrea's suggestion. The team spread out and obtained meals that were similar to those prepared for astronauts' use in space. Each member of the brigade had five of the meals, enough to provide sufficient calories for the length of their excursion in the woods. During the let up and mealtime, every member took time to venture away from the site and take care of necessary body functions. One of the men, Markus, wanted to bury their trash, but Scott and DD insisted that all refuse from meals would be carried out. Jay and Larrea agreed with the guards and nothing more was said.

Larrea stood near the center of the group and said, "We're getting close to the lake. We should be there in another thirty minutes. Then, we'll set up camp and make a fire…and have some warm drinks."

Gene Gildsmat questioned, "How do you know were getting close to the lake, doll?" A couple of the others said, "Yeah, how do you know?"

"Birds, guys, birds. Haven't you noticed more birds are around here than down by the road? The birds live around the lake for food and water."

Gene grumbled, "Birds that go fishing? I don't think so."

Jay smiled, "Some fish, normally dead ones, more commonly, though Gene, the birds eat bugs."

Markus yawned, stretched, and said, "Yeah, Gene, bugs." The other men laughed.

Todd, DD, Jay, and Larrea started moving off from the others and the rest of the brigade fell in behind the leaders.

As they trudged along someone called out, "Hey, Pops, have you got a song about a lake?" Pops had become the leader of songs as the brigade marched through the trees, occasionally breaking out with a song, usually one that was off color. Larrea didn't mind, she had heard most of the ditties before at firefighters' camps.

Pops replied, a little out of breath, "Nope! But I'll think of something when we get to the lake. I'll sing you a lullaby about counting fish and bugs." He laughed and belched. He took a few steps and called out, "Pick some of these purple berries as we hike along to the lake. I'll cook something with them, something to go with fish."

Markus, who was trailing the brigade yelled out, "It had better be good, Pops. Rotting fish will need some help."

Gene was in the middle of the pack and had started gathering a few berries, but was eating most of them, said, "I'm losing my appetite for fish, Markus."

Everyone, except the leaders, had something to say and they were yelling and clowning around as they neared the lake. They had no idea they were providing a beacon for the hunter who was gradually catching up to them, following their outbursts.

As the sun began to cast long shadows, the team's trail had become more difficult to follow, but the sounds from the brigade aided Juan. He smiled as he narrowed the distance between him and the noisy group. Before long, he would have to be careful to maintain a safe distance from the men. He had to stay hidden in the trees and never appear to be anything more than a shadow. He would camp close enough to the lake to observe the members through his telescopic gunsight. He wanted to learn each man's mannerisms in order to distinguish John from each of the others.

At six o'clock Jenny put away her art supplies and washed the colored chalk from her fingers. She wanted to get a bite of something before driving to pick up Larrea, hating her stomach growling loud enough for another person to hear. When they returned they would have something for dinner and enjoy telling each other of the day's activities.

She cut some slices of Velveeta cheese and made three soda cracker sandwiches grabbed a small bottle of water from the fridge and went out on the porch. She bit off half of one sandwich and watched some soda cracker flack fall on top of one of the packages of insulation. She grinned when she thought David would probably ask her what that stuff was. She counted the packages, ten, they were all there, nothing stolen.

Jenny finished the crackers and cheese, drank half the water, and got in her truck. When she reached forward with the ignition key she noticed bits of white cracker were on the front of her light-blue T-shirt. She brushed away what looked like dandruff and started her pickup. A minute later, she was on her way to get Larrea, something she had looked forward to all afternoon. She hoped Larrea had something funny to tell her about the men.

Her dashboard clock indicated 6:38 when she arrived at the site where she had dropped Larrea off in the morning. She knew the brigade undoubtedly made progress today and would be farther ahead. She drove past some large logs on the shoulder of the road and continued on, but slowly, afraid she might encounter someone taking a break on the road. But then she realized they would be eating dinner, so she increased her speed.

When she saw the flatbed, parked across the dirt path like a roadblock, she scanned the area as she got closer, but could see no one. She muttered aloud, "Where are they?" She stopped within ten feet of the big truck, left her engine running, and got out to look around. Nobody was there, and she was getting a little scared, David was twenty-five miles away and she had no idea where Larrea or the other brigade members were. She walked around the big truck and discovered the road ended. She took another quick look around and saw a piece of paper taped to the passenger window.

"Sour Lake?" She had never heard of it, but that was not a surprise, she was a city girl and hadn't been in Suddenly long enough to learn about the Bitterroot Range. As she climbed back in her pickup, she wondered if David had ever heard of Sour Lake.

Perhaps Julie knew about the lake.

Jenny started back toward Suddenly and saw something she hadn't seen before, a clump of bushes with black berries off to her right. Something to investigate, but not now, she was out here alone and wanted to get back to Suddenly as quickly as possible, no fooling around, it would be getting dark when she got back in town. She couldn't drive fast on the dirt roads and she constantly checked her rearview mirror to see if she were being tailed. She prayed that the motorcycle guy wasn't around.

When she entered town, she began to relax, she was safe, but it occurred to her that she was going to be alone in her house tonight and for four more nights if the note was correct. She had to talk with David. Maybe she could stay in the Wilsons' apartment until Larrea got back, but all her things were in the farmhouse. Did she want to leave the insulation unattended? Maybe David could come out and sleep on the porch.

One more turn completed, she was on David's street. She could see his car and his mother's pickup in the driveway and his stepfather's cruiser parked at the curb. She pulled in behind the sheriff's car and saw David on the porch reading something.

It was still bright enough outside to read and it was cooling off nicely from what seemed a prolonged hot day. I had finished Mrs. Willard's yard, come home, and continued reading the book I had started a week ago. When Jenny's pickup appeared coming from the wrong direction, my curiosity was aroused. I folded over a corner of the page 89 and set the book down. When I looked up, Jenny was running toward me.

"David! Larrea's gone!" Jenny was shaking and crying.

"What? Larrea's dead?" I stood up to catch her and we hugged.

"No, she's gone for almost a week. The brigade is hiking to Sour Lake. She didn't tell me." She wiped her eyes and said, "I'm sorry, I don't mean to cry. I was scared to be out there alone."

I held her at arm's length and said, "It's okay, Jen. Sour Lake? I've never heard of it. Let's go in and ask Mom what she knows about this."

Mom and Scott were in the kitchen talking about a recent homicide. They looked at Jenny and me when we came in holding hands.

Mom must have noticed that Jenny had been crying, "Jenny, what's wrong, dear?" Scott got up, put his arm around Jenny, and asked, "What's going on, Jen?"

"I went to get Larrea, but no one was at the camp and the truck was gone, so I drove to the end of the road. The truck was parked with a sign on the window that said they were going to Sour Lake and would return in five days. Larrea didn't tell me she would be gone. I was all alone and got scared."

Mom gave Jenny a napkin and said, "Here, wipe your eyes and sit down with us. I'll get my maps and we'll take a look at the location of Sour Lake. It's out of my district."

"David, get the maps from the glove compartment of my truck. Let's find Sour Lake."

I retrieved the maps and came back in the kitchen. Mom had given Jenny a glass of something, but it wasn't orange juice or milk. I looked at Mom and pointed at the glass.

Mom answered quietly, "It's lemonade."

That was news to me, I didn't know we had any lemonade. I nodded.

"Danny asked me to get some today. There's more in the fridge."

Mom spread out the map of the mountains north of Suddenly and folded back the bottom portion. All eyes scanned over the contour lines and focused on Sour Lake; a small lake that looked like a kid had tried to write the capital letter *D* without much success.

She looked at the legend and commented, "Sour Lake is about seven miles north of the end of road. That's why the brigade is going to be gone for several days, no roads or trails to follow. Oh! Now I remember why the brigade went there; they're going to clear an area for choppers to land. I got a memo about a week ago, but it didn't concern me. Sour Lake is in Ranger Drew Wylie's district."

Jenny said, "Thank you for showing me where the lake is. Since Larrea will be gone for four more days, would you mind if I stayed in your apartment?"

Mom replied immediately, "That would be fine. Do you have your things?"

"No, I'll have to get some stuff from home."

I looked at Mom and volunteered, "I'll go with her and come right back, Mom. I think we'd better put the insulation packages in the house. It should only take us about thirty minutes."

She looked at her watch and said, "Okay, be back by nine p.m."

# CHAPTER 25

We hopped in Jen's pickup and were at her place in about five minutes. While she gathered clothes from her bedroom and a few things from the bathroom, I moved the packages of insulation into the living room. On the way back to my place she said, "I saw a clump of bushes that was covered with black berries when I went to get Larrea. I wanted to stop and see if they were ripe, but I was too afraid to stay out there any longer. Do you think we could go out there tomorrow and investigate?"

"Yeah. Are you sure the berries weren't huckleberries? They're all over the place and ripe, but they're purple. Well, I don't have any customers tomorrow; we'll go after lunch. Okay?"

"It could be the berries were purple; it was getting dark out there and I just glanced at them. Black berries look different than huckleberries, right? Do you still want to do the insulation in the morning?"

"Yeah, the berries look different. We'll get busy in the attic right after breakfast. We'll be finished before Larrea gets back from Sour Lake."

"How do you think Sour Lake got its name, David?"

I chuckled, "I don't know. Someone must have taken a drink and it was sour or rancid. Something might have died, and it was rotting in the water. Maybe it was named by a pioneer back in the eighteen hundreds. We'll hike out there some time and find out."

"Five days alone with you? I don't know."

"So, you don't trust me?"

Jen laughed, "No, that's not it. I don't trust myself."

I grinned, "I'll have Mom come with us and protect me."

She tried to slap my leg, but I moved out of the way. We pulled into my driveway and I helped Jenny take her things up to the apartment over our garage. She didn't need any help, but I wanted to see if she would kiss my cheek, or better. She didn't and we said good night. I had an urge to kiss her, but I missed my chance.

When I got in the house, Mom asked, "Everything all right with Jenny?"

"Yeah, she was just alarmed that Larrea wasn't there, and she didn't want to stay home alone. I believe she was still thinking about that guy I ran off the other night."

"It's too bad that happened when Larrea had just started as her roommate. But I think Larrea can take care of herself, she's smart and capable."

"Jenny's gaining self-confidence, Mom. She's never been on her own before."

"Where are her parents, David?"

"I guess somewhere in the Far East, Malaysia or Viet Nam, but I don't think she knows. I doubt she even cares where they are. Living with Larrea will do her some good, kind of like having a mother who's interested in her daughter's welfare."

The brigade investigated the lake and surrounding area. They discovered the name was inappropriate; the lake water was fresh and had no particular taste. However, they boiled it before drinking, just to be safe. No one wanted dysentery to complicate an already tiresome journey. While they ate dinner and prepared sites for sleeping, Pops made a pie from huckleberries and a can of sliced peaches.

Pop's pie wasn't a pie, not in the regular sense. Without a pan and oven, he made a thin layer of dough in the shape of a tortilla, spooned some of his fruit mixture in the middle, rolled it, and wrapped it in aluminum foil. He cooked a dozen of them over the fire, let them cool for twenty minutes and gave one to each member of the brigade.

One of the brigade, Micky Miller, asked, "Hey, Pops, what do ya call this?"

Pops thought for a minute and replied, "It's a fruit bomb."

Everyone laughed, but most of the brigade said it was good, and he should do it again. When it was dark, the fire was extinguished, and everyone tried to fall asleep.

Laying near Larrea, Jay asked, "Did your young friend know we left for this place?"

"That's been worrying me all day. Since we didn't know about coming here until mid-morning, I couldn't tell her anything."

"Well, don't worry. She'll find the note and go back home."

"Good night, Jay."

"Night, Larrea. See you in the a.m."

Juan had moved closer to the brigade when the firefighters were eating, their attention drawn to stuffing themselves after hiking for half the day. He snuck to within thirty yards of the camp and could hear them talking. Some of the conversation was entertaining and he almost laughed out loud at one of the jokes. He was starting to recognize the voices of the brigade members and was surprised when he discovered one of the members was a woman. Juan listened to the banter for about twenty minutes, began to yawn, decided he needed some sleep, and slipped away to his own campsite.

By seven the next morning, the brigade had eaten and were beginning to clear a relatively flat area of trees and shrubs west of the lake close to the water. The sounds of the axes and saws slicing into mature trees woke Juan from deep sleep. The rest of the inmates were digging around stumps so the roots could be cut, and the ground leveled for the landing site. Since Pops had been designated camp cook, he began roaming the forest for huckleberries and any other edible plants. He carried an Army survival manual to help him identify useful and harmful plants.

As Juan got up and was moving around, he heard someone approaching. He gathered his belongings and tried to leave the area as quickly and as quietly as possible. Pops was picking berries when he thought he heard movement about twenty to thirty yards away.

He stood up straight, turned in the direction of the sounds, and yelled, "Who's there!" Pops concentrated his attention on a copse of trees and brush and began advancing in that direction. As he searched the area, he found a grassy site where the vegetation had been pressed to the ground. He looked around and commented, "Looks like a moose or a big deer stayed the night." He shrugged and returned to pick berries.

Juan had only shifted his position about ten yards away and stood behind a large fir. He peered from behind the tree and watched an older gentleman kick around the grass where Juan had spent the night. He heard the man say something and watched him walk away toward some berry bushes.

Deciding his near detection was a warning, Juan thought he should leave the area before more eyes arrived. He assumed the brigade was making a helicopter landing pad next to the lake. If that was the case, he might be spotted from the air.

Since he had not observed any large amount of provisions with any of the group members, he figured they would be returning to their previous location on the road in a couple of days. That's where he would wait; his bike was not far from the brigade's truck; access would be easy. He would watch the crew another day after they came back from the lake and then set a fire. When the brigade was fighting the fire, he would strike.

By eleven o'clock the following morning, the temperature in Jenny's attic was almost unbearable. Wearing gloves to handle the insulation and masks to keep from inhaling glass wool particles, Jenny and I were exhausted, having completed about thirty percent of the installation without a break. The job was going to take at least two more days. We climbed down from the attic and collapsed out on the porch.

I raised my left arm and took a whiff of my arm pit. My deodorant had failed. "I need a shower, bad! Something to drink, too, have any lemonade?"

"You're not the only one that smells bad. I feel like I just ran a marathon. I'll get us something to drink. I hate wearing this damned mask." Jen nearly tore the mask from her face and let it drop to the floor, jumped up and hustled to the kitchen. I heard the clink of ice cubes being dropped into glasses and the pouring of liquid. My mouth watered before Jenny appeared with two large glasses filled to the brim. She was walking slowly so not to spill on the rug.

She handed me a glass and said, "There's more if you want it."

"Thanks, Jen. This should do." I couldn't get the ice-cold drink down fast enough and almost choked.

She laughed, "Take it easy horsey."

That comment made it worse and I had a fit of coughing. A few drops of the liquid had gone into my lungs, but I knew the feeling would pass. I drank and coughed several more times before I was almost back to normal. My eyes were watering as I had a final cough. I swirled the ice cube around in the last ounce or so of the fluid.

"Jen, why don't you shower and change clothes? Then, we'll go to my place. I'll clean up, we'll have lunch and go out to the brigade's old camp and take a look at those berries."

"Okay, I won't take long." She disappeared down the hallway.

I heard the bathroom door shut and water running. I leaned back, took the last swig of the lemonade, and had a brief thought of peeking into the bathroom to see Jen in the shower. The next thing I experienced was getting poked in the ribs. I had fallen asleep for nearly fifteen minutes. A refreshed Jen had woken me.

She joked, "Hey, no naps at my house. Let's get out of here so you can shower."

I blinked a few times to make sure I was able to focus clearly; we locked up and took my car. Jen smelled great, the soap she used must have been lightly scented, I doubted she would put on perfume since we were going out on forest roads. We didn't want flying bugs to be chasing us around if she wore the scent of something like orange-flowers or jasmine.

"What's for lunch today, David?"

Her question came as a minor surprise. Jen had never asked that before, in spite of having eaten lunch at my place at least a dozen times.

I grinned and suggested, "Pizza?"

"Really? It's too greasy for a hot day, don't you think? Besides, we'll smell like pizza for the rest of the day. I'll have to shower again after."

"I was just joking. Mom will have something like waffles." I tried to hold back a grin, but it crept out.

She slapped my leg. "Okay, sorry I asked. I'll wait and see. I just wanted some conversation."

I chuckled, "We don't need to talk. A glance at you is worth a thousand words."

Jen leaned back in the seat and smiled, shaking her head. She didn't say another word until we got to my place. I looked at her several more times as I drove. Each time, I smiled, and she pretended to be ignoring me, but I detected some muted grins.

I took only ten minutes to clean up. I joined the ladies in the kitchen. Mom had stopped at the town deli, Deb's Meats and Eats, on the way home from work and picked up a salad plate with enough for six ranch hands. Jen and I were both very appreciative for the veggie feast. Scott had worked on the air-conditioning and by the time we finished lunch, Jen and I were both getting goosebumps. We thanked Mom for lunch but were glad to go outside in the warmth. I was so cold when eating, I had considered getting my light-weight jacket from my closet and a blanket for Jenny.

As Jen and I were going out the front door, I told Mom where we were going and she said, "When you guys get back, I have something to tell you."

"You can't tell us now?"

"I have to talk to Scott first. I'll tell you about it later."

Jen and I looked at each other and frowned simultaneously. I had no clue what Mom had to discuss with Scott that would affect Jen and me. Apparently, Jen's intuition hadn't toggled anything in her mind either, she didn't comment.

We got in the car and Jen commented, "What's your mom up to?"

"Haven't a clue."

I backed out of the driveway and drove to the road that led past Dexter's barn. I figured on the way back from checking out Jen's berries, we'd stop and see what Dexter was working on. I promised to help him again on the foundation for the back end of the barn, but I kind of hoped he had gone ahead with some of the work himself. I'd much rather work on Jen's house than Dexter's, Jen was much better looking and more fun to be with. There was still plenty of time left in the summer to get Dex's remodel in shape before winter arrived.

After twenty minutes of gabbing as we drove, I asked, "Where did you see that clump of bushes?"

"It's on the left about where there are some logs along the road." She sat forward as much as possible with the seat belt constraining her movement and began looking out the driver's side windshield.

# CHAPTER 26

I slowed a bit because I knew things looked different depending on the light of day and direction of travel. But Jen was observant, and I felt pretty confident she would stop me at the right place.

"There! Stop, David. See those bushes?" Jen had turned sidewise and pointed over the steering wheel to our left.

I pulled off the narrow road toward the thick growth of shrubs and parked on the shoulder, leaving room for someone to pass. Jen unbuckled and was out of the car and almost running toward the clump of bushes. I followed at a leisurely pace. I was almost one hundred percent sure the berries were huckleberries; they were all over the place in the Bitterroots.

I could hear the disappointment in her voice when she said, "Oh, they're not black, they're purple." She pulled one of the berries off and stuck it in her mouth. Jen glanced at me and said, "You were right, they're huckleberries. But they did look black last night."

"I believe you, Jen. The evening light makes everything look darker in color."

I gathered a few berries and popped the ripe fruit in my mouth. We both stood back and surveyed the growth for berries. I was estimating there must be at least half a gallon of them in front of us.

"What's that?" Jen was pointing at the bushes.

"What? More berries?"

"No, in there. It's black." She was pointing into the vegetation.

I used both hands and spread the bushes apart to see inside the thick growth. "I think we've found the bike that almost hit you the other day. I want a closer look." I went around the bushes and found a way into the middle of the vegetation. I got on my knees to check out the bike. It was an older Harley. I started to call out to Jenny, but she was right beside me.

"Do you think this is the same bike? The one that tried to run you off the road?"

"I'm positive, see the painted curls on the fenders? This is the bike. But why would it be here in the bushes?"

"Boy, you've got me there. I think I'll fix it so it won't run. That guy won't be sideswiping anyone else for a while."

"Are you going to slash the tires?"

"Nope. I've got another idea. I'm gonna get my garden clippers." We got out of the berry bushes and Jen waited while I went for my nice sharp tool. When I returned, Jen followed me to the bike and watched as I cut off the sparkplug wires and stuffed them in my pocket.

"That ought to do it." I glanced at Jen and she laughed.

"Do you think he'll have extra wires?"

"I doubt it. He'll have to come into town to get replacements. Harley is the only dealer that might have them."

Jen grabbed my arm and gave a little tug, "Let's go. What if he comes back and sees us? We'd be in deep doo-doo."

"Okay. I'll race you to the car."

"No! Didn't your mom ever tell you not to run with scissors?"

We both laughed as we walked back to my car.

On the way back home, I asked, "Care if I stop to see Dexter?"

"I don't mind; I'd like to see Skimmer again. I'd like to sketch him and paint his portrait for Dex if I can get the little guy to sit still. He can hang it on a wall."

I grinned, "You might have to wait for him to be sleeping, he's wiggling all the time when you're around."

She chuckled, "You're right. He does get excited. I think he likes me."

"He's not the only one." I grinned and wiggled my eyebrows. Jen didn't acknowledge my comment.

I was shocked when we drove up to Dex's barn. He had finished the concrete, and the ceiling joists and rafters were up. How that had happened, I didn't know. Dexter couldn't have done all the work by himself, too much had been done.

He came from the interior of the new construction and said, "Hi guys, what do you think?"

"Was one of your prayers answered? How did you do all this?"

"Remember the Springs? They arrived with a big flatbed truck loaded with preformed framing and five men came in a van. They went to work and did all this yesterday afternoon. It was a total surprise. Plus, they gave me a price I couldn't pass up."

Jen and I got out of the car and followed Dex into the interior of his new home, even though much remained to be done. I was looking at rolls of felt and several pallets of composition shingles. I asked, "When do you want me to help put on your roof?"

I almost volunteered for tomorrow morning, but Jenny's insulation project had to come first. I told him about it and offered to help after dinner tomorrow. We could get in two hour's work before the sun went down. Any earlier and the afternoon sun would bake us to cinders on the roof.

Jen commented, "I like the smell of the new wood. Where's Skimmer?"

Dex beamed, "He's in the side room; it's too hot in his saddlebag bedroom. I made a hole in the floor and he gets on the ground under the floorboards where it's cool. I'll get him."

It took a couple of minutes before Dex returned with Skimmer. When the little guy saw Jenny, he ran and launched his little body into her arms. She had gotten on her knees to play with him.

"How are you, Skimmer?" Jen let him lick her face as she picked him up, but only briefly. He squirmed so wildly, she had to put him down. She looked puzzled.

"Same thing happens with me, Jenny. He gets too warm when I hold him. He doesn't like it."

She smiled and replied, "I'll come back after it snows." Jen walked around the floor of the barn keeping an eye on Skimmer as he sniffed the pallets of shingles and boxes of roofing nails.

While Jen was exploring with Skimmer, I told Dex what I had done to the bike hidden in the berry bushes. I pulled the wires from my pocket and tossed them in a barrel of trash.

Dex snickered, "I don't think I'll be seeing him around here. I wonder if that was the bike those two visitors were on a week or so ago, sounds like it."

I told him about the woman that had been found dead in the trunk of the maroon sedan. He hadn't heard anything about it. I started informing him about Larrea and Jenny joined us when she heard her roommate's name mentioned. Jenny took over my news round-up for Dex and told him about the brigade hiking to Sour Lake. Like us, he had never heard of the place.

After we had completed our news summary, Dex told us he was going to take a nap. He had gotten up early and worked hard with the Springs' crew all morning.

Jen leaned toward him and sniffed, "You don't stink."

"I took a little scrub down with the last of the rainwater in the Hadleys' barrels. I was afraid you might show up."

Jen commented, "Sure Dexter. Nice try."

Jenny grinned, Dex and I laughed.

"The air around here is getting pretty thick, David. Let's find out what your mom wants to talk to us about."

Dex frowned. I hadn't said anything about Mom's comment before we came to check on the berries. I said, "We'll let you know what my mom's mysterious comment was all about."

I honked twice as we backed to the road. Dex waved to us as we drove away.

I turned up the AC but after a minute, Jen reached over and turned it off. She indicated that her legs were cold. We were home in another five minutes and went in the house. Mom was on the sofa in the living room with her book in one hand and cradling Gwen with her other and a pillow. She laid the book down and said, "Did you find the berry bushes?"

We told her about the motorcycle and she said, "What you did is against the law. I'm surprised at you, David." She glanced at Jenny and back at me.

I thought I was going to get further reprimanded, but Mom grinned and said, "Good work. That bike will be out of commission for a while and can be easily fixed."

"You had me scared for a minute. I wondered if you would have Scott arrest me."

"He has no jurisdiction out there and the ranger for that district is Drew Wylie. That crime comes under the title of mischief and would only get a warning. I won't rat on you this time." She grinned, leaving me with little doubt.

We sat down on the floor as Mom continued, "I talked with Scott right after you left to check the berries and he asked me to see if you would like to go to Sour Lake tomorrow after lunch. Larrea is out there with the brigade preparing a helicopter landing site by the lake. I need to inspect it."

Jenny and I looked at each other and nodded enthusiastically.

"Will we drive out and hike to the site?" asked Jenny.

"No, we won't be doing any hiking, Scott will fly us. Do you still want to go?"

I saw Jen frown; she didn't expect to be flying. I grinned and said, "Scott flew a cool helicopter when he worked for the FBI. He called his chopper Delilah. He took Danny and me up when we were hunting Megan's kidnappers. He's a really good pilot."

"Well, in that case, I'm going. I've never been in a plane or helicopter before."

"You're in for a treat, Jen. You're gonna love it."

She had that look of hesitancy and asked, "What if I throw up?"

"You won't throw up, but there are some barf bags if needed. Scott will take off slowly and it will be a little scary at first, but you'll adjust quickly and enjoy the ride. Take your sketchpad and draw something from high up; a new perspective."

Jen sat there for a few seconds. I could almost hear the gears turning in her mind. I looked at Mom and she smiled back raising her eyebrows.

"Why is the sheriff going to be the pilot? Isn't there a regular pilot?"

I couldn't answer that question. Mom took over, "The regular pilot doesn't want to fly tomorrow; his wife is in the hospital to have their first baby. He wants to be there for her."

Jenny wiped her forehead, "I think I'm getting airsick already. I'm going to lie down and rest." She stood and went out to the garage. I could hear her climbing the steps to the apartment.

Mom asked, "Is she going to be all right?"

"Sure. I think she's not used to going from hot to cold several times in one day. She might have a headache. Maybe she's anticipating her visit with Larrea but didn't expect to be flying out to Sour Lake in a chopper. I'm thinking her mind is working like a blender and has mixed up her thoughts."

"Did you guys eat anything strange today?"

"Only the salad for lunch. Oh! We had a few huckleberries, but that wouldn't be a problem. What could a few berries do?"

"I hope she feels all right tomorrow. I want her to see Larrea and know she's all right working with all those men."

"She'll be fine, Mom. I think she's been through a lot of emotional ups and downs. She's not used to life in the mountains, either."

"Oh, that's funny, David."

"What's funny?"

"You said ups and downs and mountains in the same breath."

I smiled, "I guess I wasn't listening." That made Mom laugh.

# CHAPTER 27

The morning flew by at Jenny's. We developed a system and made rapid progress with the attic insulation. Changing from nails to construction screws prevented breaking any of the ceiling paster by hammering on the attic floor boards. Jenny adapted quickly to using the drill for fastening boards with screws and I devoted my time to fitting the insulation between the joists. We almost finished the project in record time, but we had to quit with only an hour's work left for completion. Lunch was at my place and we had to clean up.

Fortunately, the workload had kept the fear of motion sickness in a chopper from invading Jenny's mind, but when we were having sandwiches, Jenny just nibbled at a slice of bread.

"Jenny, are you not feeling well?" Mom asked.

"I feel fine, I just don't want to barf in the helicopter. I would ruin everything. It would be a disaster."

"We'll give you a barf bag when you get on the copter. Don't worry about throwing up. Lots of people have problems with flying. I have some medication for nausea if you want it."

Jenny nodded and Mom went in the bathroom and came back with a little square of folded toilet paper. She handed it to Jenny and she unwrapped a round white pill, "It's Dramamine, for motion sickness; take it now with a glass of water."

Jen went to the kitchen sink, filled a glass, popped the pill in her mouth and drank the entire glass of water. She glanced at me and asked, "Is there a toilet on the chopper?"

I laughed and said, "We'll hang you out the chopper door. You can moon the forest and make yellow rain."

Mom heard what I said and reacted, "David!"

I grimaced and Jenny laughed. Mom was shaking her head; she didn't realize Jenny had experienced more gross stuff than a typical girl from Suddenly.

"We have to drive to the Ranger Station, Jenny. That's where the helicopter is. You can use the facilities there." Mom let out a deep breath.

"Mom, is Scott coming home for lunch?"

"No, not today. He's going to meet us at the ranger helipad at two o'clock."

Jen asked Mom, "May I use your phone to make a long distance call?"

"Sure, Jenny, help yourself."

Jen went to the kitchen and dialed a number, but I had no clue who she was calling. If she wanted me to know, I assumed she would tell me later, but I was still curious. Mom looked questioningly at me, I shrugged and shook my head.

I stood up and started to move a little closer to the hallway, but Mom grabbed my back pocket and said, "Sit! That's none of your business."

"Yeah, you're right. Sorry." I sat back down and waited for Jenny to return.

When she came back in the living room, my facial expression must have revealed my interest in who she called.

She looked at me, grinned, and said, "Black ops."

Mom put her hand over her mouth to keep from laughing too loudly. Jen sat beside me but made no attempt to tell me anything. I decided to keep my nose out of her business and keep Mom happy.

Mom took Gwen to Mrs. Weems's and we arrived at the Ranger Station a couple of minutes before two. Mom hated being late for anything, and I had acquired the same trait. Danny, however, liked to be fashionably late. I don't know how he ever thought being late was all right.

Scott arrived within a few seconds of 2:00 pm and disappeared into the office. He came out with the keys swirling around his right index finger and herded us to the helicopter. Scott gave me a shove and I climbed in back. Jenny followed and I showed her how to fasten her seatbelt. It was obvious and she looked at me like I was an imbecile.

I was a bit embarrassed but she touched my arm and said, "Thank you."

Mom got in the copilot's seat, strapped in, and donned a helmet with microphone attached. She surprised me with her actions. She had obviously flown before. I never knew about her knowledge of flying.

Scott got in after a walk-around, put on his helmet, talked to mom, and started the engine. Jen reached over to me and grabbed my hand, she was frightened, but I think she was being driven to ride in the helicopter by her desire to see Larrea. She was going to fly no matter what. She leaned toward me and said, "Barf bag?"

I bent forward, touched Mom's shoulder, and she glanced back at me. I made a motion like I was throwing up and Mom handed me a couple of bags. I gave one to Jen and sat on the other one. The rotor began to turn slowly and Jen tightened her grip on my left hand. I patted her hand with my right and gave her a thumbs up. She rolled her eyes and closed them. She was more afraid than I had imagined she would be. I felt sorry for her, she was going to miss takeoff.

The rotor speed increased and the chopper began to vibrate a bit, but we lifted into the air and rose above the buildings and trees. When we tilted, slightly, and moved away from the pad, Jen said, "Oh, Jesus!"

Somehow, though terrified, she opened her eyes and looked down to see the toy cars parked at the ranger complex. We picked up speed and soon were moving over a hundred miles per hour. I could see the console and watched our speed increase to a hundred and thirty. Scott banked left and followed the road that went past the Hadleys' and Dexter's houses. I pointed at Dexter's and Jen looked down and smiled. She released the wrestler's grip on my hand and began looking at the ground moving below us. I was happy she was starting to enjoy the ride and not appearing to feel queasy. The Dramamine must have helped or her system was not about to react negatively to air sickness. With her hands folded in her lap,

Jen was watching the landmarks below zoom past. In ten minutes, we passed over the brigade's truck and lost sight of civilization.

I checked my watch and did a quick calculation of the time it would take until we reached the lake: slightly more than three minutes. Nearly three minutes had elapsed when I yelled at Jen, "Sour Lake is coming up soon!"

She nodded and leaned back, smiling. I think she was happy she hadn't barfed and was actually enjoying the flight. I watched our airspeed as we began slowing and looked ahead but couldn't see the lake yet. Then, I was surprised, Scott banked to the right and I caught a brief glimpse of some water, but if that was the lake, it was ridiculously small. We circled, dropped in altitude to tree level and I could see water beneath us. Then the water was gone. I think Scott had taken a pass over the lake to see what the area looked like and spot the landing site.

We swung around like an about face and began dropping closer to the water. We moved sidewise and then we were over land. Just before we were on the ground, Jen grabbed my hand and said, "There's Larrea!"

Larrea had emerged from the trees and Jay was with her. She was standing tall and Jay was crouching to stay below the twirling rotor blades as they walked toward the aircraft. Jay didn't realize the rotor was at least four feet above his head. I remember the first time I was beneath a chopper's rotor and crouched. It was a natural response for self-preservation.

Scott shut down the engine and we released our seat belts. As soon as we could exit, Jenny dropped to the ground and ran towards Larrea. I watched them embrace. Following a long hug, Larrea stepped back from Jenny, smiled, and introduced Jay.

Jenny shook hands and said, "We met once before when I first came to pick up Larrea."

"Oh, I remember, you came with a young man. I think his name was David."

I was standing between Mom and Scott and stepped forward, "I'm back with my parents, Ranger Julie and Sheriff Scott Wilson."

Jay said, "Hi," and then, "Jenny, you have some authoritative friends."

He had broken the ice and we all laughed. The remainder of the brigade came forward in a group and Todd introduced everyone. The men all wanted to look in the helicopter and took turns sticking their head into the cockpit to investigate the instrument panel. Scott joined them and answered their questions.

Jen, Larrea, Jay, and I clustered together while Jenny told her roommate what we had been doing at the farmhouse.

Larrea commented that the insulation was a good improvement. Then she apologized for not telling Jenny about the trip to Sour Lake and she explained what happened. Our assumption had been correct.

"No apology is necessary; you had no knowledge of going on the hike. Oh, David and I found the motorcycle that guy was riding when he almost ran into me." Jen chuckled, "David cut off the sparkplug wires."

"Oh, boy. That biker is gonna be pissed."

Jenny added, "Walking several miles will be good for him; it'll give him a chance to think."

Larrea responded, "Or make him even madder. You'll have to watch out for an irate biker."

I smiled, "He'll never know who did the dirty work. I think we're safe."

Mom was talking with DD and Todd about the piles of trees and stumps that were removed from the landing site.

Todd asked, "Should all that stuff be burned?"

"Definitely not. The risk of fire spreading is too great. Leave all that material in several piles; it will be good habitats for critters. Someone will visit here in the winter and see if anything needs to be done. When are you headed back to the road?"

Todd surveyed the area quickly and said, "We'll finish up here today and leave in the morning. We should be back to our truck by lunchtime, we'll be going downhill."

Scott was walking toward Julie and heard what Todd said. Scott offered, "If you want us to fly anything out, we can do that. How about us taking your axes and shovels?"

"Good idea but leave us one of each. Never know when an ax or a shovel will come in handy." He smiled, "We might have to bury something, like an inmate."

Scott shook hands with the guards and commented, "Your team did a good job on the landing area. Julie and I will forward a complimentary note to the warden."

DD said, "Thanks, Sheriff. I'll get that equipment for you."

Ten minutes later, we were belted in the chopper and the rotor was starting to turn. Larrea was the last of the brigade to walk away from our bird, after giving Jenny a final wave. She watched us rise into the air, circle the small lake, and zoom away toward Suddenly.

Jenny sighed and wiped her eyes as if she had some tears, but it was all show. She grinned, gave my hand a squeeze, gave a thumbs up and I knew she had enjoyed the trip to Sour Lake. I don't think she'll be hesitant about flying again.

We had been in the air for less than twenty seconds when I noticed Mom pointing at something on the console and talking to Scott. All I could think of was she noticed something wrong, but Scott surely would have noticed any problems before Mom did. I loosened my seatbelt and leaned forward to see what was going on.

Apparently, Mom had turned on the Infrared Hotspot Camera and was looking at the eight by ten inch screen, but it was completely blank. She saw me leaning forward and gave me another headset.

She asked Scott, "Shouldn't I see something, anything warmed by the sun?"

"Yeah, turn up the sensitivity. I'll return to the lake and we'll monitor the brigade crew. You can count them and see if they're all present."

"Oh! What's that?" She pointed at the screen. "Is that a deer?"

"Scott glanced at the screen, "I don't think so. A deer's image would be elongated and moving. Our rotor noise would scare it. I think that's a person."

I didn't think a member of the brigade would be so far ahead of the others. "It must be a hunter."

Mom answered, "Shouldn't be. There's no hunting here this time of year, but I suppose it could be a hiker."

Jenny must have felt left out. She pulled on my arm and put her hand to her ear. I took off the headset and helped her slip it on. She smiled and nodded when she heard Mom and Scott talking.

# CHAPTER 28

Scott reversed course and returned to the lake. We climbed to five hundred feet and hovered over the landing site while Mom counted the spots on the screen. I could hear what she said by straining my eardrums.

"Twelve. That means that spot we detected was not part of the brigade. Let's go back and see if it's still there."

I had been thinking and contributed, "Possibly a porcupine?"

She answered, "I don't think so, David. Not after seeing the images of the crew at the lake. What we saw before was a person, I'm positive."

So, my next thought was maybe that person was the owner of the Harley I put out of commission. If Scott stays far enough away, we can watch to see if the guy comes out of the trees to get his bike. But then I recalled that we were moving about a hundred times faster in the air than the guy could travel through the forest. It would be hours before he got back to the road and his bike. We would be having dessert about then. No, that wasn't quite right; I would be helping Dexter with his roof when the guy got to his bike, if it's even his bike.

Scott had noted the GPS position where Mom saw that small image. When we got back to that same place, there was nothing to be seen except a few hot rocks and a couple of stumps that were exposed to the sun's rays all day. Scott decided to do some quick searches as we moved toward the road, so we followed a zigzag course. Mom's eagle eyes didn't detect anything like the image she had seen before.

As the mini-searches took place, Jenny told me what Mom and Scott were saying. I was watching the ground as we slowly returned to the brigade's truck and the road but didn't see anything but trees. I realized there were many more trees in the Bitterroot Range than stars could be seen in the night sky; millions compared to thousands.

Juan had nothing to say but foul language when the helicopter first passed over him. He knew enough about the capabilities of police heat detection equipment to realize the Forest Service would have similar, if not identical, equipment. If the chopper came back, he would be prepared. He was in no hurry to go anywhere.

As soon as the chopper was out of sight and he could no longer hear the rotor, he found a downed tree and dug a trench six-feet long beneath it parallel to the trunk. He slid into the excavation and covered himself with dirt, debris, and his camo jacket. He found the position relaxing and fell asleep.

The sound of the helicopter rotor woke him. He estimated he had been asleep for about an hour, but he didn't want to move to glance at his watch. The actual time wasn't important anyway. It sounded like the chopper was conducting a search, the sound level increasing and then fading, much like a Doppler effect. He reasoned the occupants had seen him earlier and now were looking for him using some type of grid method. They might have visited the brigade at the lake in the interim.

Juan remained hidden under the tree for another thirty minutes before resuming his trek down to the county road. He hoped his delay wasn't going to force him to recover his bike after dark. He was fearful the brigade would be arriving back about the time he would have to start his engine. The inmates would see him and be suspicious. His bike wasn't hidden far enough from the brigade truck for him to escape unnoticed. He would have to camp a safe distance away in the trees for another night.

After our search for the person Mom had observed with the infrared equipment failed to come up with anything positive, Scott started back toward Suddenly. I hadn't paid close attention, but we must have spent about fifteen minutes combing the area around the previous GPS location. Scott had resumed our cruising speed and we arrived over the brigade truck unexpectedly.

Jenny tugged at my shirt and said, "There's the truck, tell him to slow down, the motorcycle is very close." She took off the headgear and gave it to me so I could talk to Scott.

He knew we were close and asked me, "Where is that clump of bushes where the bike is hidden?"

I leaned over Jen's lap to look out to the right and she pointed my hand at the bushes. "There, David, but I can't see the bike. Do you think it's gone?"

"I doubt it." I gave instructions to Scott and he slowed the chopper to the speed of a butterfly. We dropped in altitude quickly and landed about ten yards from the bushes. He told us to stay in the helicopter while he took a look. The rotor continued to turn but slowly enough for me to clearly see the blades moving above us.

We watched Scott hurry to the site, part the bushes and glance inside the clump of vegetation. In a few seconds he hurried back, climbed in the pilot's seat, and we were airborne as the rotor blades became a blur. Ten minutes later we were on the ground at the Ranger Station landing pad. We just sat while the rotor slowed. When Mom and Scott turned around to check on us, Jenny smiled and held out the two barf bags we hadn't needed.

"Can I keep these? I'm going to start a collection."

Scott and Mom both laughed. "Sure, I'll get you some other ones. I have a few from my FBI days; I don't remember why I saved them. Maybe the logos appealed to me."

Mom, Jenny, and I arrived at our house around four-thirty, Scott stayed at the station to fill out the helicopter logbook and then he was returning to his office. Mom went across the street to the Weems' to get Gwen while Jenny and I showered for the second time today. We were surprised at how much dust we had in our hair and on our uncovered skin. The rotor always stirred up dust and debris from the ground, even when we landed and took off from concrete pads.

Jen and I watched Gwen while Mom cleaned up. When Mom joined us in the living room, Jen asked her, "Do you think the man you saw on the hotspot screen was the bike rider?"

"That's a good question, Jenny. I've been wondering about that myself. I'm suspicious now because we couldn't see him when we were searching. If he didn't want us to find him, he certainly concealed himself exceptionally well. I can't think of why that would be the case unless he has a quarrel with someone in the brigade."

I added to what Mom said, "Could be he was spying on the brigade to see if his rival is one of the crew."

"But if his foe is already in prison, what would the free guy want him for?" Jen had posed another good question.

Mom suggested, "We need to see what Scott thinks about this. He has the most experience with criminals. We should have a lively discussion during dinner."

We had an animated talk during dinner, just as predicted. Danny added some humor, even when it wasn't needed or expected. Scott's presumption was that there was an outside man who needed something from one of the brigade members and he was willing to kill for it. But that would require contacting at least one of the inmates, but which one? And how was he going to make contact?

I looked at my watch and realized if I was going to help Dexter with his roof while there was still some sunlight, I had to skip dessert. I excused myself, made sure my roofing hammer and carpenter's apron were in my car, got in and slammed the door. Jenny came running out of the house and called to me, "Can I go with you?"

I wasn't about to pass up having Jenny join Dexter and me. She would be a perfect gofer if Dex and I were both on the roof.

"Sure, hop in."

When I saw her carrying the two barf bags, I laughed, "You could have left those in the house."

She grinned and replied, "If I get on the roof, I might get air sick."

That was so ridiculous, all I could say was, "I won't let you get on the roof."

"How will you stop me?"

Now she was acting like Megan, but I was prepared, "I'll nail your pants to a floor joist. You'll need a clawhammer to get loose."

"I'll slip out of my pants, David."

"Dex and I will see you in your panties."

"How do you know I'm wearing any?"

I had to give up. We were already at the turnoff to Dex's place, so I didn't continue, although I could tell she wasn't done teasing me. I never knew Jen could be in such a flirty mood. I wondered what she would be like if she ever got mad. That entire conversation was a completely new experience for me. It kept me thinking and pondering what she looked like in her panties.

Dex was playing with Skimmer when we arrived at his gate. Jen got out of the car, the Yorkie caught sight of her, ran from Dexter and frantically barked through the wire fence. Jenny scooped him up and began scratching his neck and chest, his tail moving back and forth like a windshield wiper set on fast.

As Jen played with Skimmer, she told Dex about the ride in the helicopter.

"That was you guys in the chopper that passed over my house around two o'clock?" Dex asked.

"That was us. We were on our way to Sour Lake about twenty-five miles north."

"Why didn't you offer me a ride? I've never flown in a helicopter."

Jen smiled and said, "We didn't have enough room."

Dex commented, "I thought it looked kind of small."

When Dex glanced at me, I shook my head. "There was room, but we didn't have time. Scott took time off from his official duties to pilot us. It was kind of last minute."

Jen chuckled, "Sorry, Dex."

Dex turned around and started for the ladder leading to the roof. Jen and I followed. I was carrying my hammer and climbed the ladder behind Dex. He had nailed about half the plywood sheathing to the roof that morning before the sun forced him off the roof. We got busy and finished covering the rafters in less than an hour. Jen couldn't stand the hammering, so she took Skimmer for a walk to the road, continued to the Hadleys' and returned. Dex was a bit concerned Skimmer might run off; he wasn't on a leash. I told Dex if that happened, we'd find him if it took all night and Dex relaxed.

We covered the roof with roofing felt and had it tacked down by the time Jen and Skimmer came back from their short journey. The asphalt covering went on fast because we didn't have to deal with any valleys. It was getting too dark to continue, so we stopped working and got back on the ground.

"Are you ready to go, David?" Jen sounded eager to leave.

I replied, "All set. Dex and I are at a good quitting point and the sun is about gone."

Dex said, "Thanks for coming over. We got a lot done tonight. Can you come back tomorrow?" He was asking me.

Jen replied, "I can't, I have to pick up Larrea. Don't fall off the roof." She smiled and got in the car.

I replied, "Don't worry, I'll be back and we'll try to get the roof shingled. In the morning, see if you can get all the shingles stacked up there. It'll speed things tomorrow night."

"Okay. See you, same time, same place."

We waved goodbye and started back to my place.

Juan was worn out when he reached the road. His ankles were sore and he had several scrapes on his shins. He located his stash, dug up the items he had buried and began preparing dinner. While a small can of beans heated, he walked to the huckleberry bushes where he had hidden his cycle and ate a handful of berries. As he was chewing, he noticed two parallel ruts in the ground. He knew what created them, the landing gear from the helicopter that hunted him.

He swallowed, separated the bushes to gain access to his bike, and began to check the Harley for damage. Even though the light was dim in the bushes, he immediately detected the sparkplug wires were gone.

"Son of a bitch! Those meddling bastards are gonna pay. They had no reason to disable my bike." He furiously ate, dumped half the beans on the ground and mixed a drink with water and a package of powered fruit mix. He sat and fumed about the loss of his bike and decided to start walking toward Suddenly along the side of the road, but ready to duck into the vegetation at the first sign of traffic.

# CHAPTER 29

Jenny and I arrived at my place about a quarter past nine. Rather than go inside, we went into the back yard to avoid the illumination from the streetlights so we could observe the stars, especially the ones Larrea had identified. We sat in lawn chairs and looked into the night sky and found Vega, also known as David's star. Jenny found Polaris and I pointed out the big dipper.

Jen said, "Let's lie on the grass and look up, my neck's getting sore."

She plopped to the ground and stretched out with her feet toward the house.

I joined her so we were shoulder to shoulder. We could see where we were pointing that way.

"There's Cassiopeia," she said.

I was surprised and said, "Where?" When did she learn about another constellation?

"It's five stars that form a big *W*." She pointed but I couldn't follow her quick arm movement.

She must have seen me shake my head. She grabbed my hand and pointed at the stars. I had to turn and raise up on my elbow to follow her arm movements. I looked down at her and she was staring into my eyes. I've been thinking about it for several weeks, so I kissed her and she kissed me back.

"I've been hoping you would do that, David. Why have you waited so long?"

"I was afraid if I was a lousy kisser, you would dump me and go back to Dexter." I chuckled and gently touched her hair. That only had a hint of reality, but I didn't know what to say. I've felt like ravishing her for a long time, but I have had to maintain discipline over my body and thoughts. I continued, "I've been keeping busy and trying to keep from thinking of you all the time."

"I'm not interested in Dexter anymore. I like him but it's not the same as with you. I've been afraid you and Megan were so close I didn't have a chance."

I smiled, "So have I passed the kissing test?"

She laughed, "My opinion?"

"Shall we try it again? Maybe the second one will be better."

"Um, let's wait until we say goodnight."

I didn't know whether she was trying to make me uncomfortable, but she was succeeding.

"All right, I'll try to make the next one better. Maybe if I can hold you next to me, our kisses would improve. Say, how did you learn about Cassiopeia?" I leaned back on the grass and wondered how I was going to break up with Megan, something I had tussled with before but never found an answer. I had to come up with a logical and genuine reason. I didn't want Megan to hate me or Jenny, we still had another year of school together.

"Larrea and I were sitting on the porch the other night. We couldn't go to sleep and we were just talking about things. She's an interesting person, and very smart."

"That's why you get along so well with her, two smart women."

"Thank you. I'd better go to bed; I need to get some sleep. That helicopter ride kind of burned me out today. I think nervous energy has taken a toll."

We both got up and I followed her up the steps to say goodnight. She gave me a quick kiss on the cheek and said, "See you in the morning."

I said, "Good night," and started down the stairs. I hadn't had a chance to kiss her again; something to look forward to.

"Oh, David?"

I stopped, grabbed the railing to keep from falling and turned around.

"Yeah?"

All I heard was, "A-plus." Then she closed the door.

I laughed and went in the house.

Mom asked, "What are you so happy about?"

"Jenny, she makes me laugh."

Juan walked at a steady pace for two hours without seeing any vehicles along the dirt road that led to Suddenly. He sat and estimated the distance he had travelled at approximately six miles since eating. His watch read 11:06 pm.

As he hiked along the road, he planned the next step of his plot. In addition to elimination of Jay, he wanted the inhabitants of Suddenly to suffer the consequences of disabling his bike. They had to pay the price for messing with him. The fire was going to be much bigger than he had originally considered, maybe the whole town would go up in smoke.

As he continued walking, he kicked at rocks and pinecones, pretending they were inhabitants of the cussed town, punching them in the face and hurling them to the ground. He didn't care who the victims were, male or female, old or young. When the forest was ablaze, he would be observing at a distance, firing from a bunker at anyone trying to fight the blazes, especially the guy they called Jay.

By 1:00 am, Juan had covered half the distance to the town and decided to rest for a few hours. He would steal an ATV sometime in the morning. He knew of two locations where the little vehicles were, but he had to see the roads in the daylight in order to find the small four-wheelers; there weren't many landmarks to follow in the forest and he had only driven the area a time or two. He set the alarm on his watch to wake him at five o'clock. He stretched out behind a small clump of trees, used his saddlebag as a pillow and closed his eyes.

When he woke, the sky was beginning to turn from black to gray and the stars were vanishing in the eastern sky. He stood, yawned, and flexed his arm, neck, and leg muscles. He began to walk again until he came to a turnoff and realized it was this sideroad that led to one of the ATVs. When he last saw the machine, it was parked in the perfect place, next to a garage and out of sight from the residence.

Juan tried to remember how far the property was from the main road, but he only knew distances and times from riding his bike. However, it couldn't be far to walk, no farther than a quarter mile. Once he saw the house, his plan was to move into the forest, circle around toward the garage and take his prize. Juan hoped the ATV was not locked with the brake set. Anyone living out here would not worry about vehicle theft; neighbors were honest and looked out for each other.

He had walked what he estimated a quarter mile, but still no buildings. Was he wrong about this place? Another twenty yards and all doubts vanished, there it was, the machine was parked just as he remembered. He figured it was too early for any of the inhabitants to be awake, but he still ducked into the vegetation and began moving away from the main residence using the forest as a screen.

Juan stopped periodically to observe the house and garage from between the trees. When he could no longer see the house, only the garage and the ATV, he crept toward the defenseless machine. If a dog barked or a rooster crowed, he would have to back off until everything was quiet again. He had to move as silently as possible, push the vehicle away from the house down the road, start the engine and escape without getting shot in the back. If he had any luck at all, he would get away unscathed.

When he reached the machine, a Honda, he moved quickly, checking the vehicle in ten seconds. He was able to push the ATV without much effort. Fortunately, it was rolling on a slight downhill grade and the balloon wheels made little noise. He was fifty yards away when he heard a rooster. He froze for a second, then hustled to get the booster cables attached to start engine, hopped on the seat, and sped away, smiling.

He didn't look at the gas gauge until he was on the main road. A glance was all he needed; the tank was more than half-full. His plan was taking shape. All that remained now was to set multiple fires and wait for the brigade to arrive. He would ride a little closer to the town, turn away from the road and find a spot in the trees to organize his thoughts and check his fire igniting materials. He wanted to set fires good distances apart so the resources of the firefighters were stretched. He even hoped a helicopter would get involved so he could take a shot at the pilot, the guy that had hunted him previously and sabotaged his bike.

When Juan was about a mile from town he turned off the road to the west and entered a heavily forested area, riding the ATV like it was a mechanical bull. Darting around trees and densely growing bushes kept his mind and reflexes synchronized at top speed. After threading his way for about a mile, he parked and walked to the edge of the trees to observe his location with respect to the town. The only buildings in proximity were a small structure with a new roof and a larger residence about fifty yards away. He had to go farther, at least another quarter mile parallel to town.

His watch was counting toward 6:30, time to find his first site of three widely separated locations to set ablaze. He would start the fires at twelve o'clock noon when everyone was eating and was not expecting to quickly react to a forest fire. Momentum of the fire growth was important. He anticipated shooting at least one firefighter and during the commotion escape into the western mountains of Idaho. When he ran out of gas, he would simply junk the ATV and start hiking.

Scott had arrived in his office a couple of minutes after 8:00 am. Ginny had already made fresh coffee and turned on the air-conditioning before her boss arrived. Scott filled his coffee mug and sat down to look at the overnight Faxes when the office phone rang.

Ginny exclaimed, "It's for you, Sheriff. It's Mr. Berwyn, he's upset."

Scott picked up the receiver, "What can I do for you, Bert?"

"Someone stole my son's ATV this morning."

"Did you see anything?"

"No, not a damn thing. None of us were up yet, not even the roosters."

Scott went to his wall map and measured the distance Berwyn's place was from the end of road. "You're about ten miles from end of road, is that right?"

"Yeah, so what?"

"I think I might know who took it. Don't go out confronting people, I think the guy that took it is dangerous. Let me take care of it. Okay?"

"All right. My son and I were gonna go look for it, but we'll stay home. I want that machine back, it's almost new, just bought it from Harley."

"So, it's a Honda?"

"That's right, red and silver."

"Sit tight, Bert. I'll call you."

"Thanks, Sheriff."

Mr. Berwyn hung up and Scott asked Ginny to contact Deputy Doureline so the deputy could be informed of the theft and the suspect. Then Scott called the Ranger Station to notify the agents of the situation. Scott wanted Julie to know of the potential danger. Scott decided to take a ride out to the Kincaids' to tell David and Jenny about the theft.

Scott pulled into Jenny's driveway and parked his cruiser behind David's SUV. When he got to the front door, he could hear faint voices from David and Jenny. Scott entered the house and approached the ladder leading to the attic. He called out, "David! Got a minute?"

There were a few seconds of silence before David's masked face appeared in the recessed opening in the ceiling.

"Hey, Dad, what's going on?"

"I would have phoned, but I don't have Jenny's number. Can you come down here for a minute?"

"Sure, we're finished up here. We were just going to bring the tools down."

I pulled my head up from the attic access hole and told Jenny to start down the ladder. If she slipped, Scott would catch her. While Jen descended to the first floor, I loaded my hammer, utility knife, nails, and measuring tape into my tool belt. When Jen was off the ladder, I started down, reached up and dropped the trapdoor into position then continued to the bottom of the steps.

Jenny had taken off her gloves and mask and was in the kitchen with Scott pouring three glasses of our favorite drink, lemonade. I took off my equipment belt, mask and gloves and joined them.

I had to ask, "Why did you come to visit, Sheriff?"

Jenny laughed and I grinned when I referred to him as Sheriff.

"I wanted you guys to know Mr. Berwyn's ATV was stolen this morning. I think the thief is probably the motorcycle owner. I'd like you to lock up here and go back home. That guy might be the one you chased off and he could return. I think he's a killer, so I don't want you out here until he's behind bars."

# CHAPTER 30

I wasn't too concerned about myself, but I worried about Jenny. Scott had made a good suggestion.

"Well, I'd better get back to the office. Deputy Doureline and I are going to drive the streets and see if we can find that ATV."

I didn't think the guy would come in town with the stolen vehicle, but he probably wouldn't be doing anything we expected. Jen and I would go back to my place, but first we should probably take a side trip and let Dexter know about the theft. Chances were better for Dex to hear the little four-wheeler than us since he was on the outskirts of town where it was relatively quiet. There were few competing vehicle noises out there except for those of the Hadleys' and Megan's jeep, but Megan wouldn't be at Rick's until early afternoon.

As we followed Scott out to his cruiser, Jenny said, "I'll lock the house and we can leave. Let's tell Dexter about the ATV."

Scott got in his cruiser and told us to update Dex, then go straight home.

"Okay, David, if you see that ATV, I don't want you to do anything. Leave the guy alone. He's probably still mad about the loss of his bike."

Jen joined us as Scott started his car. "Thanks for the drink, young lady."

She giggled, "You're welcome, Sheriff."

He backed out of the driveway and drove away. Jen and I got in my SUV and started toward the main drag that led out to Dexter's place. As we passed Harley's New Cars and Trucks, Jen touched my right arm.

"Hear that?"

"Yeah, it's an ATV in Harley's shop. Don't worry, if it follows us, we can easily outrun it."

I kept an eye on my rearview mirror all the way to Dexter's place, but no one followed us. We arrived at Dexter's at 9:53. He was on the roof making some measurements but hadn't started nailing the composition roofing in place. He had one of the labels from a bundle of shingles and yelled at me as I cut the engine.

"Hey, David. Get your butt up here. I don't know how to get started."

Jen got out and slammed the door. "Can I bring my rear end up there, too?"

Dex yelled back, "There's no limit to the asses on my roof."

I was laughing as I started up the ladder. When I got off on the tar paper, I steadied the extension ladder for Jen and helped her onto the roof. I could see in her facial expression that she felt uneasy, so she sat down next to Dex and me.

"Dex, we have something to tell you. Let's sit for a minute."

Dex and I joined Jenny on the warming tarpaper at the roof ridge where Jen and I told him about the stolen ATV and what Scott had warned us about.

"Thanks for the info, guys, but I'm not gonna try to run him down with my bicycle."

Jen chuckled at his reply and shook her head.

I smiled and said, "Good. Let's get going on the first row of shingles."

It was nearing eleven o'clock when we finished the first square of shingles. We were starting to get awfully warm on the roof.

Jen said, "I have to get down, David. Can you help me?"

"Sure. I have to get down, too. C'mon, Dex, let's get off the roof. We can do more later."

I steadied the ladder while Jen went down and then for Dexter. He held the ladder for me as I descended. When I reached the ground, Dex said, "I've been thinkin'. I might have heard an ATV engine this morning when I was on the roof before you and Jen arrived."

"Yeah? What direction did the sound come from?"

Dex pointed at the trees a couple of hundred yards to the west. "Over there, I think. It wasn't a continuous sound, more like someone gunning the engine to go over hills, you know, an intermittent sound, kind of off and on. I didn't think anything about it until after you mentioned the theft of that ATV."

I looked at the edge of the forest where Dex had pointed and wondered why the ATV would be over there. It would be a difficult place to ride for fun, the trees were in a dense stand and no streams were in that area. If it's the stolen ATV, the rider has something other than fun in mind. I'd mention it to Scott at lunchtime.

Juan had set the first digital timer for 12:00 noon and was moving on to the second location, the one that would start at 12:10. He set the timer and moved nearly a quarter mile to the top of the closest ridge to the west of Suddenly. He wanted to get the fire travelling on both sides of the hogback to give the firefighters a bit more to keep them occupied. He placed the last two ignition sources with timers set for 12:05, then he rode the ATV to an adjacent hill, roughly five hundred yards to the northwest. From that position he could easily monitor two of the sites using the scope on his rifle.

With everything in place, Juan could relax and have an enjoyable lunch. He would just settle back against a warm boulder and wait for the smoke to rise and the activity to begin. He had planned for the fires to merge before any of the four could be even close to being extinguished. If Jay's little group weren't within range he would adjust his position to get a good shot, but he had ammunition enough for all twelve members of the brigade. He smiled as he wondered how many shots it would take before the firefighters would realize they were targets. He imagined someone would react after three shots were taken, maybe before, depending on how many men were down. If possible, he would get Jay first and leave the woman for last. Juan didn't think any of the fire crew would figure out the source of the gunfire. Juan took out the last of his cheese, unwrapped a candy bar and began enjoying the beautiful scenery while he ate what he hoped to be his last lunch near Suddenly.

By 8:00 am, the brigade had packed their equipment on the truck and were ready to ride back to town. Todd and DD had arranged through the warden for the group to stay at the Shady Lake Motel until time for dinner. The penitentiary office had called Mrs. Nash, the proprietor of the motel, to rent six of the ten units for ten hours, but she was wary of the group. Sheriff Wilson had guaranteed if any damage resulted, the state would reimburse Shady Lake Motel and arrange for repairs. After the sheriff had talked with her, she agreed to the arrangement.

The inmates had earned some time off and a chance to take showers. Following their evening meal, they would pack up and head for another site ten miles south of tower seventeen. As soon as everyone was cleaned up, Todd and DD would go over the next assignment.

They would stay at an abandoned campsite formerly used by construction workers when the fire towers were being erected several decades in the past, around nineteen-fifty. The site was at the end of road, but there was an ancient logging road two miles before they reached the camp site. The brigade was to investigate the logging road and clear it from fallen trees and undergrowth.

The crew arrived at the motel about 9:40. The sheriff met with them to return the equipment from Sour Lake he had flown out in the chopper. He also informed them of the ATV theft, asked them to report any vehicle of the type he described, and warned them of the potential danger from the man suspected of the crime. Scott asked Larrea if she would rather clean up at his home than stay at the motel, but she declined, saying she would share a unit with Jay.

"Does Jenny know where to pick you up tonight?"

"No. I think she can meet me wherever we have dinner. Let me check with the bosses." She talked with Todd and mentioned to Scott, "We'll be eating at the Ax Handle Pub and Grill, but it's a little too seedy for her. I'll be waiting for her outside, about seven-thirty."

"All right, I'll let her know. Thanks, Larrea."

When Jen and I arrived at my place for lunch, we changed our pants so we wouldn't transfer stains from Dexter's roof to the furniture. A few minutes after twelve Scott came home and sat with us in the dining room. He gave Jenny the message from Larrea while we started lunch: sandwiches of our own construction, an apple or banana, potato chips, and a can of pop.

We were having a lively conversation about how hot it was and no sign of rain in the forecast, when the phone rang. Mom was in the kitchen and grabbed the receiver.

"Hello."

She must have pressed the speaker phone button, because the next thing we all heard was a man's voice, "We've got a fire, Julie."

"Oh, no. Where?"

"Looks like three of them in quads nine and thirteen."

"Jeez, Leonard, those areas are just west of town. Have you called the brigade?"

"Yeah, just got off the line with Todd, but they only have a truck, and there's no road out there. Another chopper is coming in from Dillon. It should be on site in about ten minutes. Can you report in and meet it?"

"Sure, I'll bring Scott. If we need another pilot, he can handle it."

"Ten-four."

We were all quiet during the conversation, but when we heard the signoff, I said, "Mom, Mr. Hadley has a caterpillar tractor and can make a road for the brigade truck."

"I know, David, but that would take too long. We've got to get on this right away. The crew can hike in, it's only about a quarter mile to the tree line. Scott and I need to go right now. You, Jenny, and Danny can take care of Gwen while we're gone. If you need help, go across the street to the Weems's."

"Okay, Mom."

Scott was at the door waiting. "Let's get over to the station, Julie."

Mom grabbed her work belt and ran to the door, waving, as she pushed Scott ahead of her. A couple of seconds later, I heard the doors of the cruiser slam shut and the wheels laying rubber as they took off down the street.

Jen raised her left eyebrow and commented, "Pretty serious stuff, huh?"

"Yeah, just what we didn't need this summer. We're fairly far from the flames, so I don't think we need to worry much. Luckily, there's no wind today. With two choppers dropping water and retardant, the fires won't burn long. The brigade will be out there to mop up in no time."

Gwen was strapped in her highchair and starting to hit the plastic tray that kept her from falling forward and out of the chair if she slipped under the waist belt. When she purchased the chair, Mom had made sure it wasn't one of the recalled type.

Jen leaned down to Gwen and asked, "Are you ready to get down, Gwen?"

Gwen drooled something, partly audible, and Jen wiped the baby's smiling chubby face with a wet napkin. Jen tossed the napkin to me and started unbuckling the cherub from her chair. I watched the operation, wondering if Jen would have trouble releasing the tray so Gwen could be lifted from the chair. But I was surprised by my new girlfriend, she put her hand beneath the tray, released the lock, and slid the platform off the chair arms.

The next thing I knew Gwen was sitting between Jen and me, waving her little arms and making funny noises.

I glanced at Jenny and said, "She's thanking you for getting her out of the chair."

Jen grinned, "I figured you would understand babytalk."

I chuckled, "I don't get all of it, just the important words."

"Like what?"

"All that stuff from below the equator." I wasn't going to elaborate to give her the satisfaction of embarrassing me and I was saved by the bell. Not the bell, really, it was the fire alarm for the town. I hadn't heard it since the last big fire that came close to Suddenly, the one my dad died in six years ago. There had been a few tests but nothing to make everyone in town take notice.

Jill looked at me with her head tilted and said, "Is that what I think?"

"Yeah, it's not for an air raid. The volunteer fire department will be meeting to help out where needed. Most of the guys have fought forest fires before."

# CHAPTER 31

"You're being silly. I didn't think it was for an air raid." She smiled, "Maybe a tornado, a volcano, or a tsunami?"

I had to laugh when she said tsunami. And when I started laughing, Gwen started, and then Jenny.

"Hey, you're not supposed to laugh at your own jokes."

"Seriously, David, how are we going to know what's going on with the fires?"

"We have to stay near the phone. Mom and Scott will tell us what we need to know."

"What about TV coverage?"

I had to think for a minute. "Uh, the ABC station in Butte might send a crew down in a chopper. They might have live coverage, but they probably won't show up for another thirty minutes to an hour."

Jenny was anxious and said, "Can we turn on the TV and watch for news bulletins?"

"Sure. You can have the remote."

She looked at me as if I were reluctantly giving her command of our flat screen. I was going to ask her to scan the local stations, but I decided to keep my trap closed and let her do whatever she wanted. If we were going to be together for at least the next year, I had to give up trying to make all the decisions. The remote was sitting next to me on the arm of the sofa. I picked it up and handed it to her. She turned on the set and a news break from Butte came on relaying a note passed to them from

Dillon, thirty miles to our northeast. I wondered who had called them from Suddenly.

I didn't have to ponder long, the newscaster said that Director Turner at the Ranger Station in Suddenly had reported a fire to the west, a quarter mile from the town. That wasn't anything new to us, we had heard from Mr. Turner before Mom and Scott ran out the door.

The ranger station had contacted the brigade as the crew was beginning to eat lunch. DD and Todd were huddled together in a booth listening to a voice on their walkie talkie.

Todd stood up and called out, "Take one more bite, we've got a fire to attack. It's not far from here and we'll be hiking in. We'll drive to the edge of town and go cross country to the flames. We'll have two choppers dropping retardant and water. The local fire department will back us up. Larrea, I want you to act as ground coordinator."

Chairs skidded across the vinyl flooring and at least half of the crew was griping, not about the fire, but about the interruption of their meal. There was a small jam up of bodies at the door as everyone tried to get out of the restaurant simultaneously. Before all members of the team were on the truck, it was beginning to roll toward the main road leading out of town. Two of the crew members had to run to catch the arms of men leaning over the rails to hoist them aboard. Larrea had gotten into the cab with the guards to access one of the walkie talkies.

Todd was driving and DD was advising Larrea about the use of the communication system. In less than ten minutes, the truck pulled into the lane leading to Dexter's property. As soon as they stopped, the clothes lockers on the truck bed were opened and the crew began suiting up. Dexter came out of his side room shack holding Skimmer who had started barking when he heard the truck arrive. Dexter swung open the gate and asked Jay, the closest crewman, "What's going on?"

Jay replied, "There's a fire about a quarter mile from here. Can we drive the truck across your property?"

"Sure, my property only extends fifty feet back from this gate, the city owns the rest, out to the trees."

"It looks flat. Are there any obstacles to avoid?"

"Not that I know of. I've walked out there and the only things I noticed are gopher holes, weeds, and a few small bushes."

"Thanks, that's good information."

Jay walked over to Todd and told him they could drive to the trees without danger speeding access to the fires.

Todd mounted the running board and called out orders, "We're gonna ride to the trees, so pile on the truck. You drive, Jay."

Jay climbed in the cab and started the engine, checked his rearview mirror for stragglers, heard some hands bang on the roof, and started moving the crew toward the trees at about ten miles an hour. The rough landscape forced him to keep the speed limited, but still three times faster than the brigade could hike. Larrea was in the cab with Jay and gave him another set of eyes to help avoid rough spots.

Two minutes later, the brigade was afoot entering the trees, carrying axes, shovels, and two chainsaws. Larrea had taken off into the forest moving as quickly as possible, darting through the undergrowth and trees that towered overhead. Jay grabbed one of the chainsaws and tried to follow, but soon lost sight of her. He kept moving in the direction she was headed when she disappeared. Gene and Markus were right behind Jay when he heard, "Follow the noise, Jay. You can hear the burning."

The two men following were carrying shovels and all three of them forged ahead as fast as they could through the dense underbrush. Larrea suddenly appeared and yelled, "Start cutting an east-west break, Jay. Fell the trees toward the south. A chopper will be here in a few minutes to drop water. We've got three class B fires, but I want to keep them from merging."

Jay asked, "Where are we with respect to the other fires?"

"We're just north of the northernmost fire, It's about thirty yards wide, moving west and a water drop will knock most of it down. Tell the shovels to start tossing dirt on hot spots. After the drop, we'll try to cross the burn and work the other side."

Larrea was speaking into the walkie talkie as the three men moved toward the flames. Jay could feel the air temperature rising and smell the fire before he could see it. He heard the rotor blades of a chopper approaching and stood with Markus looking up through the branches at spots of blue sky. Gene was working his way toward the fire paying no attention to anything overhead. He removed his helmet and wiped his forehead with his undershirt pulled up from around his neck.

The chopper was passing nearly overhead when the water drop occurred. It wasn't the helicopter the sheriff had flown to Sour Lake; this one was bigger and even sounded much larger. When the water came down, Jay thought of the sound of a thousand toilets flushing simultaneously, and a change in noise from the fire was evident. Jay looked at Larrea and heard her say, "Another drop on this one and we'll be in great shape. My guys can handle what's remaining. Make your next run overlap to the south."

She held the walkie-talkie at her side and walked over to Jay. "It looks like this fire has only burned three or four acres. We're making good progress. As soon as the guys can work the edges, we'll go for the center fire, it's almost twice as big and it's gone over the ridge."

"Where are the choppers getting the water?"

"About a half-mile from here on the southwest edge of town, a small puddle of water called Cowpiddle Pond."

"You're kidding me."

"No, that's a real name. A farmer named it a long time ago. Ranger Julie told me about it, but it can't supply much water."

"You hear that engine?"

"Yeah, I got a message about a logger. Name's Hanley. He's got a D4 caterpillar tractor. He's coming to help make the breaks."

"I'd better get busy, that D4 isn't a big machine. He might need help with trees."

The second water drop extinguished nearly three quarters of the remaining burn and the men were controlling small breakout flames so they couldn't spread. Larrea determined that she could move on to the larger fire and was directing two choppers to drop retardant and water. The eastern expanse of the fire had been knocked down and the brigade had started hiking to the ridge to work the western downslope fire.

Juan was waiting, listening to the crackling of the fire closest to him and noticing the reduction in the smoke rising above the treetops. He had resisted shooting at the aircraft, fearing the pilots would report the gunfire and he would be hunted. He had yet to see any of the brigade members, but the engine noise from the D4 tractor led him to believe men would soon appear coming over the top of the ridge.

The burned area had left open spots where he could watch the firefighters as they fought the blaze. Juan was becoming impatient; he was anticipating Jay's image in his sight. The first sign of movement along the ridge was a tree tipping toward him and then the appearance of the caterpillar blade pushing burning undergrowth.

He focused his telescopic sight on the driver but passed up taking a shot. Juan thought the heavy wire cage around the operator might deflect the bullet. But then he noticed the driver was not alone on the D4, there was a rider carrying a handset. It looked like John. He didn't have to lead his target, he could aim for the torso and as the tractor began its descent, the slug would also make a great head shot. He wanted to see the white helmet explode when the slug struck home.

Juan took aim, held his breath, and squeezed off his first shot. But in the time the bullet travelled across the valley, approximately twelve hundred feet, Larrea had turned and raised the walkie-talkie to her face, only to have it explode, knocking her helmet off and sending her tumbling off the tractor.

Hadley was shocked momentarily, but then he realized what had just taken place. He stopped the tractor and raised the blade into the air to offer protection for himself and the injured firefighter. He hadn't noticed the person on the radio was a woman until he saw her on the ground without head protection, red streaks developing in her disheveled hair.

Just before he jumped off the D4 to assist the woman, he sounded the horn on the tractor, three piercing high frequency blasts. Hadley had altered the original equipment of the caterpillar so his logging crew would respond at a sudden alarm.

Jay had just glanced at the tractor and saw Larrea using the walkie-talkie, but he hadn't seen her fall to the ground. When he heard the three sharp blasts, he dropped his saw and ran to the tractor. At first, he thought Mr. Hadley had a problem, but as he got closer, he saw Larrea laying on the ground. She wasn't moving and Jay was confused, what the hell had happened?

Jay dropped to his knees and saw the blood in Larrea's hair. "What happened? Did she fall?"

"No, someone shot her!"

"What?"

Jay sat beside Larrea and carefully began checking her head for an entry wound, but he only found facial scratches and one deeper bloody crease about an inch long two inches above her right ear.

He shifted his legs so he could put her head on his thigh and she began to move her arms. He folded her arms across her stomach and said, "Don't try to move. You've been shot."

She began blinking her eyes and asked, "Is that you, Jay? What happened?"

"You're just over the ridge of fire two. The walkie-talkie must have deflected a bullet that was meant for you. It knocked you out. You've got a cut in your scalp that needs some stitches. I've got to get you off the ridge and to the hospital."

Hadley spoke up, "I can help with that. I've got a CB on the tractor; I'll call the sheriff and he can arrange for someone to get her to the hospital."

"Great! But I'd like to get her to the other side of the ridge and out of sight. I'm assuming the shot came from over there." Jay pointed across the valley.

Hadley said, "I think you're right. Someone is hunting us from the next ridge to the west. I'll let the sheriff know." He climbed back to the driver's cage and used his radio.

Markus and Todd arrived and were informed of the added danger. They began spreading the word for the brigade members to keep hidden behind trees and undergrowth as much as possible.

Five minutes later, the smaller chopper appeared overhead and set down on the eastern side of the ridge. Staying out of sight of the shooter's suspected position, Hadley and Jay carried Larrea over the ridge to the chopper. After a quick discussion with Jay, Hadley wrapped Larrea's head with gauze from a first-aid kit and went with her to the hospital. Hadley had more medical experience than Jay because of Rick's many hospitalizations.

# CHAPTER 32

Jenny and I were watching a news broadcast of the fires at two o'clock when the phone rang. I jumped to my feet, darted into the kitchen, and snagged the phone off the wall cradle.

"Hello?"

"David, is Jenny with you?"

"Hi, Megan. Yeah, we're watching the firefighting progress on TV."

"Tell Jenny that Larrea was just admitted. She's been shot."

"What? That's a cruel joke, Meg. I'm surprised you would say something like that."

"I'm not kidding, David. She was flown in from the biggest fire. Mr. Hadley rode in with her. Let me talk to Jenny."

"Okay." I called to Jenny, "Jen, Megan wants to talk with you." I thought it was better to have Megan tell Jenny what had happened rather than me repeating Megan's words. It took a few seconds for Jenny to join me. I gave her the phone and stepped back to listen.

"Oh, no! What happened? Is she going to be okay?"

I watched Jen nod her head slightly and hang up the phone.

"I've got to go to the hospital, David. Can I take your car?"

"Um, sure. I can't go with you; I have to stay with Gwen."

I wrestled my key ring from my pocket and gave her the car key. Jen ran out the door and in what seemed record time, I watched my car speed down the street and disappear around the corner. There was nothing I could do but return to watching TV and keeping an eye on Gwen as she slept in her playpen.

An anchorwoman announced the arrival of another large chopper from Butte. It was capable of dumping several thousand gallons of water and was attacking the third, southernmost fire with success. Reports were the water had been taken from Sour Lake. I felt that things were coming under control, but I wondered how Larrea was doing. I wanted to call Megan but decided against it; she was probably helping the doctors and nurses with Larrea. Besides, there were probably other more important calls coming to the hospital. Maybe Meg would call again and give me a progress report.

The phone rang again. I got it on the second ring, hoping the noise didn't wake Gwen.

"David?"

"Yeah, Mom, what is it? Where are you?"

"Scott and I are at the Ranger Station getting ready to go after the shooter. We think we know his approximate position and we'll be using the infrared hot spot locator used before on the flight from Sour Lake."

"Why isn't the regular pilot flying you?" I asked.

"On his last water drop, the shooter took a shot at him. He refuses to fly anymore until we get the guy responsible for the shooting."

I was starting to worry about Mom and Scott, but they were just doing their jobs. Scott didn't have to pilot the chopper, but I'm sure he didn't want Mom out there on the ground alone hunting a guy with a rifle who was probably a killer.

"Be careful, Mom. We all need you and Scott."

"We'll be fine, David. How's Gwen?"

"She's still sleeping. I'll give her a bottle when she wakes up."

"Sounds good. We'll talk to you later, bye."

As I said "Bye," I heard the phone click off.

Jenny pulled into the hospital parking lot, and in her haste to see Larrea, parked haphazardly occupying sections of two spaces and ran to the emergency entrance.

Nurse Berg was shutting the rear door of the ambulance and asked, "Miss Kincaid, can I help you?"

"Yes, I came to see Larrea Wisdom. How is she?"

"She's in room one-twelve. Dr. Rennick just closed her head wound. She was extremely lucky."

The nurse ushered Jenny into the hospital and pointed down the long hallway, "Room one-twelve is on the right, don't run."

Jenny would have broken into a run if it hadn't been for the nurse's warning. Jen moved as fast as possible without running and found room one-twelve. The door was open and another nurse was giving Larrea an injection. Megan was standing to the left of the nurse and glanced at Jenny.

Megan said, "Come in, Jenny. We're giving Larrea some antibiotics. She's awake."

Megan stepped aside and Jenny took her place, reached out to Larrea, and grasped her right hand. "I'm so glad you're going to be all right."

Larrea smiled, "I guess my head is too hard for a bullet to do much damage. I'm glad I wasn't talking on a cell phone, that wouldn't have deflected the slug. Have they caught the shooter yet?"

"I don't know. I was at the Wilsons' and David let me take his car to come see you. I can't understand why anyone would want you dead."

"Maybe the same crazy that started the fires. I'd like to know the reason."

"Do you think it was a mistake? Could he be after one of the men?"

"Could be." Larrea leaned back into her pillow and closed her eyes. Jenny glanced questioningly at the nurse.

The nurse glanced at Larrea's vitals on the monitor and said, "She's just sleepy. We'll keep her here overnight. There's nothing you can do, but you can sit with her if you like."

"Thank you. I'll just stay a few minutes. When will she be released?"

"Well, we usually observe concussions for twenty-four hours, so tomorrow about three o'clock, if no problems arise."

"Okay, I'll pick her up at three. Thank you."

"You're welcome. I'll tell Ms. Wisdom you'll be here to get her. I'm sure she'll want to leave by three."

The nurse left the room and shut the door. Jenny held Larrea's hand for a few minutes, moved quietly out to the hallway and walked slowly to the parking lot. After getting in the car, she dabbed her eyes with a tissue, started the car and drove back to the Wilsons' residence.

The helipad at the ranger station was alive with activity. A city firetruck had loaded 200 gallons of water into the small chopper's drop tank. As Scott and Julie came running from the station, the driver yelled that it was ready to go.

Scott signaled with a wave that he got the message. He and Julie climbed into the front seats, buckled up, and took off toward fire two.

Julie commented, "Would we fly better without the load?"

"Yeah, but I want this to appear as a normal run at the fire."

"Good thinking. Our killer won't expect anyone shooting back. Any special tactics?"

"I'm going to approach from the west so we can get a good look at the close western ridge before we make the dump. That's the ridge where we think he's located. It will be awkward for you to watch the IR screen and move quickly into the cargo hold. Then, I'm going to climb, do a one-eighty and return west. You'll only have a few seconds to lay down some fire. If you don't hit him, you'll at least give him some doubts."

"What if he shoots at us?"

"The underside of our fuselage is remarkably rugged and we'll have gravity on our side. After we make our first run, I'll climb to two-thousand. I don't think a bullet will penetrate our underside at that altitude. Make sure you have your safety harness secured, there might be some unexpected g-forces."

Julie gave Scott a shoulder pat, climbed into the cargo area, checked her rifle, made sure she was secured by a cables and belt and called back to Scott, "I'm ready, let's find our shooter." She slid back the right cargo door and gasped when she looked down at the ground flashing by beneath her. She focused her eyes back inside the chopper and leaned over the front seat to see the IR screen.

Ten seconds went by before Scott said, "I'm starting our run, watch for our target."

Julie had her long gun in her left hand and was holding tightly onto the back of the copilot's seat with her right. She watched the screen like a hawk looking for dinner on the ground as they approached the burning, half-orange-half-black landscape. She saw movement and switched the screen back to visible to locate landmarks, then hastily moved to the open cargo door and unbuckled her belt.

Scott reversed course suddenly, causing Julie to grab at the fuselage wall to keep from falling out the door. She regained her balanced and was ready to fire when they passed over the dump area and headed toward their target. Scott had slowed to give Julie an extra second or two to shoot. She squinted and found the target location, fired five shots, and moved away from the open cargo door, slamming it shut.

She could feel the chopper rising and heard Scott, "We're at eighteen, nineteen, two thousand. Going back, get ready. I'm going to circle over our target. Watch the IR screen."

Julie appreciated, but didn't need Scott's instruction; she was already watching the hot-spot screen for movement and was rewarded. When she saw motion of a single individual, she moved into the cargo area, and opened the door. It was difficult to target an individual from that altitude, especially when moving, so she yelled at Scott, "Drop down to a thousand for a few seconds. After I shoot, climb back to two thousand."

Scott didn't like being only a thousand feet from a man with a rifle shooting at a large target, when the chopper was the man's prey, but he thought Julie could end the hunt with only one good shot; he descended to one thousand and approached from the west.

Julie saw movement, got off a quick three shot burst, and noted something red in the trees as they passed overhead: it had to be the stolen ATV. When they regained altitude, she said, "See if you can get us between the sun and that last target, I think I see the ATV. I want to disable it. Hold us steady so I can't miss."

Julie watched the chopper's shadow slowly creep across the trees but when she was going to shoot, the chopper rotated and she lost her target.

"Scott, hold us steady!"

He heard the frustration in Julie's voice, but there was nothing he could do, the rear rotor was not working properly and he headed toward town. Scott had to set the craft down to inspect the tail rotor, if he lost complete control in the air, they could spiral into the ground. He began descending as he drifted the chopper toward the Hadleys' property. If he needed tools, chances were Hadley would have something he could use to fix the problem, otherwise they were done for the day.

"I've lost almost all power on the tail rotor, Julie. I've got to set us down."

Julie rejoined Scott in the cockpit and watched the ground slowly approach but with their rotation slowing. Scott commented, "It's the rear rotor cable system. Something is preventing the cable from controlling the pitch of the tail rotor blades, it's only working sluggishly at low main rotor speed."

"You think you can fix it?"

"Depends, but I'll sure try. I need to have full control if we're going after that guy."

As they touched the ground, Julie said, "Hurry, Scott."

He looked at his wife and laughed, "Now you want me to hurry?"

They were both on the ground in seconds. Scott opened the fuselage side panel and began inspecting the tail cables.

"Get in the pilot's seat and press on the floor pedals as hard as you can."

Julie did as asked and Scott said, "Okay. I know what's wrong. I need a four-inch C-clamp; can you get one at Hadleys'?".

Julie abandoned her seat and was running as Scott yelled, "A large vise-grips might work."

She yelled back, "I'll get both, —and Mr. Hadley."

As Scott waited impatiently, he tried to correct the metal impeding the cable's movement, but his fingers weren't strong enough. He had to give up and leaned against the chopper for about a minute before he saw Julie and Mr. Hadley approaching. Hadley was carrying something, much larger than the tools Scott had requested.

Hadley carried a small stepladder, something Julie had mentioned when she asked for the tools. Scott would have better access to the cables when using the ladder.

Hadley recognized the problem immediately and asked, "What could have caused that tear and warpage?"

Scott answered without hesitation, "A high velocity bullet."

Hadley shook his head, "Jesus, Sheriff, I believe a bullet like that nearly killed Larrea."

"That's why we want to get back in the air. We need to get this guy before he kills someone." Julie gave Scott the clamp and vise-grips and watched Scott bend a metal cable guide back to allow free movement of the tail cable.

Julie had anticipated Scott's request to operate the foot pedals and was already in the pilot's seat when Scott called out, "Try the pedals, babe."

"That's it!" He replaced the access cover and dropped to the ground, thanked Hadley for his assistance, and climbed into the chopper. Scott restarted the engine, waved to Hadley, who watched the rotor speed increase as he backed away toward his house. A minute later, they were back in the air headed for the burned area they had left when tail rotor trouble started.

# CHAPTER 33

Juan had expended all but two of his cartridges and was beginning to worry about the helicopter that had attacked him. He had taken two shots at the chopper and was sure he hit it both times. When he watched it disappear from view, it looked to be in trouble, spinning slowly about the main rotor axis. He was unhappy about not being sure he shot Jay, his planned target, but he had gotten one kill, conceivably Jay, the walkie-talkie operator.

He was irritated with himself for not carrying more ammunition. He could have taken all the cartridges with him on the ATV, so now he decided to return to his stash and reload. He would cut across open ground to the road and in half-an-hour would be ready to resume his hunt for Jay. The brigade would still be working hot spots into the night, a perfect time for him to stalk.

He moved quickly to the ATV, secured his rifle, and started weaving through the trees and descending to the valley floor. Time was being wasted, but Juan could finally see across the open expanse to the kid's barn and his neighbor's house, and surprisingly, the chopper he had supplied with two holes. To keep from being detected, Juan cut the engine before emerging from the tree line. He would wait until the chopper was gone, ride to the house and steal some gasoline.

Rick Hadley, wheeled out on his back patio, was watching his dad assist repairs to the helicopter and wishing he could be involved. The craft had been on the ground for only twenty minutes before Rick heard the engine start and the rotor begin to turn. His dad was slowly walking back home after waving toward the chopper. Rick was loaded with questions about the helicopter's brief visit near his backyard.

Dexter's and Hadleys' houses receded as the chopper climbed above the nearest trees. Julie had begun watching the forest below when a flash of red appeared at the edge of the tree line. Her immediate thought was the shooter had left the fire area and was retracing his steps, but why? She broke the silence and said, "Scott, I think our man is behind us. Go back toward the Hadleys'."

Without hesitation, Scott reversed course and Julie moved to the cargo area, attached safety straps, and checked her rifle's ammunition; she was ready. They were at a thousand feet when the ATV could be seen halfway between the trees and the two houses.

Scott flew sideways so Julie could take a clean shot at the ATV and rider from the cargo door. She saw the guy look up as she squeezed off her first shot. Scott hovered the chopper and said, "Take two more shots so he'll know we mean business. Take out the ATV."

Juan had no defense, but the occupants in the chopper didn't know that. The ATV was out of commission. Shots from the chopper had killed the engine. He was getting ready to seek refuge in one of the houses but before he could turn around to run, he was knocked to the ground, struck with a bullet from behind.

He was in a crossfire and struggling to throw out his rifle. He wanted to crawl away from the no longer functioning machine but that made little sense. His left shoulder was on fire as he lay spread-eagled in the dirt. Juan wondered who had shot him from the house abruptly ending his plan for getting rich. He began preparation for a series of questions, he wouldn't admit anything, especially his real name.

Scott landed about ten yards from the ATV and the ranger and sheriff approached the guy with their side arms drawn. As Julie read him the Miranda rights, Scott ran to the chopper and got the first-aid kit. When he returned to the suspect, Mr. Hadley had appeared.

"Great shot, Mr. Hadley."

"It wasn't me, Sheriff. Rick shot him with his twenty-two. He uses it to shoot crows and hawks from our back patio. I don't think Rick meant to hit him, just scare him."

"Well, this guy has several charges: murder, attempted murder, vehicle theft, setting fires, and probably several others. I'll take him to the hospital and then jail. Thank your son for us."

Hadley inquired, "You gonna leave the ATV out here?"

"You can do me a favor, sir. Roll it to your driveway. I'll have Mr. Berwyn come and get it."

Scott and Julie had flown the suspect to the ranger station, transferred him to the sheriff's cruiser and driven to the hospital. Deputy Doureline volunteered to remain at the hospital overnight to keep tabs on the prisoner. In the morning he would be transferred to jail.

Scott called it a day and went home to relax at five o'clock. After leaving the hospital, Julie had gone to monitor progress extinguishing the remaining small fires. She met with Director Turner, who had taken over ground operations when Julie was flying and wasn't available to direct ground activity.

"How are we doing, Leonard?"

"Looks like we'll have everything under control before dark. Six of the town firemen and all of the brigade will stay overnight to monitor things. We certainly don't need any flareups. Shovels and water should do the trick."

As the director and Julie conversed, Todd and Jay joined them. Both men were covered with smudges of soot and dirt but were smiling broadly.

Julie had never seen firefighters worn to the bone exhibit such behavior. She queried, "What's the joke, gentlemen?"

"No joke, ranger. We have a present for you. Hold out your hand."

Julie frowned, glanced at the director, hesitated, and extended her right hand, palm up. She didn't know what to expect and the director seemed equally wary of what was coming.

Jay put his fist with fingers down over Julie's palm and opened his fingers. Julie felt what she thought was a small pebble strike her hand, but she looked closely and recognized a slightly deformed lead slug.

Mildly shocked, Julie asked, "Where did you get this?"

Jay replied, "It was under the left side of the cushion on the D4 tractor. I hope it will help convict the guy who was shooting at us. The rifling should be reasonably clear for matching with bullets from his gun."

"Thank you. This will help immeasurably. Much of our evidence is circumstantial but this is direct and convincing. By the way, we have arrested the suspect."

Todd asked, "Who is it anyway?"

"We only know his name, Juan Martinez. We'll probably have you attempt to ID him. He might have been incarcerated before. A DNA profile will be submitted to try to find a match. That's done for all gunshot victims."

Jay smiled, "Who shot him, you or the sheriff?"

"Neither of us, a citizen shot him with a twenty-two."

Jay and Todd snickered. Todd commented, "Good for him."

"Thanks for the bullet, gentlemen. I'll give it to the sheriff. And you've done admirably with the fire suppression."

Jay and Todd turned away and began trudging back up the hill. Turner commented, "That was a fortuitous event, huh?"

"Sure was. Scott will be surprised and pleased to have the evidence. I'll put it on his plate at dinner tonight. If you don't mind, Leonard, I'm going home to get dinner ready for my tribe."

"What are you having tonight?"

"Spaghetti and meatballs."

Leonard started up the hill behind the two men and chuckled, "Don't burn anything, Julie!"

Julie placed the slug in her pocket and for some security, buttoned the flap. She started walking back toward the Hadleys' where she had parked her truck.

Julie was thinking of taking a shower and donning clean clothes that lacked the smell of smoke and sweat as she drove home. When she arrived, she was greeted with hugs and kisses. Scott had started dinner and was in the kitchen drinking a beer. He followed Julie into the bathroom and enjoyed a more sensual embrace before going back to the kitchen and his beer. The younger generation returned to the sofa to continue watching the summary of the firefighting events, including the report of the shooting of one of the brigade members. When the newscaster mentioned Larrea, Jenny shifted closer to David and grasped his hand. David put his arm around Jenny, holding her tightly.

A reporter had been on the scene when Larrea was taken from fire number two and flown to the hospital. Danny was watching eagle-eyed and calling out the names of everyone he could identify.

"There's Scott, and hey, that's Mom! I almost didn't recognize her wearing that hard hat. That's Mr. Turner with some of the brigade members."

Dinner went quickly, discussion of the fire and apprehension of the suspect were the main topics. When Scott mentioned the suspect had been shot, David asked, "Did Mom shoot him?"

Julie grinned and replied, "Why would you think I shot him, David? Why not Scott?"

"Wasn't Scott flying the chopper?"

"I guess that was the most obvious conclusion, but no, I didn't shoot him."

"Who did? Was it Mr. Hadley?"

Julie smiled and shook her head, letting David stew a little bit. She watched David's forehead furrow, pleased to be teasing her eldest, the one that normally had most of the answers. She was proud David was so bright.

"So, who was it?"

"I want you to figure it out, David."

I was stuck. I realized Mom was teasing me, but who could have shot the suspect? I was thinking logically, or so I thought. I looked at Jenny for assistance. She shrugged; she had no idea.

I gave my best guess, "Was it Mrs. Hadley?" I thought that had only a slight chance, I knew Mrs. Hadley didn't like guns. It couldn't have been Megan; she was at the hospital. It couldn't have been Dexter, either. He didn't have access to a gun. Then it hit me, it had to be Rick! No wonder he was my last guess, I didn't think he could shoot from his wheelchair, but maybe he was strong enough to stand.

"I've figured it out, Mom, it was Rick Hadley."

Mom clapped her hands, "You got it! Rick shot him with his twenty-two."

"In the butt?" When I said that, Jenny laughed.

Scott had been listening and smiled, "No, in the left shoulder. We took him to the hospital. Deputy Doureline recognized him. A couple of weeks ago, the deputy stopped a motorcycle. The driver had ignored a red light. It's the same guy, Juan Martinez, from California."

I had several questions, "Why is he in Suddenly? Why did he start the fires and why did he steal that ATV?"

Scott chuckled, "I have the same questions. I asked him those things, but he remained silent, not a peep. After the bullet was removed he laid down and went to sleep."

I wondered if this guy, Juan, had ever been in prison, so I asked Scott, "Will you run his DNA through the prison system files?"

"His DNA is being processed, but it will take some time."

I remembered when Megan and I had our DNA analyzed and it took a couple of weeks. I wasn't sure Scott could hold this guy for that long, so I asked, "When will you get the results?"

"I sent a blood sample for FBI rapid processing. I should have the results late tonight or tomorrow."

That was a major surprise. I wondered if that was a result of Scott being a former member of the FBI, or it was just modern progress. I imagined the DNA results would take two weeks or longer.

Jenny had been quiet for some time. I thought she might not be feeling well or was thinking about Larrea lying in a hospital bed overnight.

I gave her a little nudge and asked, "Are you okay? You're awfully quiet."

"Un-huh." She forced a smile, "I need to talk to your mom."

When Scott and I were talking, Mom went into the kitchen for some unknown reason. I glanced at Jen and said, "Mom's in the kitchen, you can talk privately in there."

I assumed the face-to-face was a private matter, but when Jenny got up, she pulled me off the couch and jerked my arm so I would follow. I began to wonder what was going to transpire. I never knew what to expect when Mom was in the kitchen and adding Jenny made the possibilities almost endless. However, I was only a step behind my new love interest.

# CHAPTER 34

When we entered the kitchen, Mom had just gotten the popcorn popper from the cabinet to the right of the sink. Her head swiveled slowly and she ordered, "Get the bowls, David."

Before I followed instructions, I voiced, "Jenny needs your advice, Mom."

"Oh, well, sit down and let's talk. What is it, dear?"

"Larrea's mother and daughter are arriving in Butte tomorrow at noon. I bought them plane tickets a week ago so they could come visit. They haven't seen Larrea in over two years. I don't know what to tell them about Larrea."

Mom was excited about what Jen had done, as was I. That was such a nice thought. Just thinking about what Jen had done almost brought tears to my eyes. My judgement of Jen's heart had just risen to enormous heights. I wanted to give her a giant hug, but Mom beat me to it.

Mom released her arms from around Jen and said, "Just tell them the truth. Explain what happened and tell them they can come with you to the hospital when you pick up Larrea. That's a good place to reunite the family. Larrea will be overjoyed."

Jen asked, "Should I put them in a motel or take them to my place? I have enough room, but my house is so old."

I believed Jen wanted them to stay at her house, but she wasn't sure it was the best idea. She had so many thoughts swimming in her brain, she was confused and was asking for help.

I offered my thoughts, "I'll bet your place is as good as any, Jen, and you'll have more freedom. If you want, you can borrow my car; you'll have two extra roommates. Your truck can only seat three people comfortably."

I watched Jen's face mutate from a frown to a big grin. "David, will you go with me to the airport? I'll buy the gas."

I couldn't decline, I relished any time I could spend with Jenny. "Sure. When do you want to leave?"

"How far is it? I've never been to Butte."

I knew the mileage, about eighty-five, but we'd have to take our time on the mountain roads until we reached Interstate 15. I ventured a bit of a guess, "About two hours, so we should leave around nine o'clock."

Mom nodded, "That will give you extra time, in case there are any delays."

Jenny chuckled, "How much time does it take you to fix a flat, David?"

I wasn't sure she was serious, so I answered truthfully, "I don't know, I've never had a flat. But now that you've mentioned it, I'll make sure the spare is properly inflated."

After the corn was popped, buttered, and salted, the bowls were heaped and we adjourned to watch the report of the Suddenly fire. We had to laugh at the reference. We thought the blazes should be called the Bitterroot fire, but we decided the Bitterroot designation was perhaps too general for Montanans. When the phone rang, Danny reacted quickly, beating me to it before the third ring.

Danny placed his hand over the mouthpiece and whispered to me, "It's for Scott. It's deputy Tim." Scott had followed us to the kitchen. I figured he was expecting a call about the DNA results. Danny handed the receiver to him and sat down at the kitchen table to eavesdrop.

"C'mon, Danny. Scott's call is none of our business." Danny gave me a dirty look, stood up to return to the living room, but Scott stopped him.

"It's okay, Danny. You can both listen."

Danny dropped back in his chair and I sat adjacent to him.

Scott pressed the speaker phone button so we could hear the deputy.

"We received an email from the FBI. They received the sample and will get the results to us tomorrow."

"Thanks for the call, Tim." Scott grinned, "Don't bother to tuck in the prisoner. Good night."

I watched Scott replace the phone in the wall cradle and stand there for a moment scratching the back of his neck. He glanced at Danny and me and said, "Let's join the ladies and watch the news wrap-up."

We talked with the women for about a half-hour while we watched a roundup of the news regarding the fire, but nothing new was reported. Before we realized it, the hands on our wall clock were converging on ten o'clock. Gwen was already in bed and I caught Jenny with her mouth open, yawning.

She poked me in the ribs and muttered, "I've got to go to bed, tomorrow will be a busy day. Come with me and say good night."

She didn't need to drag me out to the garage, I was confident a kiss would be waiting for me at the top of the stairway. Side by side we slowly climbed the twelve steps to the apartment door, the darkness preventing Megan from seeing us. I hadn't broken up with Megan yet, but it had to happen in the next few days. The deck at the top of the stairs was a perfect place to kiss and say goodnight, the kiss lasting for more than a couple of seconds, it was a passionate ending to an exciting day.

It was after midnight when I finally fell asleep. I had twisted and turned for more than an hour trying to think of what to say to Megan. Everything I thought of sounded juvenile and hollow. I had a feeling Meg knew what was going to happen and I hoped there wouldn't be any tears. I couldn't believe she would have any ill feelings toward Jenny, Megan had more character than that.

As usual, whenever Jenny stayed in our apartment, she joined us for breakfast. Jen was wearing an outfit I had never seen before, cowboy boots, tan slacks, and a short-sleeve light-yellow blouse. She was gorgeous and I whistled at her, making Mom give me the evil eye. I had jeans and a blue T-shirt on and I reasoned Mom thought I didn't represent the Wilson and Drum families appropriately. I wasn't going to change, I wanted to be comfortable on our trip to Butte.

Mom had to leave early for a meeting at the Ranger Station, leaving Jen and I to get Gwen across the street to the Weems' household. Mrs. Weems was a bit surprised when Jenny and I showed up at her door with Gwen, but I explained the deviation from the norm.

As we walked back home Jenny asked, "Have you checked the spare yet?"

"Not yet." I checked my watch. "We've got another hour before hitting the road. I'll do it now."

I approached the cargo hatch of my Subaru, unlocked the door, and removed the back floor to get the extra tire. Jen watched as I took the car apart to access the spare. I rolled the replacement tire into the garage and checked the pressure; it was fifteen pounds low, so I added air until it was at optimum.

Jen was following me around, trying to keep from getting dirty. When I was replacing the spare in its nest, she said, "I can change a tire in fifteen minutes."

I dropped the tire in the cargo depression, reinstalled the floor, and slid in the rubber floor mat. I turned to look at Janny and realized her statement was not only a statement, but also a challenge.

I stated, "I can change a tire in twelve minutes." She couldn't beat that time; I was positive, but everything would have to go right, no wasted moves could occur.

She grinned, "I can change a tire in eleven minutes."

It suddenly donned on me that Jen was playing Name that Tune with me and I started laughing. "Okay, Jen, change that tire." I expected her to say she couldn't do it today, because we didn't have time to fool around with changing tires. But that wasn't her excuse, she had a better one: she would have to change clothes, she didn't want to get dirty today. I had to agree with her and said, "Okay, but when we are dressed appropriately, we'll have a contest. The loser buys ice cream."

She chuckled, "Okay, but I use my truck and you use your car."

I thought for a moment and decided she would have a slight advantage; her spare was loose in the back of her truck. She didn't have to take her truck apart to get the replacement tire, I had to work to get mine out of the back of my SUV. But this was going to be fun and I wouldn't mind losing to Jen. I'd buy her some ice cream if we weren't competing. It would be a fun date.

We were on the road to Dillon at nine o'clock, just as planned. Jen didn't want to drive until we reached the freeway, so I drove the first leg. Dillion is a thousand feet lower in elevation than Suddenly, but the downgrade isn't pronounced; it takes place over a distance of thirty miles. That thirty mile trek took us nearly forty-five minutes; the mostly dirt and gravel roads prevented freeway speeds.

I pulled over at a gas station in Dillon, filled the tank and Jen took the wheel. I was a slight bit nervous for a few minutes, but her steady driving was admirable, so I relaxed, leaned against the door with my head touching the window and fell asleep. Having only driven to Butte a couple of times with Mom, I didn't recognize the surroundings when I woke up nearly an hour later. I blinked my eyes, glanced at Jenny, and apologized, "Sorry, I left you for a while, you doing all right?"

"That's okay, sleepy. I'm fine, your car drives like a dream. We passed a sign about a mile back; the airport is ten minutes away. A jet was off to our right a few minutes ago. Our visitors might be waiting for us at the terminal."

I sat up straight, stretched my arms and legs even though I was constrained by the seat belt, and said, "I'm hungry. I think we should buy them lunch before we head back. What do you think?"

"That's a good idea. When we get back to Suddenly, we'll probably need to go to the hospital and pick up Larrea. I can hardly wait to see her surprise when she sees her mother and daughter."

I figured when I saw them meet up, I would have some tearful moments. "Yeah, we need to take a camera and get some candid shots. We'll plan a reunion dinner or something on the ride back home. I wonder if either of them resembles Larrea."

Jen commented, "I gave them our descriptions, so they can find us when we go to the arrival area. I hope there's a place to eat at the airport."

"There's gotta be, I think it's a reasonably new building; I haven't been to the airport in a long time. They should have more than hamburgers or cold sandwich machines."

"Let's start back and stop in Dillon. There's a nice place to eat near the Interstate. Grams and I went there once."

"We can see what your guests would like to do. I can buy a candy bar to tide me over."

"What's your favorite?"

Jen was watching the road and signs, so I didn't answer her question. When I get in traffic, I turn off the radio so there is no distraction. I assumed she might have the same preference. I refrained from telling her it was a Butterfinger.

From a distance, the terminal wasn't obvious, but as soon as we were on Airport Road, the futuristic looking terminal building was breathtaking. I immediately wanted to see what the shell of the building enclosed. Parking was free. We entered the building and our questions about the restaurant service were answered. The Payload Restaurant was located on both sides of Security. Jen and I stood in the open and our eyes swept the patrons, looking for two women, one young and one elderly.

"There they are!" Jen said excitedly, pointing toward the restaurant.

I directed my gaze and saw two tall dark-haired women moving toward us, smiling. I guess Jenny's description of us had done the trick, apparently, they had recognized their ride before Jenny had caught sight of them.

# CHAPTER 35

According to Jen's knowledge of Larrea's native Indian genetics, her mother would be one quarter Navajo and Larrea's daughter one sixteenth, but that assumes the fathers were white and possessed no Native American blood. Since the ladies were living on the Navajo Nation, that was probably a stretch.

As I watched them walking toward us, I searched for facial similarities to Larrea, but that quest was quickly discarded, however, the two were nice looking. The only thing I could compare was their stature; if all three women were walking away from me, I would have difficulty determining their identities; they were all tall and slender, the elder's genes were passed down successfully.

Jenny, responsible for the travelers coming to Montana, stepped forward to the older woman and said, "Hi, I'm Jenny. How was your trip?"

"It's so nice to meet you, I'm Susan and this is my granddaughter, Spring." They shook hands and Spring said, "We had never been on a plane before and were scared the first few minutes, but the attendants were nice. I think they knew we had never been on a big plane before."

Susan added, "Yes, big eyes and white knuckles tipped them off." Susan looked at me and said, "Is this your boyfriend?"

I upstaged Jenny and said, "That's right. I'm David Drum, the sheriff's stepson, so no scalping."

I could see that Jenny was shocked at what I said and reacted, "He's trying to be funny."

Susan chuckled, "Don't worry, David, my scalping knife is hidden in my luggage. It's made of rubber."

We all laughed. That gave me a way out of my dumb comment. "Let's pick up your luggage and get out of the terminal." But then I thought to ask, "Are you hungry? We can get something to eat before we start back to Suddenly."

"Our luggage is at the restaurant. We didn't want to have to go through security again to get it." Spring glanced at Susan, who gave a slight nod. Spring responded, "We could eat a sandwich, something light. All this traveling has upset our normal routine."

I was happy because my stomach was starting to growl and I didn't want that to be a topic of conversation as we drove on the freeway. A growling stomach was always embarrassing. We went back to their luggage, sat in the booth, and ordered. I ordered soup, a cheese sandwich, and a strawberry smoothie and the ladies had a blueberry muffin, a small fruit bowl, and various coffees.

We were out of the terminal after approximately thirty minutes. Susan and Spring climbed into the back seat and Jen rode shotgun. I had no choice but to drive while the ladies talked. Jenny had turned sideways so she could see her guests without contorting her neck muscles, and the powwow began. I tried to hear what was being said, but the road noise and the women's quiet voices kept me from hearing more than a few words now and then. When we arrived in Dillon, I stopped to top off the gas and we all used the facilities. The last forty-five minutes of our trip were more entertaining than the first hour's travel, I could hear the exclamations about the forests and the rock outcroppings that decorated the landscape.

As soon as Spring mentioned her desire to sketch the trees, Jen was in artist's heaven. She had found a kindred spirit. I think Jen knew Spring was an artist, but she waited for her guest to bring up the topic.

When we entered the outskirts of Suddenly, I could see in the rearview mirror a giant smile on Susan's face. I had been listening to the younger women discussing their interests in art, but nothing they were saying would have generated such a smile.

I spoke over the younger women, "Did you see something entertaining, Susan?"

"Yes, our little town is surrounded by rocks, yours is surrounded by trees, but other than that, things are similar. I believe we will like being here."

Before driving to Jenny's house, I took a few minutes and passed through our downtown streets. Jenny pointed out the few things of interest, so it was a short exposure to Suddenly. It was a quarter past two when I pulled into Jen's driveway, we had nearly an hour to get ready for the big surprise. Jen and I helped Susan and Spring move into their bedrooms, then showed them around the house. They were somewhat shocked to see everything looked so clean and smelled good. Jenny confessed that we had recently repainted the interior of the house.

Following the house tour, Jen showed them the yard, which was going to be reestablished, it had not been replanted since it had been excavated in search for buried lawn ornaments. More than a handful of weeds had sprouted in random sites, but Jenny didn't want to replant lawn until after the summer drought had ended.

When the guests were acquainted with everything, Jen glanced at her watch and announced, "I'm going to get Larrea now, so get ready. Hide your luggage!"

Originally, Jen was going alone to pick up Larrea at the hospital, but she asked me to go with her in case Larrea needed someone to steady her as she got in the car.

We got there a couple of minutes before three and parked close to the front entrance. Larrea must have seen us drive up because before we had gotten out of the car, the automatic front door to the building slid open and Larrea, wheelchair bound, came out pushed by Nurse Berg.

Jenny ran to Larrea and gave her a hug and helped her out of the wheelchair. Larrea, as most patients do when leaving the hospital, stood ramrod straight and began walking apparently with little assistance. It almost looked like Larrea was helping Jenny walk to the car, the patient could only be identified by the bandage above Larrea's right ear. I walked toward them but could see they didn't need my help.

When Larrea was entering into the back seat, she hesitated for a moment and stated, "I must be hallucinating, I just got an image of my mother, a whiff of her scent. Isn't that strange?"

I tried to hide our involvement in the coming reunion by commenting, "I've done that before, too. When I smell my sweaty socks, I have an image of the football equipment drying room at the gymnasium, but it's not pleasant."

Jen laughed, "That's disgusting, David. Now I'll be getting that image. Get in the car and let's go home."

I grinned as Jen and I got in the front seat. When Jen started the car, she gave me a thumbs up and a wink, but out of Larrea's field of vision. As Jen drove us, she asked Larrea, "Do you have to work tomorrow?"

"No. The doctor ordered me to have a week off and avoid anything strenuous. I guess that will be my summer vacation."

"I know you will have a great time; I have a feeling," Jen said, smiling.

I had to keep from laughing and almost choked. I think Larrea was the only one in the car that wasn't excited. She had no clue of what was coming in a few minutes.

When we arrived at Jen's place, she turned in the driveway and drove very slowly. I wondered what she was thinking. I guessed that she was trying to keep from jostling Larrea as the car passed over the ruts, but she might have been giving Susan and Spring extra time for preparation. I felt like a kid on Christmas morning, getting ready to find out what Santa had left me under the tree.

Larrea exited the car without any help, climbed to the porch and was waiting to Jen by the door.

"It's open, Larrea, go on in."

Jen and I were arm in arm as we moved toward the front door, listening for excited voices. It didn't take long.

"Mom! How did you get here!"

Then we heard crying for a few seconds before another outburst, "Spring! You're here, too! Oh, my gosh!"

Then more crying as we entered the house to see the three women hugging and sobbing in the middle of the living room.

I heard some sounds that must have been Navajo mixed with English as they all seemed to be talking simultaneously. I think I heard Susan say, "Can we sit on the couch, Larrea in the middle?"

The ladies moved a few feet to the sofa and sat down holding hands. Larrea looked at Jenny and me and said, "You guys arranged this?"

I had to deny any involvement. "It was all Jenny's idea. I didn't know about it until yesterday. You scared us when you were getting in the car, making that comment about your mother. For a moment we thought the surprise was lost."

Larrea turned to her mom and explained about the faint scent she had detected.

Susan said, "My daughter has always had a sensitive nose, almost like a dog's."

Larrea reacted, "I'm shocked, Mom. You gave me the name of a wildflower, not a dog."

We all had a good laugh and I invited everyone to have dinner at my place. Mom had told me to bring all the ladies for a get-together. I was curious to find out what we would be having for our evening meal, but I was afraid to ask Mom, for fear she might strangle me. I didn't want her to think I wasn't confident in her choice of what to serve.

We expected the reunion at Jenny's place to go on for more than an hour. Jen and I listened for a few minutes and then stepped outside to give the ladies some privacy. Jen and I strolled the outskirts of her property and I was presented with several ideas Jen had been pondering. She must have been thinking about things for some time because she had more ideas than I would have ever thought possible. I wondered if she had sketches of her yard in her idea book.

When five o'clock rolled around, we returned to the house to find the girls still talking, Susan and Spring quite animated, and Larrea sitting between them, smiling in silence. I reasoned she had held back speaking her mind for two years in prison, so had plenty of practice remaining quiet, but she would undoubtedly be released before long. Of course, she might possess a reserved nature and just be a quiet person.

I interrupted, "Well, ladies, I want you to meet my parents and brother at dinner. If you have any freshening up to do, please do it; we'll go as soon as you're ready." Fifteen minutes later, I was driving a carload of women through the streets of Suddenly.

Mom had gone out of the way to prepare supper. I had never thought of dinner as a feast, but this meal certainly qualified. She must have spent all afternoon in preparation, but I suspected that someone had helped, maybe Mrs. Weems.

It didn't take Mom and Jenny long to be accepted into Larrea's family conversation and the five women moved outside to the back patio after cleaning up the dinner table. Scott, Danny, and I went out front and played with the dogs while the women visited until a few of the brightest stars began to flicker. Megan never made an appearance. She must have seen our guests and didn't want to butt in.

We all gathered in the house for some dessert when the sun was completely gone for the day. Following generous portions of orange sherbet, Jen asked me to drive them to her home. Jen ran up to the garage apartment, tossed her clothes in a pillowslip and in a minute, climbed into the front seat holding the stuffed bag like a tackling dummy. While taxiing the group to Jenny's, I could see the backseat ladies' eyes slowly closing, and frequent yawns; the excitement of the day finally catching up with them. They would probably sleep soundly, even though in strange beds.

When I got back home, Mom was taking care of Gwen. I had forgotten all about her during dinner, and Mom hadn't said anything about my little sister.

"Where was Gwen during supper, Mom?"

"Mrs. Weems took her for the evening. I couldn't tend her and have a big dinner gathering." She smiled and said, "Rangers plan ahead, David."

We all laughed and after picking up the dessert dishes, went to bed.

Scott was the first to rise the next morning. My alarm woke me at seven and I could tell he was already dressed because of the footsteps, much heavier than Mom's, were shuffling about in the kitchen. I dressed quickly and joined him. His pancakes were something Danny and I always requested when he had the time to cook for the entire family. I was a bit surprised when I discovered he was mixing the batter and no one else was up.

"Good morning, David, glad you came down this early. I'm making pancakes."

"Morning, Scott. What's the occasion?"

"Oh, nothing special. I'm not going to the office until nine today so I wanted something to do to keep my mind off the fire reports and the guy we locked up."

By eight o'clock, Mom, Gwen, and Danny had joined Scott and me in the kitchen and were removing pancakes from the stack that had been growing higher every few minutes. I had been eating, but the cakes were big and fluffy. I could only eat two at a time to prevent syrup from overflowing onto the table. My limit was six, but I had to wash down the last two with cold milk and water. Today I stopped after four.

Mom skipped the pancakes. She said last night's dinner was still being digested. She talked with Scott for a few minutes, gave him a kiss, picked up Gwen, and waved goodbye as she went out the front door. It was a regular workday for her.

# CHAPTER 36

Danny made a few complimentary comments about yesterday's guests, then asked me if the Navajo Indians were famous fighters. I had no clue, nor did Scott. We sat in near silence with the only sounds coming from utensils and chewing until the phone startled us.

I was closest and reached over to remove the phone from the wall cradle.

"Hello."

I recognized the deputy's voice when he asked for Scott. I pressed the speaker phone button.

"We received the DNA results, Sheriff. This guy, Juan, doesn't have a criminal record, but he's got a close relative in the pen."

"What's his name?"

"John Allen Young. He's a member of the brigade work crew. He goes by Jay."

"I've met him. His record says his only brother, Tom Clyde Young, died in an auto accident. There must be some mistake."

"So, you think the FBI is wrong?" Tim questioned.

"Could happen, mistakes are made occasionally, even at the FBI. I think we'd better have Jay take a look at our prisoner. I'll visit the brigade this afternoon and bring Jay to the jail if he's not involved with some other work detail."

"Okay, Sheriff. Ten-four."

Scott scowled and hung up the phone. "Another wrench added to my day. I'd better get to the office and start flipping through a pile of papers that are attracted to my desk." He looked at me, smiled, and asked, "Is paper magnetic? The top of my desk is."

"I don't think so, but that was rhetorical, wasn't it?" I hadn't used that word before, but I remembered it from last year's English class.

Danny was puzzled and said, "What does rhetorical mean?"

I grinned, "Look it up, Danny." I thought he would complain but he went to the living room and grabbed the dictionary off the coffee table.

Scott said, "What are you guys doing today?"

Danny answered, "I'm looking up big words. After that, I'm gonna ride over to Carl's and give him some tips on piloting his new drone. I'll probably eat lunch over there. His mom likes to feed everybody."

Scott and I laughed and I said, "I'm going out to Dexter's to help with his roof. I'll check on Rick Hadley, too."

As Scott went to the front door, he said, "All right, I'll get out of here. See you for dinner."

Scott's desk was as he expected: mail to be opened, emails to reply to or delete, and reports dealing with procedures when flying over the fires. He was busy with paperwork and didn't relax until halfway through the lunch hour. At 12:30, Scott radioed Deputy Doureline and told him they should meet at the Dairy Queen, but Doureline had already eaten. Scott said he would buy him a cone, and the deputy said he'd be there in five minutes.

Scott wanted the contact with his deputy to be private, he never knew who would be listening in on the police frequency. The sheriff wanted Tim to observe the prisoner when Jay appeared to ID the detainee. In addition, they discussed the return of the ATV to Mr. Berwyn. Scott wanted Tim to inform Berwyn personally that the city would pay for the repairs. In the meantime, Scott would visit the brigade and ferry Jay to the courthouse to view the prisoner. Scott and Tim scheduled the meeting to occur at 3:00 p.m.

Scott was unsure where the brigade was camped, but assuming they were somewhere near their previous encampment before they hiked to Sour Lake, he drove past Hadleys' toward the end of road. He found the men scattered around their truck where they had been when Guns was injured. Some of the men were partially clothed, sitting in small groups drinking coffee after trying to clean up. Todd stood and approached the sheriff's cruiser.

"We're taking some time off, Sheriff. What can we do for you?"

"I need to talk with Jay. I don't see him."

"Huh. He's using the latrine. I'll tell him to come see you."

"Thanks. Can I borrow him for about an hour?"

"Ah, sure. We're not gonna work today," said Todd. "Want some coffee?"

"No thanks."

Scott got out of his cruiser and leaned against it for about five minutes before he saw Jay walking toward him, tucking in his shirt.

"What can I help you with, Sheriff?"

"We caught the guy that shot Larrea. I'd like to see if you can ID him."

"I hope you've got him where I can't get to him."

"He's in a jail cell, but you won't be seeing him from a one-way mirror. You'll be just outside his cell."

Jay was becoming incensed, "Just keep him away from the bars or I'll grab him and pull him through."

"Get in, I'll take you into town. We'll meet with my deputy and the suspect at three. Afterward, I'll take you to see Larrea, her mother and her daughter."

"What? Larrea told me they were in Arizona on the Navajo Nation."

"I think you met Jenny Kincaid. She had them flown from Arizona to see Larrea."

"Jeez, what a nice kid."

Jay was wearing a worn-out T-shirt and jeans and wanted to put on something more presentable, so he said, "Just a minute, let me get a shirt."

Scott slid into the driver's seat and waited about two minutes for Jay to reappear wearing a clean but slightly wrinkled short-sleeve plaid shirt. Jay climbed into the passenger seat and they headed back to Suddenly.

Jay was quiet for about two miles, but then asked, "What have you found out about this guy you arrested?"

Scott hadn't decided what to tell Jay and what to hold back, for fear the knowledge might influence the identification, but he said, "He's about your size. He gave his name on a citation as Juan Martinez from California. He was riding a Harley and staying in one of the old fire lookout towers when he first arrived in town. I think he killed his wife, strangled her."

Jay said, "Real nice guy. He doesn't sound like anyone I would know. The guys on the brigade are pretty harmless, no killers that I'm aware of. We joke around a lot. Some guys get a bit heated, but not enough to even throw a punch."

"Have you figured out what you're going to do when you're released?"

"I'm interested in motorcycles. I'd like to have a shop: sell and repair 'em but first, I want to tour the country and see the sights, you know, visit national parks, monuments, stuff like that. I'd like to see what I've been readin' about all these years. But I'll have to earn some coin before I do anything."

"Would you like to work for the Forest Service? You might qualify for some of the positions."

"Maybe. I hadn't thought of that. But it would only be temporary."

Scott said, "I'll ask my wife if she knows what you might pursue."

"I'd appreciate that, Sheriff."

The men entered the outskirts of Suddenly and went directly to the Sheriff's Office. As Scott entered his small office room, he glanced at Ginny and heard, "Five minutes to three, Sheriff," as he removed his side arm and locked it in his desk. Jay had waited outside the office and the men walked together to the jail cells.

Deputy Doureline sat in a fold-up chair six feet from the prisoner's cell, thumbing through a travel magazine. He stood, watching the prisoner, when Scott and Jay entered the cell area. Scott motioned with his head for Jay to step nearer the cell and take a close look.

Jay was shocked by what he saw. The prisoner, Juan, who was laying down on the cell bunk, was actually Thomas Young, Jay's older brother. But Jay questioned what he was seeing and turned to the sheriff. "He looks like my brother, but Tommy is dead."

The prisoner grimaced as he sat up favoring his shoulder, and said, "Well, hello John. Where have you been all these years? I'd give you a hug, but you know…"

"You should have stayed dead, you worthless piece of crap. I can't believe I once admired you. I bet you're responsible for Erica's death. You probably caused the wreck and ran away. Where'd you go, Mexico?"

"Hey, the wreck wasn't my fault, the guy in the other car crossed the center line on a bridge. I couldn't avoid the crash, no place to go. Just two lanes on that narrow bridge. Yeah, I went to Mexico."

"So, where'd the guy that died with Erica come from?"

"Erica and I gave the guy a ride. He was in the back seat and didn't want to wear the seat belt. Erica asked him to buckle up, but he just laughed. He said he'd take his chances. He lost and I was able to get out before the fire started. I put him in the driver's seat and gave him my ID. He was really mangled; his face was a mess. I checked Erica, but she had no pulse."

"I don't get it. Why'd you put him in the driver's seat?"

Scott was paying particular attention to this part of the conversation. He leaned against the bars of the cell behind him and watched Jay tighten his fingers into fists.

"Ah! That's because of something you never knew about. I discovered Mom invested Dad's life insurance money and when you get out of the slammer, you'll get nearly half a mil. If you don't live long enough to get the money, it goes to me. You know what half a million bucks would do for me?"

"But you're officially dead. How would you get the money?"

"With you gone, all I have to do is show up and prove I'm not dead. That shouldn't be much of a problem, DNA, and all. I'm related to your kid."

"So, you thought I'd die in the fires?"

"Well, Johnny boy, I was gonna push you along with a helping of lead. I thought that was you on the tractor with the walkie-talkie. I believed I nailed you, but it was that woman."

"You're gonna be put away for attempted murder. If you ever get out, you won't have a cent. I hope you enjoy prison." Jay glanced at Scott and said, "Get me out of here. I'm tired of breathing the same air as this stinking garbage."

Scott, Jay, and the deputy withdrew from the jail cells and went back to the office. As the men passed by Ginny's desk she said, "There's fresh coffee waiting for you. I assumed you would have a discussion after the prisoner interview."

"Thanks Ginny. You read my mind—again." Scott stopped abruptly, turned toward his secretary, and said, "I'm going to recommend you for a raise, or at least an extra Christmas bonus."

Ginny grinned, "Thanks, Sheriff, but which Christmas?"

Scott and Tim had a good laugh. Ginny resumed typing at her keyboard and the grin gradually faded. Jay had dropped into a chair and seemed oblivious to the others. Finding that his brother was still alive after thinking he was dead for close to ten years had been a shock. Being told when he got out of prison he would be a rich man had put him in a mental tornado. He was now rethinking his future, his thoughts about his son were rapidly changing, as were reflections concerning Larrea. He now had something to look forward to and offer a woman.

Scott and Tim had fresh coffee and were sitting quietly watching Jay, who seemed to be in a trance. After half a minute, Scott spoke, "Did you want some coffee, Jay?"

Jay was staring at the vinyl flooring between his feet but his mind was a mile away in the clouds. He hadn't heard Scott.

Scott repeated, "Jay?"

Jay blinked, looked at the sheriff and said, "Could you take me to see Larrea? I have to talk to her."

Scott grinned, "I guess you don't want any coffee?"

"Ah, no thanks. I need to see Larrea. It's important."

Scott stayed in his office to write up the results of the brothers' conversation and Deputy Doureline drove Jay to the Kincaid farmhouse. The four women were on the porch talking as the deputy's cruiser turned into the driveway.

Jenny was the first to react, "The sheriff is paying us a visit. He probably wants to talk with you, Larrea." Jenny was sitting on the steps, got to her feet, dusted off her pants and began walking toward the car before it stopped. She saw that the driver was the deputy and called out to Larrea, "It's not the sheriff, stay put." Then she saw Jay and exclaimed, "I think you have a visitor, Larrea. It's Jay."

Jay was out of the car before it had completely stopped and running to Larrea, who was still sitting in a large yard chair with her mother and daughter. She got up slowly and Jay threw his arms around her and said, "How are you doing? Are you going to be all right? I was going a bit crazy worrying about you."

"Yes, Jay. I'm going to be fine. I'm supposed to remain calm for a few days. The bullet creased my scalp but the scar will be in my hair where it can't be seen."

"We were given the day off and I had to see you. The guy that caused all the trouble is my brother. I thought he was dead. I just talked with him. He's in a jail cell."

"I remember you told me that he died in an auto wreck years ago. You'll have to tell me all about him, but first I want you to meet my daughter Spring Rain and my mother, Susan Charles. I've told them you are my brigade partner."

# CHAPTER 37

Jay took the initiative and introduced himself. He shook hands with Susan, saying, "Hello, I'm John Young. Happy to meet you. Larrea has told me all about you." He held Susan's hand with both his hands and smiled, "I see why Larrea is so nice looking."

Susan chuckled, "Thank you. I remember my grandfather told me once about compliments. Some men will tell you how many horses they will trade for you, but they have no horses."

Jay laughed with the women and said, "But my comments are not hollow. You are all fine looking women." His eyes drifted to Spring, "You should be extremely proud of your mom. She has taught me how to stay alive in forest fires and how to help my coworkers do their jobs. She's very smart."

Spring stood, shook hands with Jay and said, "She told me you are a quick learner."

Jay couldn't think of what to say except, "I try." Then he remembered Spring was an artist. "Have you and Jenny talked about your art interests?"

"We haven't had much time yet, but I want her to show me around the country here. The forests are beautiful. At home I just have rocks to draw," she grinned.

Jay said, "Well, I hope you enjoy your stay in the Bitterroots. But if you stay through winter, be prepared for several feet of snow."

Spring said, "I don't think we will be here that long, but thanks for the warning. It was nice meeting you, Mr. Young."

The deputy was known to be shy around women. He didn't get befuddled when he talked with only one, but there were four here, so he stayed at or in his cruiser while Jay met with the ladies on the porch. He watched the time go by and was getting impatient. He wanted to get Jay back to the sheriff.

He leaned out the window and called, "Jay, we gotta get goin'. You about done here?"

Jay had positioned himself a few feet from the women and motioned for Larrea to join him away from the others when he heard the deputy. He waved to Doureline and held up and waved his forefinger to indicate one minute.

Larrea asked, "What is it, Jay?"

"I need to talk to you about my son. I want you to come with me to see him. Can you do that?"

Larrea hesitated, "Ah, I guess so. When?"

"I hope tomorrow morning. I'll ask the sheriff to take us to see him. You and the sheriff can back me up when I tell Dexter who I am. I'm afraid he might not believe me."

"What time do you want to go?"

"I'm sorry, I don't even know if I can go. I'll have the sheriff call Jenny's number.

If you don't want to, I understand. I'll figure out something."

"Oh, I'll go with you. Don't worry, it'll work out." She grasped his shirt collar, pulled him down and gave him a kiss.

He returned the kiss and said, "Thanks, I needed that," and smiled. He stepped in front of the other women and said, "Pleased to have met you. I have to go."

Back in the cruiser, Doureline asked, "Did you get your business taken care of?"

"Not entirely, but I've thought there's always tomorrow for what I have to do."

As he backed to the street, the deputy gave Jay a glance, "And what is that?"

"If you don't mind, it's personal, but I'll need the assistance of the sheriff."

"You don't think I can help you?"

"That's right, it's a family matter."

"Oh. I guess you're right, that's beyond my experience." Jay wasn't sure if the response was serious or sarcastic, so he let it go.

The next morning, Dex and I were on the roof of his remodeled barn, nailing the ridge caps in place when we saw Scott's cruiser moving toward us from the highway. Dex tossed the last piece of shingle to me and I nailed it in place. We heard two car doors slam and then a third, which got our full attention. I stood up and saw Scott, Jay and Larrea approaching the gate.

Scott called out to me, "David, would you and Dexter please come down here?"

We tossed our tools to the ground and Dex climbed down the ladder with me right behind. Dex waited for me to touch the ground before asking, "What do you suppose they want?"

I shook my head, "I don't know, maybe something about the fire."

"I didn't see anything but the helicopter landing next door."

I brushed the sand from my jeans and followed Dex around to the gate.

I knew Jay and Larrea but I didn't know if Dex had ever met them. I said, "Dex, this is Larrea Wisdom and I only know this gentleman as Jay. They're part of the fire brigade."

Scott stepped forward, put his hand on Jay's shoulder and said, "This man is John Allen Young, your father."

Dex rubbed his nose, frowned and responded, "This is a joke, right? My father is dead."

Jay looked Dex in the eye and said, "No, that's what your grandmother told you. I've been in prison all this time. I made a deal with her so you wouldn't have to grow up knowing your dad was in prison. I should be out in about two more years if I'm lucky."

Larrea spoke up, "I'm gonna be waiting for him. He's a good man, Dexter."

"So, what did you do to be sent to prison?" said Dexter.

"I tried to rob a bank to pay for your mother's cancer treatments. It was a stupid idea, but at the time, it sounded good. We had little money."

I stood there listening, but I could tell Dex still wasn't sure this guy was his father. Dex asked me, "How can I know if what he's saying is the truth?"

"Ask him something only your dad would know, something that wouldn't be on the Internet," I said.

Dex nodded and asked Jay, "When I was eight years old, my dad gave me something. What was it and what color was it?"

Jay smiled and didn't even blink. "I gave you a twenty-inch bike. It was blue and white. You loved that bike. You rode it everywhere."

Dex reached out to me and grabbed me around the neck, pulling me close and whispering, "He's right. Only my dad would know that."

"I think you two should have a talk, Dex."

Dex moved away from me, extended his hand to Jay and said, "I guess you are who you say. Come in my house and talk with me."

I watched the father and son shake hands. Then, Jay opened the gate and followed Dex onto the floor of the house under construction. The roof and the subfloor were complete, but the walls were only studs open to the elements. The father and son sat on sawhorses and began talking.

Larrea and I watched for a moment and she said, "I think they will both be okay."

I said, "Yeah, Dex has family he didn't know existed. Are you serious about waiting for Jay?"

Larrea nodded and said, "He's an honorable man, nothing like my ex. I'll find a job and we can start a new life when he's released."

"I guess you and Jay have made some plans. Working together has allowed you to become more than good friends, you've grown close."

Larrea commented, "Speaking of good friends, Jenny and you have become good friends, too. How's that going?"

"I hope we have a future, but I know we're young. We'll have to finish school before we make any definite plans. We both want to go to college and I know getting married before we finish would make things difficult."

"You're thoughtful and dependable, David. Jenny likes that about you."

"She's said that?" I asked.

"Yes, we've had some long talks. You're both thinking ahead. That's good, but Jenny's worried about your present girlfriend."

"She doesn't need to worry any longer, Megan and I are finished."

I said that with certainty, having lost enough sleep thinking about how to break up with Megan. A year ago, breaking up would never have entered my mind, but after working so closely with Jenny through good times and murky ones, my allegiance and love had slowly changed. Megan was planning on moving to another state to attend college and that had sent me a strong signal, her future wasn't in Suddenly. Megan was headed for a big city and glitter.

Jenny, however, had moved away from the lights and noisy activity of a big city and found serenity and great enjoyment in the mountain forests, the opposite environment that Megan desired. I concluded that Jenny and I were much more compatible than I was with my next door neighbor.

The time for my discussion with Megan was tonight, I wouldn't put it off any longer. I'll bet Megan was wondering when I would pull the plug, she had seen me too many times with Jenny and I had denied being interested in Jenny too often, but I was just lying to both myself and Megan.

Larrea had accompanied Jay to give moral support and verify Jay's statements, but she hadn't been needed. I was glad she and I talked. She hadn't said much, but I was forced to think of where I stood with Megan and Jenny. I stopped fooling myself and had made an important decision.

Larrea, Scott and I leaned against the cruiser and watched Jay and Dexter, stand up and embrace, each patting the other on the back. They parted, shook hands, and began walking toward the police car. It appeared that Dexter had enthusiastically reunited with his father. I didn't know what, if any, plans had been made for their futures, but Dex would no longer be alone in the world. I would find out more with regard to Dex's relationship with his father in the days to come as I assisted with the construction of his home.

Holding hands, Larrea and Jay scrambled into the back seat, and Scott, smiling, said to me, "I'm running a taxi service today, but it looks like good things are happening in Suddenly." Scott slid into the driver's seat and backed to the road. He beeped twice and we watched the cruiser accelerate toward town.

# AFTERWORD

That evening, I walked slowly across my front lawn to visit with Megan next door. She came outside and we took a seat on the porch swing listening to the crickets and the sounds from the Isaacs' TV. We sat without speaking for a minute or so before Meg spoke up.

"What do you want to talk about, David?"

"Us. I think we should call it off." I bit my lower lip. "But I still want to be friends. That will probably be forever if you want. I just think we have different goals that we have to pursue, but we can't be happy if we're together."

"Oh! I'm so glad you feel that way. I've been trying to figure out how to say those words. I agree and I think you and Jenny are better suited for each other than we are. Of course, I still want to be able to study with you occasionally." Megan smiled and stood up, "I've got to get back to a program, it's a special from Carnegie Hall. Thanks for coming over."

"You bet. Good night."

"Night, David."

I was relieved that breaking it off with Megan had been so easy. The cloud on my brain had been lifted and I felt like yelling, but I didn't want to scare any of our neighbors or alarm Mom. What would people think if they heard carrying on at the sheriff's house?

When I got inside, Mom said, "Jenny wants you to call her. She sounded all excited."

I punched in her number and Jen answered after only one ring. She must have been next to the phone.

"Hi, David. I have something to tell you. You can use the speaker phone if you like—so your family can hear."

I pressed the button to enable the speaker and heard, "Larrea was notified by registered mail today that she's a free woman. She doesn't have to go back to the pen. She got recommendations from your mom and dad, DD, and Todd, and even the ranger director. The warden signed her release papers day before yesterday and they arrived today. What do you think?"

I was happy that Jenny was so excited, "That's awesome! Is she still going to stay with you?"

"Yes, they all are. We're going to keep fixing the house and Larrea knows where we can get lots of free firewood to get ready for winter. Susan and Spring are excited about staying here over the bad weather months. They want to see what three feet of snow in the mountains is like. Then they'll decide if they want to return to the desert climate."

I snickered, "Ha, I think I know what they'll want to do. Say, why don't you bring Spring over to Dexter's tomorrow. She might like him. I know he'll like her, and they're about the same age. She might have some ideas for his house."

"Good idea. I already told her about Skimmer. She loves little dogs."

I turned off the speaker and picked up the hand set. I couldn't keep the lid on about my breakup with Megan so I blurted out, "I broke up with Megan tonight. I thought you should know."

Jenny didn't react immediately. I could hear her breathing. After a few seconds, she said, "I know that was difficult for you, but it makes me happy. You know how I feel about you."

Jen had just made me a happy camper and I said, "That's my feeling, too. Good night, Jen. See you at Dex's place tomorrow."

She said, "I'm going to sleep great tonight. Good night."

The trial of Tom Clyde Young took place a week before the fall semester of school began. Most of the jury was selected from inhabitants of

Dillon who had little knowledge of the suspect's activities in and around Suddenly. The courtroom was packed to capacity and incontrovertible proof of his guilt was presented. He was sentenced to life plus twenty-five years in prison with no chance of parole. His brother, John Allen Young was released early due to good behavior and admirable work with the forest fire brigade.

In the summer months of July and August, the population of Suddenly had grown by four. The new residents were excited to see what the future held.

# Books by Donald F. Averill

The Bitterroot Diamonds
The Bitterroot Fire
The Kidnapping of Megan Isaacs

An Iceberg's Gift
Detour in Oregon

The Kuiper Belt Deception
The Antarctic Deception: A Sequel of "The Kuiper Belt Deception"

The Lighthouse Library
The Lighthouse Fire

Glacier Fires and Ornaments of Value

Missing Notes, Hidden Talents, and Other Stories

Wolves' Hollow Murders

The Niffits

A Professor's Affair

CPSIA information can be obtained
at www.ICGtesting.com
Printed in the USA
BVHW030856100521
606949BV00001B/21